CURSE OF THE DARK PRINCE

PRINCE'S ASSASSIN #3

ARIANA NASH

Curse of the Dark Prince, Prince's Assassin #3

Ariana Nash - *Dark Fantasy Author*

Subscribe to Ariana's mailing list & get the exclusive story 'Sealed with a Kiss' free.

Join the Ariana Nash Facebook group for all the news, as it happens.

Copyright © 2021 Ariana Nash

Edited in US English.

Version 1 - March 2021

www.ariananashbooks.com

CHAPTER 1

𝒩iko

KILLING HAD ALWAYS COME EASY. Living with the blood on his hands was the hard part. But as Niko stood breathless among the bodies, he felt nothing. He couldn't even be sure the carnage strewn about him was by his hand. He held a sword, its edge dripping, but only vaguely recalled swinging it toward Alissand's men. Some of those men had wielded the flame, tossing it at him like a lifeline. He remembered that. Remembered how their dark swirl of magic had washed over him, no more effective than cool mist. He'd felt that. But little else.

It seemed important that he feel *something* and perhaps more important that he didn't, but as his eye was drawn to the Yazdan crest on the door of a nearby carriage, all thoughts and reason left him. Glossy black paint, no windows. A prison on wheels. His prize. His target. The very carriage he'd been tracking south for days now.

He trudged through the churned earth and over the dead. Ten days knowing Vasili bled inside this same carriage. Ten days of torture, waiting for Alissand's guards to thin out, waiting for the right time to strike.

He grabbed the carriage door and flung it open.

The metallic taste of blood laced his tongue. Feeling seeped back into his muscles and bones. Rage came first. Roaring back to him like a beast from the shadows. The moment Vasili had given himself to Alissand outside the Bucland Manor, this was always going to be the outcome. The Yazdans didn't care about alliances or deals, like the one Vasili had struck. Alissand Yazdan— his uncle—wanted blood.

Grabbing the handles, Niko hauled himself inside the gloomy carriage.

Vasili's spread-eagled body lay on a mattress—wrists tied, veins weeping. He glowed in his paleness. So like when Niko had saved him before. History repeating. Niko lunged for Vasili's bound right wrist. Vasili's hand lay limp and cool in his. "No, no, no." He had to cut him free *now*.

Heart lodged in his throat, Niko dropped Vasili's wrist and lifted his sword. *Cut him free. Get away.*

A fragment of wrongness snagged his thoughts, freezing him still. Vasili's shirt lay open. His smooth chest rose and fell with every breath. But where was the old scarring, where were the countless, savage marks the elves had given him? He lifted his gaze to Vasili's face. Two closed eyes, lashes fluttering.

This man was not Vasili. The hair was too short, the face too angular, the clothes all wrong.

No, no!

Niko recoiled.

Yes, Master.

The man tied, his veins gaping, was Amir.

But he'd died at the end of Vasili's blade. He'd died in the Loreen street. He *couldn't* be here. He was a phantom in Niko's head, nothing more. The flame was making him see things... *wrong* things.

Sickness roiled in Niko's gut. He clutched at the wagon wall and then at his head, trying to squeeze the madness out. His gaze found the prone body again. Unable to look but unable to look away. *Amir.*

Ten days tracking Alissand's men. Ten days watching the wagon from afar, thinking of Vasili inside, knowing he was being bled and tortured. Ten long days and nights, and all for... Amir?

Not dead.

Not even close. The wrong Caville.

Blood dripped from Amir's veins, pooling and congealing on the carriage floor. *Drip, drip.* Tap, tap. Amir's heartbeat, his life, his power. Niko's skin crawled, itching. The hot, damp interior of the carriage tipped and swayed. His tongue dried, suddenly thick in his mouth. Every drop of blood was a waste. If he could just taste it, take it into him again, where it belonged. That was right, wasn't it?

His knees thumped to the floor. *Drip, drip.* His veins

burned, his body hot and alive, cock hard and thoughts spinning. A madness. A relentless need to feel the dark flame filling him up once more. He just had to crawl across the floor, seal his lips on the wound, and drink. He *craved* it.

Flashes of memories struck like whip lashes. Amir pouring poison between his lips. Amir demanding he kill Vasili. *Yes, Master.*

He groaned out a moan. What had he come here for? The sword in his hand, coated in blood. Blood all around. In the air, on his tongue. Power. Amir was that power. Within Niko's grasp.

No. This was wrong. What was happening to him? He'd come for Vasili. To save Vasili. To free Vasili.

You're safe. He heard Vasili again now, felt the brush of his lips against his ear. Amir had done something terrible to him, something unforgivable, something Vasili never would. Spice had taken the memories, but not the sickening sensation—the weight of wrongness.

He could kill Amir right here, drive the sword through his chest and make his death stick. Fuck freeing the flame. Amir would be gone from this world, and that had to be right.

Niko tightened his grip on his sword, thrust its tip into the carriage floor, and heaved himself to his feet. He staggered forward and loomed over Amir's vulnerable body. Amir's eyes were still closed, lids still fluttering.

Drip, drip.

Niko raised the sword. His thumping heart burned up his throat. The smell and taste of blood blurred the

sight of Amir's sleeping face. He didn't look dangerous, didn't look like the king who had forsaken his city,
his people, for the flame. He just looked like a fresh-
faced man, hardly older than a boy, cut open and
exposed.

Don't stop, dog.

Yes, Master.

A shining droplet of blood trickled down Amir's
forearm, and suddenly it was all Niko could see. To taste
it again, to feel it filling him up and pulling him down.
He lowered the sword to his side and skimmed the
fingers of his left hand through the blood, smearing it
across Amir's pale skin, scooping it to his lips. The elixir
sizzled on the tip of his tongue.

A boom sounded outside, startling him back into his
own mind.

Blood shimmered on his fingers. He tasted it on his
tongue and staggered back. Disgust chilled his blood,
dousing the madness and desire. Gods, what in Etara's
fresh hell was he doing?

"Niko!" Yasir's yell startled him some more.

He clutched the sword to his side and cast Amir a
long final look. "Rot here forever. It's all you deserve."

Yasir's gun boomed again outside, and Niko jumped
from the carriage, stumbling a little in his haste to get
away from the nightmare it contained.

At the tree line, Yasir waved him on. With the long
gun at his side and his hat at a jaunty angle, Niko
choked on a sob to see him. He couldn't fall apart here.
Just because Amir was in that carriage didn't mean
Vasili wasn't nearby. It wasn't over yet.

"Where's Vasili?" the captain asked, glancing behind Niko toward the carriage.

"Not there. Decoy. Retreat and regroup." How easily the lies came. He plowed back through the undergrowth, hearing Yasir quickly fall in behind him. The questions would come, but not until morning. They could still do this.

They dashed through fat, wet leaves, retreating to the high ground and its outcrop of overhanging rocks. Liam was on his feet, big brown eyes lit by moonlight. "What happened? Where's the prince?"

Torch flames bobbed in the distance, highlighting the rest of Alissand's men. Their line snaked through the dark. Reinforcements. Alissand's wagon train had split into two during their journey southward, with the wagon holding Amir at the end.

"The carriage was empty," Niko grumbled. Blood sizzled on his tongue, burning like his lies. "Vasili must be among the others."

Yasir frowned at Alissand's mobilizing forces. "We scouted that camp. He wasn't there."

"Then Alissand has him disguised. He's there." Niko grabbed Adamo's reins and swung into the horse's saddle. Adamo snorted and stamped the ground, ready to bolt at the slightest twitch of the reins. Niko had returned to the abandoned Caville palace and retrieved Vasili's devil horse, despite Yasir's pleas to find another. They needed Adamo for when Vasili would be with them again. Niko had needed him too.

"Niko, wait." Yasir grabbed his horse's reins but hesitated. "We planned to take the carriage when the guards were few and far between. We didn't plan for the main camp. It's heavily guarded. If Vasili is there, he could be anywhere among them. We need a better plan than just running in and—"

"There will be no better time than now." Adamo pranced and chewed on his bit like he *knew* this had to be done, whereas Liam and Yasir both looked at Niko like he'd lost his mind. Perhaps he had. He could still taste the blood, sharp and metallic, still feel the sharp points of the memories lost to him and hear Amir's laughter. "I'll go alone. Stay here, both of you."

Moonlight made the shadows gathering around Yasir's frown cut deeper. "Niko, don't be a fool. I can assist—"

"Alissand will close ranks around Vasili if he hasn't already. It has to be now."

"You're just going to take on twenty, maybe thirty guards alone? Niko, you're not prepared—"

"No, *you* are not prepared," Niko snapped back. "It's now, or we lose him. I'm not taking that risk." The words rang around them in the hollow, leaving Yasir staring and Liam's face etched with concern. They'd seen something in him. Niko felt it too. The sizzle of the flame biting at his nerves, sparking his desire to hunt, to kill, to seed chaos and unleash the monster slithering through his veins. Did they also see his eyes flicker black? There was no time to think on it now.

He turned Adamo toward the tree line.

This night would end with Vasili at his side, whatever the cost.

CHAPTER 2

 asili

DISTANT, sharp, and short explosions startled roosting birds and woke the men asleep on their bedrolls. Vasili watched them leap to their feet, gather their weapons, and at Alissand's command, they plunged into the night.

Alissand hung back, catching Vasili's gaze. "Guard him." Then he mounted his horse and raced toward the source of the gunfire.

Vasili eyed his new contingent of guards. Five men, each of them built like bears. Probably trained by Nikolas in Seran. There was exquisite irony in that. Five men were a formidable force, but not enough should he unleash the flame. They wouldn't last more than a few minutes against its torrent of power. But then... neither would Vasili.

"I'm not going anywhere," he told them, not that

they'd listen. They'd all been forbidden to speak with him. He'd spent the last ten days in silence, riding among the guards. Not restrained, at least, not with ropes. But they'd kept him close, *observed*. Alissand had even dressed him like a guard, in light leather armor, to better hide him among their number.

He picked up a stick and tossed it into the campfire. Flames quickly turned it to ash. Despite the lack of restraints, he was still a prisoner. But a prisoner of honor, as he'd given his word to Alissand that they would work together. Honor was a new concept for him. Nikolas would be... surprised to learn he intended to keep his word, once he recovered from his disbelief. Vasili had no intention of leaving Alissand. Whatever ruckus was happening in the dark could stay there. He needed the alliance with the Yazdans if the elves were ever going to be stopped, and just so long as he wasn't tied, every step alongside them was progress.

He picked up another stick and turned it over between his fingers. The stick's fate was in his hands. Drop it and it went on unchanged, but toss it into the fire and it wouldn't last. Nikolas's fate had rested in his hands too. Left alone, he'd have survived whatever the gods threw at him. But Vasili had tossed him into the fire.

He flicked the stick into the fire. It twisted and bent before finally succumbing.

Shouts barreled through the camp. Vasili shot to his feet, but the guards sprang into motion, blocking Vasili behind them and obstructing his view. A glimpse of white flashed, and a thundering of hooves shook the ground. The guards suddenly scattered, revealing a charging, riderless white stallion. The horse knocked down two guards and whirled, kicking out and striking a third in the head so hard he flew back and lay twitching.

Adamo?! But how? They were weeks from the palace, where Vasili had last seen him.

The guards drew their blades, but the metallic scrape of metal seemed to enrage Adamo more, and with the whites of his eyes showing, he trampled a fallen man into the dirt. More guards tried to fence him in, their shining armor and shouts serving only to worsen Adamo's rampage.

Movement along the farthest reaches of the firelight caught Vasili's eye. A single figure emerged from the darkness, bloody sword in hand. Shadows flocked to him, as though the night itself had sent him forth to do its bidding. Vasili blinked, trying to clear the swirl of power smudging his sight.

A guard barked a warning, but it was already too late. The shadowed figure cut down three men before they'd had a chance to raise their blades. A fourth lunged but fell, screaming, clutching his hacked leg. Others raced in, and he dealt with them as though they were no more bothersome than flies, his sword swinging, his body a masterpiece of movement. Glorious and brutal, like he'd always been. But now that he was fueled by the flame, he'd become the very monster he'd most feared. Nikolas.

The remaining guards saw sense and fled in Alissand's direction. A thick quiet befell the camp, broken only by Adamo's panting.

Shadows peeled from Nikolas, turning to dust, like a dream upon waking. Vengeance burned in his dark, flame-touched eyes.

Vasili's heart tightened. A small fearful voice at the back of his mind urged him to flee. The voice of fear, his constant ally and nemesis. But that voice did not control him. He'd never backed away from Nikolas and wouldn't begin now. Spine straight, he planted his boots and lifted his chin.

Nikolas extended a bloody hand. "Let's go." The command resonated through the air.

Vasili batted his hand aside. "No."

"Don't try me, prince." Nikolas's white teeth flashed.

This man was infuriating. What was this, some ridiculous attempt at a rescue he didn't need and hadn't ordered? "I gave Alissand my word—"

Nikolas stole a step closer. "Your *word* means shit, and we both know it. Take my hand or I'll throw you over my damn shoulder, Vasili."

Considering the determination on his face and the bloodlust that was likely running through his veins, the threat was entirely real. "I need the Yazdans."

He moved another step closer. The odors of smoke and metal and war came with him. Scents that reminded Vasili of eight years in hell, until Nikolas had entered his life and changed everything. Stubborn and rough, smelling of hot metal, horse, and wood smoke. It was the wood smoke that did it—reminded Vasili of the cabin in the woods. Of the short life Nikolas had made for him. A life with Nikolas at his side.

Nikolas sighed, and the blazing righteousness in his

gaze dissipated. His fingers twitched, hand still offered for the taking. "I swear to Etara, I'm not leaving here without you. So, you either come with me now, or when Alissand returns with his entire contingent of guards, he'll kill me."

Something dangerous and sharp caught in Vasili's chest, making his heart stutter. He wanted to go with him, that was the torture in all of this. He'd always wanted to be the man who could walk away, and Nikolas kept damn well tempting him—torturing him with a dream he could not have.

"You shouldn't have come," Vasili said, more softly now. "I need Alissand. I need control and power if I'm to claim a victory over the elves. With the Yazdans, we have hope of regaining everything we've lost. Loreen... its people. It's not that I don't want to go with you, Nikolas. I simply do not have a choice."

Niko wet his lips, licking them clean of blood, and glanced about the camp and the writhing wounded, as though only now seeing the chaos he'd wrought. With every body he noticed, the more his brow pinched. "I'm not leaving you."

"You must."

"No."

So stubborn! "Nikolas!" This fool and his wonderfully stubborn denials would ruin everything. "One man's want is not enough to abandon the war."

Nikolas thrust a pointed finger in Vasili's face. "He will hold you down and cut you open, just like—" He bared his teeth, cutting his own words off. "I don't give a shit what grand scheme you have planned, prince. I don't care what you want or the thousands of little lies you've told to get here. You're leaving with me on your devil horse, *right now*. That's an order."

He was impossible. He always had been. Vasili closed his eye and bowed his head, working his jaw around all the arguments, none of which Nikolas would listen to. The ex-soldier didn't reason, he didn't *think*. Vasili should have known he'd come, and perhaps buried somewhere in all this insanity, he had truly hoped he would. But his being here didn't change what had to be done, and it did not erase everything *already* done to him. "If I go with you, then what happens?" He looked up. Nikolas's dark eyes spoke of all the anger and fury he'd always carried with him, but also of more, now that Vasili cared to look. Nikolas cared. Even now, after everything Vasili had done to him, *he cared*. "Where do we go? How do we beat the elves, the flame? *How Nikolas?*" Vasili hissed the last, as furious with himself as Nikolas. How many times had he told him that whatever he wanted, whatever life he built, it wasn't for them?

"It doesn't matter."

"Everything matters!" Vasili twisted away, folded his arms, and stared at the spitting fire. Impossible, stupid man, dangling freedom within his grasp, knowing he couldn't damn well take it.

Nikolas's fingers looped around Vasili's arm and tightened. A dart of fear struck Vasili in the heart. A memory, the past, the pain. Rough elven hands on him, holding him down. Instincts had him jerking away, but Nikolas's strong arms came around him, trapping Vasili against his chest, but also freeing him. Wood smoke and metal. Strength and compassion. By Walla, Vasili did not deserve this man. He sighed, surrendering only to him. In Nikolas's arms, like this, there was nothing else in the world. No war, no agonizing past, no relentless betrayals, no grim future. He wanted this. He ached for it so badly that it tortured him anew every time he was forced to let Nikolas go.

"I can't go with you," he whispered, hating every word.

"Then I'll make this choice for you, Your Highness." Rough whiskers scratched Vasili's cheek. Hot fingers gripped his arm tighter. "Get on the fucking horse."

Nikolas reached for Adamo's reins and drew him alongside.

Vasili shouldn't go with him. A thousand reasons told him not to, but as Nikolas swung into the saddle and reached down for Vasili, there was no force in the world strong enough to keep Vasili from taking his hand. It was a weakness, choosing Nikolas. He'd fought it for so long, but he was tired of fighting. Perhaps the choice would seal all their fates, and perhaps Vasili no longer cared about fate, about the war or his inevitable part in it. Perhaps he just wanted to live in Nikolas's world for a short while, where the answers were easy and the right choice obvious.

"Hold on," Nikolas said. His deep voice rumbled through them both as Vasili folded his arms tightly around him. "Yar!"

Adamo reared and launched forward, and then there

was nothing but the race of Nikolas's heart and the thumping rhythm of Adamo's hooves.

∼

YASIR and his lover met them several miles from Alissand's camp. Vasili offered the pair a silent nod, and they rode alongside until dawn. Few words were spoken between them. Nikolas's relentless pace carried the troop through the following day and into a second night, until reaching an old coaching inn squatting at the side of the stony, exposed road. Weak morning sun highlighted steppelands of a boulder-strewn wilderness, interrupted by snowcapped peaks.

Every muscle ached as Vasili slid from Adamo. A heavy cloak, given to him by Alissand, had kept him warm, but his breath misted in the cold and his ungloved fingers had stiffened. Nikolas dismounted and cast him a concerned glance, his expressions always moving, betraying his every thought. Vasili shared a small smile, enough to ease his concern so he could concentrate on stabling the horses in the inn's nearby barn.

"Liam and I will see if the landlord is awake," Yasir said, heading for the small main doorway.

Lazy spirals of smoke drifted from the chimney. A limp sign above the door read *The Callovorn*. Vasili had never heard of it, but he'd never been this far north. Or, similarly, never been west for that matter. He only knew the east because he'd fled the elves with Julian at his side. And he knew the south because, well, Yasir had told him all the tales before they'd set foot on Seran's sunbaked streets. His experience outside the Caville palace was limited. The palace library books taught him geography and languages, but words on a page could not describe the sensation of standing on a windswept ridge, staring into the northern mountains. What was beyond those great peaks? Aura herself, perhaps.

Nikolas emerged from the stables, expression rigid, his jaw-length, dark hair wet and swept back from his face. Ever practical, he'd found a well or a pump and washed the blood from his face, but his dark eyes and intense frown were as permanent as always. "You can stay pissed at me all you want," he said. The first real words he'd spoken to Vasili since attacking Alissand's camp. "It changes nothing."

"I'm not angry." Oh, he was more than angry. He was furious. And he'd grown more furious with every mile they'd traveled *north*, abandoning his responsibility. But he couldn't blame Nikolas for all of it. He reserved half the hate for himself, for taking Nikolas's hand and agreeing to this foolish expedition.

"Liar," Nikolas said, passing by and heading into the inn.

Vasili plunged into the inn's warmth after him, but as Nikolas veered left, toward Yasir speaking with a stout older woman near the back of the low-ceilinged room, Vasili gravitated toward the fireplace and the large, well-worn chair beside it.

He sank into the chair's embrace. The fire's heat thawed his fingers and soothed the aches from his muscles. The flames danced, content in their iron grate.

There would be no alliance with the Yazdans after this. The only thing he'd had left to bargain with was his word, and now that was as worthless as his name. No army, no lands, and with just frayed strings of control left over the dark in his veins, his chances of claiming any victory for Loreen or his people had never been worse.

And now Nikolas had brought him here, to the middle of nowhere, for reasons he could not fathom.

"Hello." Yasir's lover smiled down at him and offered his hand. He had a mop of chestnut hair and a smattering of freckles that made him look younger than he probably was. His smile was the honest kind, his clothing patched-up remnants of typical Seranian wear. "We haven't officially met," he added breezily. "Although, of course, I know who you are. I'm Liam."

Vasili ignored the extended hand and resumed gazing at the fire. "What *I* don't know is how you ended up at Bucland Manor or why you're here now." The man's smile faded in his peripheral vision.

Liam loitered, caught between his desire to leave and whatever he thought he was going to gain from this conversation. He chewed on his bottom lip. "Alissand used me as leverage to coerce Yasir into giving up Nikolas." He paused, perhaps waiting for some kind of acknowledgment. Vasili had none he could speak without offending the man. "If you hadn't gone with Alissand, he'd have killed me and probably Yasir. So, thank you... for saving us."

Vasili drummed his fingers on the arm of the chair.

18

"Some advice, Liam. Leave. Take a horse and go. If you don't, you'll get Yasir killed."

Liam blinked his big, innocent eyes and clearly thought Vasili an asshole. Liam was a liability. A loose end. Alissand had seen it, used it, and someone else would too. He wasn't a soldier. Or a sorcerer. He wasn't useful. He was baggage. Yasir's baggage. Vasili glanced over his shoulder at Yasir and Nikolas deep in discussion. With his wet, tousled hair and crinkled clothes, Nikolas looked like a barbarian, one twitch away from rage. Yasir leaned against the wall, wrapped in a riding cloak, his attire no worse off for their ordeal, gem earrings glinting. Yasir didn't look as though he could command shadows or shoot a coin from between his fingers at a hundred paces, and that was what made him so dangerous. Yasir was useful. He did not need distractions.

"This..." Vasili waved a hand for Liam's benefit. "Whatever this is, it's not for the likes of you."

Liam folded his arms and tucked his chin in. "I see you're the type who pushes everyone away."

Vasili smiled. "Just the weak."

Liam's cheek ticked. "Are you really this horrible or are you trying to ensure my safety, in some strange Caville way?"

Vasili let his thin smile grow some, knowing it looked predatory. "Your life is inconsequential to me. Don't expect to be saved again. Does that answer your query?"

Liam huffed a sharp, humorless laugh and left the fireplace to join Yasir and Nikolas.

The hypnotic flames drew Vasili's gaze back to them again. Red embers dallied upward, unlike the ash in Loreen that had fallen like snow, settling on Amir's motionless body.

Only, that moment was not as it appeared to be. And the flame...

He could not think on it. He couldn't change the past.

"—rest up."

Vasili jolted away from the touch at his shoulder, alarmed to find Nikolas beside him.

Nikolas snatched his hand back. "Sorry. I—"

"You said something?" Vasili's voice cracked some. He cleared his throat. The flightiness wasn't Nikolas's fault. It never had been.

"We have a room for the night. Liam and Yasir have their own. We should retire and rest up. We'll think better tomorrow."

His shoulder sizzled from the ghost of Nikolas's touch. Every brush, every skim felt like elf-blades reopening old wounds. They'd left him with many scars, but those in his mind were the worst. "I'll rest here a while."

"I'd prefer it if you came up," Nikolas tightly replied.

Concern had etched into his face again, making his lips turn down and his brow crease. "Fearing I may leave?" Nikolas's expression was answer enough. Vasili glanced at the door. "Would you stop me?"

Nikolas arched an eyebrow. If he walked through the door right now, would Nikolas restrain him? There was something raw and savage in having Nikolas's rough hands on his skin, but the lust his touch summoned often shattered, quickly turning to revulsion.

"You know the answer," Nikolas grumbled.

"From one prison to another," Vasili muttered.

"That's not what this is." Nikolas softened his voice. "Come up, please. I... It's been... difficult. I'd like you with me."

The longing in his tone whittled Vasili's resistance to nothing. He could never resist a begging man, and certainly not one such as Nikolas. If Nikolas knew the effect his reluctant surrender had on Vasili, he'd no doubt deliberately lose every argument. "Very well."

The room they'd rented had one small bed, a wash-basin, a lit fireplace, and a wonderful view of the mountains through tiny, fogged-up windows. Vasili headed for the fire first. He'd struggled to get warm since Loreen's fall, even on the road south. His fingers had trembled at night, so he'd taken to huddling close to the campfires, where the dark and the cold couldn't reach him.

Nikolas stripped the pillow off the bed and dumped it on the floor, clearly assuming he'd be sleeping there.

Vasili hid the quirk of his lips. "You may take the bed."

"You need sleep," Nikolas groused.

"You've spent the last two weeks on the road, tracking Alissand, and before that, what you experienced in Loreen under my—" *Brother*. Nikolas's sharp glance cut him off. "You need the rest more than I, Nikolas."

"Another night on a hard floor won't kill me." He tore at his belts and jacket buckles, angrily stripping off all the frayed layers. His defiance tugged at Vasili's smile and spiked Vasili's veins with the sweet bite of lust. If only Nikolas knew how he so easily tripped Vasili's thoughts. It had always been that way, since the first time they'd met in the Stag and Horn bar. The ruffian, ex-soldier whom Vasili knew to be an important Yazdan had roused in Vasili a desire he hadn't felt since before his years *away*.

"Take the fucking bed, Nikolas."

Nikolas threw Vasili a powerful glare. His cheek flickered. Barely restrained rage shorted every breath filtered through gritted teeth. Vasili swallowed and narrowed his eye and attempted to ignore how his heart raced and his body responded to Nikolas's fury like it was an open invitation to fuck.

This wasn't about the bed. This was about them. And the fact Nikolas was on the verge of breaking something, or someone. When he got like this, he was too easy to push over the edge. Vasili had reveled in it before—the picking at Nikolas's edges, making him come undone. He'd made quite the sport of it in the palace and had greatly missed the game when Nikolas had left. But there was a line, and Nikolas was teetering on it, his nerves beyond frayed. Vasili might have offered him some comfort if he knew how to go about such things. Whatever action he took, Nikolas was likely to misinterpret it.

Vasili strode across the room, grabbed the pillow off the bed, and returned to the fireplace with it.

He stretched out in front of the hearth, resting his head on the pillow, his back to Nikolas, and waited for his response, whatever form it took. A resigned huff came moments later, then the sounds of clothing hitting the floor, followed by the splash of water as he washed himself at the basin and the creak of the bed frame.

The soft sounds of snoring came when the fire had died down to embers.

Vasili watched the fire throb in its grate and resigned himself to a long night of fighting nightmares.

iko

Whispers woke him. Foreign words. Summoning words. The same words he'd heard on Julian's lips, but this time they were on his own. He touched his lips, tasting blood, and tried to lick them clean only to find the blood had vanished, if it had been there at all. His heart pounded, like he'd fled a fight. He was losing his damn mind.

"Nikolas?" Vasili's soft query fluttered to him in the dark.

The firelight was low, barely more than a soft orange glow about the room, but enough to silhouette Vasili sitting up.

"I'm fine." He dropped his head back and stared at the shadows on the ceiling.

"You were speaking sorcerer's words."

He didn't even know any sorcerer's words, not really, or what they did. Like he didn't know the living thing he'd consumed in Amir's blood and that now lived in his veins. Whatever it was, it burned through his skin now, making him hot and breathless and hungry for things he should not desire.

Turning on his side, he put Vasili and the fire at his back again.

The bed dipped moments later, the frame creaking.

"Give me your hand," the prince demanded in his royal voice.

Niko rolled onto his back and glanced at the prince beside him. Vasili stared at the ceiling, but his hand lay between them. Nikolas lowered his over Vasili's. Smooth, lean fingers folded into his rougher touch.

"I saw the dark in your eyes when you came for me," Vasili said. "And in Loreen, when you cut down the elves. It's not gone."

Shame made him want to pull away and leave the room. How was he supposed to reply? That yes, he'd let Amir poison him? That other things had happened too. Spice had stolen the memories, but not the feeling of wrongness. The desire for more blood. The *desire* for Amir. Gods, it made him sick.

"When your mind is quiet, that's when it whispers," Vasili said.

Regret clogged Niko's throat. Even if he knew what to say, he wasn't sure he could speak it. He had been feeling these things, and the last weeks had been like a waking nightmare, like he was losing his mind. He'd thought he was, because Amir was dead, so it couldn't be the flame. But Amir was alive and the flame was inside his veins, like it had been in Julian. He hadn't wanted any of this. Amir was alive, which meant the flame was still divided between the princes, and Vasili didn't know.

He squeezed Vasili's hand and turned his face away so the prince didn't see the tears.

"I am sorry I made you go to him," Vasili said. "I'm sorry for what he did, and I'm sorry we're here now, with none of it having made any difference."

He didn't have the energy to argue. It *had* made a difference. It had brought them together. And that had to mean something. At least, it did to Niko.

Niko woke in a cold bed and colder room. He reached to his side, expecting to find Vasili resting beside him, but his half of the bed was cold too. Vasili had *left*. He pulled on his clothes and boots and hammered down the rickety staircase.

"Ah, sir." The landlady met him in the narrow hallway. She had kind eyes and a face creased by age. "Breakfast is in the lounge. Would you like some tea?"

"My companion. Tall, white-blond hair, is he there?"

"Oh yes." She gave him the kind of smile probably reserved for hopeless souls and nodded toward an open door. "I'll bring you a hot drink. You look as though you need it."

Nikolas nodded mutely and entered the room, finding the kind of scene he should have expected. A roaring fireplace, Yasir telling a raucous tale, Vasili chuckling in the chair next to him, and Liam laughing along. They all heartily tucked into a generous spread of toast, sausage, and eggs, like yesterday hadn't happened —like *the past year* hadn't happened.

Vasili hadn't left. He was leaning back in the chair, a glass of water in his hand. His damp hair had been swept back, darkening it from pale blonde to silver, complementing the icy blue of his eye. He wore Alissand's leather garments, all laced and looped to tightly fit his slim form.

Relief almost had Niko reaching for the back of the nearest chair. Instead, he gathered his wits and the pieces of his sleep-addled thoughts and approached.

"Ah, Nikolas." Vasili gestured at the empty chair to his right, his gaze lingering on Niko's face before sliding lower.

Niko sat and cleared his throat, garnering long looks from them all. He looked down at himself. He was barely dressed, his shirt gaped, and his hair was likely a ruffled mess. He ran a hand anxiously through his locks. In his haste to find Vasili, he hadn't lingered to check he was properly attired.

"Are you well, Niko?" Yasir asked. "You look a tad... startled."

"I left a note inviting you to breakfast," Vasili said.

"I didn't get a note." He reached for the pitcher of water and poured himself a glass. His wretched fingers shook.

"Did you look?"

Niko slid his glare toward Vasili and saw the prince's

tiny, corner smile. The smile he always tucked into his cheek, like a secret. He hadn't damn well left a fucking note. He'd known Niko would rush after him like a fool.

"Did you forget how to dress?" Yasir asked with a barely restrained snort. "You, er..." He gestured toward Niko's middle. "Missed a few buttons."

"Laugh it up." He poured himself a drink while fighting his own traitorous smile. "I thought *he'd* left," he admitted.

"As if I would do such a thing," Vasili scoffed.

"But you were all here enjoying yourselves."

"They argue over everything," Yasir told Liam. "Vasili will call a box square and Niko will argue it's round."

"Because he knows I'm right." Vasili grinned a true smile, and after so long without it, Niko's heart skipped. He cleared the knot from his throat and drank from his glass.

Liam and Yasir chatted between them, Yasir telling of how some marauders had once attempted to kidnap Vasili. Niko caught sight of Vasili's crooked smile. Bastard. Although, if he was back to his usual manipulative self, then perhaps other things were back to normal too. Like whatever their relationship was. They hadn't talked about it, hadn't really dealt with anything from Loreen. The dark flame, the fallen city, Alissand's bargain. And then there was the contents of Alissand's carriage.

Niko's smile faded some, but as Yasir dove into a fresh tale, he listened along, watching Vasili. The prince's stiff Caville persona was slipping away, revealing the true man beneath. More human, less Caville.

The landlady brought coffee and closed the door behind her, giving them privacy. With the food consumed, the air warm, and the coffee flowing, the discussion turned to menial topics, such as Yasir's new string of hoop earrings, which Liam disliked, and, for a while, the laughter and warmth in the room was a welcome distraction.

Niko's thoughts inevitably turned to where they'd go next, to the flame, and Liam. He knew too much, but unlike Yasir, he could still escape. Liam would not survive among them. But Yasir would not let him go. Was it better to abandon a love to save it or to hold it close as it died? Niko discreetly lifted his gaze to Vasili. The prince sat slanted in the chair, at ease. He softly laughed at something Yasir had said. Delight made his eye bright. His mouth—when not wrapped around a snarl—was soft and forgiving, and Niko knew exactly how those soft lips felt when skimmed across his.

Niko cleared his throat. "Liam should go south," he said, severing their conversation. "He's not safe with us."

Vasili dipped his chin and stroked his fingers down his glass. If he disagreed, he'd speak up. The fact he hadn't made his thoughts clear.

"There's nothing left for me south," Liam said, after glancing at each of them in turn. "Seran is all but ruins." He leaned back in his chair and folded his arms. The man had a strong will and clearly had smarts, but those things would only get him so far. He wasn't a soldier. And he wasn't touched by the dark.

"Can you fight?" Niko asked, already knowing the answer. "Swords, pistols?"

Liam's lips pressed into a line. He looked to Yasir for support, but Yasir lifted a shoulder in a halfhearted shrug. He knew what was coming.

"No," the young man admitted. "But I have other skills."

"Niko." All the good humor drained from Yasir's face. "I'm not sending him south."

Niko glanced to Vasili, but he stared out of the window where ash had begun to bump into the glass. No, not ash. Lazy snowflakes.

Niko cupped his hot drink in his hands and fought back the memory of ash falling in Loreen and where that ash had come from. Yasir had helped save him that day, of that there was no doubt. Helped saved him many a time. Niko owed him much. Yasir stared across the table, as though he could stare Niko into relenting.

"It's not too late. Liam can escape the flame."

"I'll protect him," Yasir replied. Of course he would. He'd die for him. But it didn't have to happen if Liam traveled south, found himself some shelter, and stayed out of the flame's way until whatever was destined had passed him by.

"There's something else." All eyes turned to Niko. He should tell them about Amir. Tell them the king lived, that Alissand was bleeding him, making the Yazdans stronger with every drop. But to do so, he'd have to admit how he'd found him, and how he'd left him there, still alive. They'd think him compromised. Think him weak. Perhaps he was. "We need to discuss what happened in Loreen. Specifically, what I did that has Yasir so terrified."

Yasir winced. "You really don't remember?"

"I know you've not looked at me the same way since. Even you, Vasili, see me differently."

Vasili shifted in his chair. "The flame had you." His glaze flicking to Liam, he added, "Speak a word of this to anyone, and I'll—"

"Vasili," Yasir interrupted, anticipating the threat to come. "Please. Liam isn't a fool."

Vasili arched an eyebrow. "Amir saw in you, Nikolas, what I refused to. Bucland and Yazdan. A forbidden union, if you will. It's obvious your exiled mother and Lord Bucland didn't fall in love for love's sake. They planned this. We've learned how the three keys are in the blood of three families. Two are combined in you. Clearly, after what we all saw in Loreen, a powerful combination."

"I didn't see anything in Loreen, just ash. Tell me," Niko said.

"You are a sorcerer, perhaps the strongest there is. You're also able to control the flame. Julian..." A crack in Vasili's voice gave him pause. He took a drink before continuing. "The flame drove him to madness, as it does everyone it touches, eventually. But not you."

"Why?"

"Likely because of your Bucland blood. It makes you a formidable vessel."

Niko ignored Vasili's awe-filled tone at the fact he'd

finally gotten the sorcerer he'd always wanted. "If Bucland and my mah, Leila, planned this, what was their reasoning?"

"You are power *and* control. And the flame despises control."

"I didn't feel in control." The words choked him. He winced and took a sip from his mug, washing a new acidic taste away with cold coffee.

"Did you find anything useful in Amir's books, Yasir?" Vasili asked, changing the subject.

Yasir shook his head. "Hearsay and myth. References to the three keys, to the sorceress who began all of this as she battled the nasdas, eventually bottling it inside the Caville bloodline. No solutions. But there was something unusual in Bucland Manor. Nikolas saw it first. The limestone fireplace with the three family seals. There are more clues in that house, I'm sure of it, but I didn't get a chance to search for more before we followed you south."

"You should not have followed me at all," Vasili said firmly. "Alissand will come looking. He needs the flame to protect Seran, and now he knows he can't trust my word. Should he find us, his retribution will be swift and devastating. He'll kill you, and none of my promises will stop him from bleeding me anew."

"He won't suspect we've trekked north," Nikolas added.

"We can't hide here," Vasili said, looking Niko in the eyes. "As tempting as the thought is. We must move forward."

It was tempting, but riding north had always been a

temporary pause between getting Vasili away from Alissand and what came next. "Then are we to return to Bucland Manor and whatever knowledge it holds?"

Yasir snorted. "Alissand will surely look there."

"Eventually," Niko agreed. But he knew Alissand already had a source of the flame. His need to find Vasili was likely not as immediate as everyone assumed. "So we mustn't linger."

"Yasir should take Liam south," Vasili repeated.

"No," Yasir replied. "There was a library in the house, albeit moth-eaten and water-damaged. Liam can read old Seranian. If we're to find anything of use, we'll need his eye."

Liam glared like he could buckle Vasili with looks alone. "Let me help."

"Yasir asked the same," Niko replied. "And he now carries the flame in his blood."

"I've not lost my mind yet," Yasir said cheerily, earrings glinting.

Adding a fourth to their doomed number seemed like the height of foolishness.

Vasili dipped his chin, conceding to whatever Nikolas decided. "My thousands of little lies—as you so well described—have not steered us well to date. If you believe Bucland Manor holds answers, then we should look for them. I certainly have none to offer."

Bucland Manor was a riddle, one Yasir was well-equipped to solve. If the price of that was Liam's safety and he was willing, then perhaps it was a price worth paying. "We will encounter elves in Loreen. Winter will slow them down, but we'll need to be careful. We'll stay

34

at the house for a few days, but no more. If the house and its library give us nothing, then we'll head south. There may be some potential allies displaced from Seran."

Nobody argued. Even Vasili seemed in agreement. He caught Niko's glance. "There is potential in your newfound power, Nikolas. Perhaps I can assist in your control of it?"

"I don't think that's wise." Just the thought of inviting the power to his fingertips had his throat drying in anticipation of Amir's elixir. Shame tried to crawl across his skin. He gritted his teeth and turned it to anger instead.

"You are potentially our greatest weapon in all—"

"I said no, Vasili."

Vasili stiffened, and now Nikolas felt like a dick for snapping. He pushed from the table and retreated to his room to wash up and fix his clothes, leaving the others to their murmuring.

He'd succeeded in what he'd set out to do these last few weeks. He'd brought Vasili back, so why then did he feel more lost than ever? Only after returning from the war to find his home was rubble and his life gone had he felt anything like the same emptiness inside.

Julian had been a large part in filling that void. And that had not ended well. But then there was Vasili—the man who had filled his dreams and occupied his thoughts since trying to buy him in the Stag and Horn. A prince he had once despised, who hid the truth of himself beneath layers of lies. Vasili was the real reason Nikolas was still here.

What if they took Adamo and rode north until there were no more roads to follow?

A foolish thought. Vasili wouldn't run from his destiny, and really, would Niko? Wasn't that Vasili's point this whole time? A prince trapped by the curse in his blood. If only there was a way to remove it.

"The horses are ready," Vasili said, entering the bedchamber to find Niko at the window, watching snowflakes bump against the fogged glass. The prince's blurred reflection hovered ghost-like in the window. Niko wiped away the condensation, revealing a sharper image of Vasili.

There was no way out for them. He'd always known it, but it hadn't mattered before, because Vasili hadn't cared and neither had Niko. They'd hated one another. Everything had been easier.

He should tell him Amir was alive. But the words wouldn't come, because whatever Amir had done to him, he'd *liked* it. And he couldn't tell Vasili that. Not after everything he'd been through and how he looked at him now, his guard down.

Vasili stopped behind Niko. Their reflections stared back from the snow-speckled greyness outside. Vasili didn't touch him but might as well have for Niko's racing heart.

Niko braced his forearm against the window frame, leaning forward to catch a glimpse of the distant mountains.

Vasili's touch, when it did come, branded Niko's hip. His hand stroked down and around the back of his thigh, where his fingers dug in. Niko froze.

"I find distractions help." Vasili's words fluttered close to Niko's ear. The brush of his lips spilled shivers down Niko's spine. His hand lifted from his thigh, caught Niko's wrist, and bent his arm behind his back.

The shivers quickly turned lustful, hardening Niko's cock. It didn't take much for Vasili to *distract*. It never had. Niko had wanted to fuck him since pinning him against the Stag and Horn bar and breaking his wrist. He'd told him as much. That hadn't changed. They hadn't changed either. Not really. Vasili was still a manipulative prick, and Niko was still the stubborn soldier, but together they were something else. Something beautiful. And powerful.

Vasili shoved him hard against the wall. His rigid body was plastered to Niko's back and ass. Like this, he was fire and heat and unafraid of touch, but if Niko turned and tried to seduce him in return, Vasili would shut down. And that fucking killed Niko every time.

Having Vasili focused on him—feeling Vasili's cock pressed against his ass and knowing he wanted this just as much as Niko—it was everything, and by the three, Niko would take it all while he could. Because there was no doubt in his mind that this precious connection was fleeting and fragile. And, like most things, it would not survive the dark flame.

Vasili's fingers stroked Niko's hair back from his cheek. "I hate that he had you."

Oh gods. Niko clenched his jaw. Need made him ache.

"I hate that he hurt you." Vasili's soft lips skimmed Niko's neck. His fingers dove around Niko's waist, between Niko's belt and skin, and eagerly found Niko's erection, stealing a gasp from his lips. He fought to keep from thrusting into the prince's fingers. Trapped as he was, not giving Vasili everything he wanted was all the control he had left. He could make the prince wait.

"You are mine to touch." Vasili punctuated that with a dig of his hips, grinding the telltale hardness against Niko's ass. The fingers of Vasili's left hand clasped the back of Niko's neck, holding firm. "Mine to hurt." His dry grip on Niko's cock tightened.

"You walk a dangerous line, prince," Niko growled. He could throw him off. Vasili wasn't physically strong enough to do anything Niko didn't want, but he had no intention of fighting him. The fantasy of Vasili fucking him had been a surprising one, a new one, and one he was willing to make a reality. Almost as much as he wanted to fuck Vasili, but that fantasy was unobtainable.

"Would you take me in?" Vasili whispered into his ear, grinding his cock harder against Niko's ass. "If we had the means?"

"Yes," he conceded, breathlessly. Gods, yes.

A shudder ran through Vasili, and, pressed close as he was, Niko felt his quivering. "I didn't think..." Vasili paused as his voice turned rough. "I didn't think you would."

Niko turned his head and fixed the prince's shining eye in his gaze. "Only for you." His soft, pink lips parted, and his look of surprise spoke of a man who didn't know how to be loved, and it choked Niko to see him so fucking vulnerable.

A knock at the door startled them both. Vasili was quick to step away and run a hand through his ruffled hair, leaving Niko hastily adjusting his trousers and desperately clearing the lustful thoughts from his head.

He cracked open the door an inch to find Yasir waiting, eyebrow raised. "We're losing the light. Any longer and we'll have wasted a day."

Vasili opened the door all the way and marched past Niko into the hall, layered in his thick riding cloak, boots clipping the boards. "Your timing, Yasir, is atrocious."

Yasir's eyebrow arched some more as he gave Nikolas a knowing look. "Please tell me you've fucked, or he'll be in that mood until you do."

Niko grabbed his coat and joined Yasir in the hall. "Like he said, your timing is shit."

CHAPTER 4

asili

THE RIDE back to Bucland took longer than it should
have due to deteriorating weather and building snowfall.

Bucland Manor's approach hadn't improved in the
time they'd been away. Boarded windows and a
collapsed section of roof told a sorry story of neglect.
Fresh snowfall had softened the corners and angles, but
it was still a grim and uninviting place.

The cold continued to gnaw on his bones inside the
house. He couldn't tell if it was the weather or the flame
punishing him, and as Yasir set a campfire on the
polished floor of the grand hall, Vasili took the opportunity to warm himself through. Smoke soon filled the
ceiling space, evicting a pair of roosting pigeons.
Nikolas had taken himself off to scout the immediate

area for any sign of elves and set traps, leaving Yasir and Liam with Vasili.

"Why not light a fire in the fireplace?" Liam asked, approaching the limestone monolith.

"Elves will see the smoke from the chimney," Yasir replied while nursing the small campfire's flames.

"I see what you mean about the crests." Liam stood at the fireplace, arms folded, looking up at the enormous carvings. "Once you see them, they're hard to miss."

Yasir joined his lover by the cold, gaping mouth of the garish fireplace. He placed a hand on the man's lower back, and Liam leaned into him, seeking his touch.

A spike of jealously pushed Vasili into motion toward the nearest boarded window. He peered through a slit in the wood. Moonlight bleached all the color from the overgrown approach road. The trees beyond made excellent cover for any elf stalking them. This house was not the best of sanctuaries. The sooner they moved on, the better.

"There's definitely more to it," Yasir explained. "Like there's more to this house. A Yazdan and a Bucland left this here for a reason. We just have to find that reason. We'll check the library in the morning."

Liam muttered something Vasili missed and Yasir whispered back. A glance revealed their heads bent together, hands entwined. Yasir's gentle smile was full of warmth. The love they shared was real.

Vasili peered through the window board again. Alissand had come from those woods and might again.

Twice Vasili had escaped his clutches. He'd not get a third chance.

A shadowy figure skimmed the tree line and vanished out of sight around the side of the house. He'd know Nikolas's outline anywhere. He'd seen it in his dreams a thousand times. When he did sleep, he dreamed of Nikolas driving a blade through his heart. Those woke him more often than the rest. There were other dreams. In those, Nikolas's touch didn't hurt or make him want to recoil. Those were good dreams, until he woke and had them wrenched away.

"Keep the fire low," Nikolas's grousing order announced his return. Carrying a bundle of logs, he stomped across the room to the firepit and dumped the logs beside it. "There doesn't appear to be any sign of elves, just deer tracks in the snow. I've set up some strings. We'll hear if anything is out there. I'll take the first watch."

Some old chairs and crates lay scattered about the hallway from their last visit. Yasir arranged them around the fire, creating an indoor camp. Vasili continued to watch the monochrome view outside.

Nikolas approached and leaned against the window boards, making the old wood creak under his shoulder. He glanced behind him to where Yasir and Liam were getting comfortable, then faced Vasili again. Whatever was on his mind, he kept it sealed behind his lips.

He'd always had an intensity about him, likely from his years at the battlefront. The things he'd seen and done would have changed him from a naïve blacksmith's boy to the man Vasili had met in the pleasure-house.

The same man who had somehow crept beneath Vasili's defenses and coaxed out a part of him he thought he'd lost.

He had not meant to fall in love with Nikolas Yazdan. Use him, yes. But never love him. He'd been so long without love, he hadn't seen it stalking him until it had struck. And now he was defenseless against it.

Under the weight of Nikolas's silent gaze, he stared outside again, into the frosted moonlight. He'd looked at him with hate in his eyes for so long that Vasili had become accustomed to it. So accustomed, he hadn't noticed when it had changed from hate to something else. The specter of Julian was still very much between them, joined now by whatever torture Amir had subjected Nikolas to. A torture Vasili had knowingly facilitated.

"They're good together," Nikolas said.

Vasili watched the woods. "Hm."

"Liam is patient and understanding, Yasir is... well, Yasir is Yasir."

Yasir was a friend. One Vasili hadn't expected to find. From his tales to his colorful personality, the captain was an unexpected joy. Vasili had told him too many truths in the time he'd known him, most of them during spice- and wine-addled nights.

"Are you jealous?" Nikolas asked, lowering his voice so they weren't overheard.

Vasili glanced at Nikolas. "Not at all, I'm..."

"You spent months with him at sea."

"Nothing happened between us, Nikolas, despite your continued suspicions."

Nikolas laughed a deep, dark chuckle and stepped closer, filling the space between them. "Defensive, prince?" He reached out a hand and stroked a lock of hair away from Vasili's scarred eye. Anyone else would have received a merciless backhand for daring to touch him, but Nikolas's brazen familiarity momentarily stole all Vasili's thoughts, even the bad ones. He'd spent so long afraid, lashing out whenever anyone strayed too close, that trusting Nikolas was terrifying, but also freeing. "I'm concerned," he admitted, returning his attention to the slit in the wood and the shadows outside, giving himself room to breathe around Nikolas's presence. Nikolas was woefully unaware of how he filled any room he entered or how, when he spoke, people listened. Only Nikolas could have spoken to King Talos as though they were equal and earned himself imprisonment for the crime.

"The ice prince has a heart?" Nikolas asked, clearly enjoying himself. Perhaps this was retribution for Vasili abandoning him in the inn's bed.

Vasili faced the man again and folded his arms. "Aren't you supposed to be on watch?"

"Yes, Your Highness." Niko dipped his chin, his grin growing. He sauntered past, and Vasili stole the opportunity to slide a hand down his ass and quickly dig his fingers in, making him trip.

"Tease," Nikolas growled. If they'd been alone, he'd have likely turned on his heel and come back for more. Vasili distinctly recalled how Niko, on the deck of Yasir's ship, had threatened to *milk you until you cry my fucking name.* Nikolas had worded it as a threat, but

45

Vasili chose to think of it as a promise. He'd thought of having Niko on his knees often enough, preferably bound.

Truly, in a life mostly devoid of joy, he reveled in provoking Nikolas.

Pulling up a chair, he sighed into its dusty cover and slouched low. Closing his eye, he let his thoughts drift. The whispers crept in slowly. They began as dark thoughts, urges, needs, disguised as his own. Carlo, as a boy, had succumbed too easily to the voice, doing its bidding like the puppet on the end of his master's strings. Amir had uncannily and unwittingly denied it purchase until Talos's death, after which it had clearly taken hold. Vasili couldn't recall a time without the voice. It hadn't spoken when he was younger, not in any language Vasili knew, but it had needs. It influenced his mood, tipping him further one way, making anger turn to rage, making impulses reality. Spice helped muddle his mind now he was older, keeping the voice at bay, but spice wasn't an option now. Only his iron will held it back.

When Vasili next opened his eye, the fire had burned low. Yasir and Liam lay tucked together on a pile of sheets they'd salvaged from somewhere in the house. Moonlight continued to leak through the cracks in the window boards.

Nikolas would return soon.

He breathed out slowly and tilted his head back, absently enjoying the quiet. The campfire's warm glow made patterns swirl in the ceiling's old, ornate, plastered cornice and cove, turning smooth lines sharp. The design was ugly and unsymmetrical, like a child had scrawled on a piece of paper and some fool had thought to preserve the chaotic marks, but something about those manic swirls had Vasili's gaze lingering. The turns and curves seemed familiar, like a jigsaw puzzle before its image was revealed.

He cocked his head, following a line in the pattern. The sprawl of lines suddenly fell into meaning. He sat up in the chair and tried tilting his view another way.

No... it wasn't possible.

He stood and walked the room from wall to wall, scanning the ceiling with every step. It wasn't a pattern at all. The switches and flicks in the plaster, the stepped angles and spirals, like seashells tossed into a pile of boxes. It was a map.

"Vasili?" Yasir croaked.

"Look up."

Yasir threw off the cloak acting as a blanket and blinked sleepy-eyed up at the ceiling. "What am I—"

"The east wing, you see it there?" Vasili pointed, chasing the outline. It was so obvious now. "The library, the kitchens, the receiving hall, the towers, it's all there."

Yasir yawned into his hand and mumbled, "I don't understand."

"The palace." The entire ceiling was a map of the Caville palace, and at its center, where the heart of the palace should be, the plaster lay flat. Unfinished. It might have been a repair patch, if not for the deliberate way the corridors butted against its edges, abruptly cutting off. All but one. That single corridor led from the kitchens straight inside the void. An entrance. One way in, one way out. A chamber. Or a prison.

"You were right," Vasili whispered, then demanded, "Where's the library?"

"You want to go now?"

"Show me."

"Niko isn't back yet, and—"

"Now, Yasir. This cannot wait."

"All right, fine." He grabbed his long gun and hastily made a torch from a chair leg and a half-rotten sheet, then plunged its end into the fire to catch it ablaze and gestured for Vasili to follow. The spluttering torch did little to fend off the shadows, but its dim glow was also less likely to shine through the hallway's boarded windows. Yasir walked him through a collapsed section of house where vines had worked their way inside, until finally reaching high double doors. One hung crookedly off its top hinge.

Vasili followed Yasir around a teetering door and ventured inside a high-ceilinged room. The limited glow from the torch revealed floor-to-ceiling shelves, but most of the books lay in mounds all about them, as though someone had tossed them all aside.

"We should come back at first light," Yasir said. "We'll never find anything in the dark."

Vasili narrowed his eye. He wasn't looking for a book. That would be too obvious. Whoever had left the clues had done so in such a way as to hide them in plain sight. The fireplace. The ceiling. It would be in the walls.

"This is foolish," Yasir muttered.

"Hush." Vasili maneuvered around the fallen books and lifted the torch, casting waves of light across the empty, cobweb-strewn shelves. Something out of place?

He walked along each wall, scanned each dusty shelf and corner, but found nothing, just Yasir's exasperated face after making a full circle. "We should go back," Yasir said.

"It's here." Vasili backed into the middle of the room. Uninteresting plaster coated the ceiling. No maps there. And the fireplace was just a small, plain cast iron fireplace.

"And we'll find it, in daylight. Niko will rage if he returns to find you vanished."

"Let him." Vasili's boot brushed a book, one of the hundreds tossed to the floor. He scooped one up. Pages fell from its spine and fluttered to the floor. Moth-eaten and water-damaged, just as Yasir had said. Tossing it with the others, he brushed the mold from his fingers and regarded the books again. The books were mostly piled high in one spot. Why throw them together? Why not toss them anywhere or burn them for warmth? He used a boot to brush some of the pile aside, sweeping dust and debris across an intricate parquet floor. A wooden tile appeared lighter than the others. Vasili crouched and drew the torch closer. Shoving a few more books aside revealed more of the lighter color and what could be a line or pattern in the design.

A sharp cry sounded through the house.

"Liam!" Yasir held out his hand. "The torch. Vasili, give me the torch!"

Vasili looked again at what could be a pattern. All

the books would have to be moved, but that was easily done. A pattern in the floor would align with the clues they'd found so far. Ceiling, fireplace, floor. This house was indeed a riddle.

"Vasili!"

"Fine." He handed over the torch, and Yasir bolted, taking the bubble of light with him.

The darkness suddenly grew thick, and the quiet swallowed the library with Vasili in it. He froze, closed his eye, and listened. His sight would adjust to the dark soon enough, he just had to wait. Stumbling about, blind, in a half-collapsed house was likely to result in injury, and what was a little darkness on the outside when he lived every day with it inside him?

The silence listened back.

Something small and light scurried nearby.

He opened his eye. Still dark, but with more shades of darkness, some heavy, some like smoke.

Soft shuffling sounds drew closer from behind. Then a sudden, hollow clunk sounded against the floor. So loud in the silence. Vasili slowly reached around his waist, slipped his fingers beneath the inner hem of his under-corset, and eased the small, thin, hidden dagger into his hand. If it was a shadow beast, the dagger wouldn't slow it, but the sigh of soft leather suggested elf. As did Liam's earlier cry. If they'd been watching, they'd know to strike when Vasili was separated from the others.

Closer still, the rustling sounded, within a few strides now.

Vasili whirled, dagger pinched and ready to fly, only

there was nothing to aim at. Shadows layered over mounds of rotting books. But he'd heard... something. The shuffle came again, and again the clunk, from behind. Slowly, he turned toward the noises, staring into the mottled dark. What was this? Ghosts? He'd heard of such things. The palace staff were forever twittering about the palace's haunted chambers, but he'd never witnessed such a thing himself.

Clunk.

He tilted his head. The sound, like the grand hall and its ceiling, was *familiar*. He reached for the meaning, but his memories fled, hiding from the truth.

"My darling, treacherous son."

The voice... it didn't belong here. *He* couldn't be here.

Clunk. The sound of his cane striking the floor. He'd heard it every evening, knowing his father would soon arrive. Talos had ignored Vasili as a boy, until the flame had gotten hold of him, turning his mind to madness.

"Fulfill your wretched destiny by dying!"

Vasili whirled again. The outline of his father loomed from the shadows. Closer, those shadows came, rising up like one great wave, making Vasili smaller, *drowning him.* Fear had him in its grip, freezing his body uselessly to the floor. There was one way to stop this, to silence it, to drive it back, and it was always the same.

Vasili pressed the tip of his dagger to his wrist. His skin parted, blood welled. Laughter bubbled inside his head, or outside of it, he couldn't be sure who it belonged to. He just knew for this to end, he always had to *bleed.*

CHAPTER 5

iko

LIAM'S SHOUT rang like a pistol shot through the house. Taking two steps at a time, he flew down the hallways, down the old staircase, and charged into the grand hall, sword drawn. The windows were still boarded, no threat from there. Liam knelt beside the dying fire, brushing down his thighs.

"Gods!" he cursed.

"Are you hurt?"

"A rat—right by my face." He raised a hand to his face, demonstrating its closeness, and shuddered. "Big too."

Niko laughed, and, sheathing his blade, he squeezed Liam's shoulder. "Yasir is surely the better bedfellow. Where is Yasir?" And where was Vasili?

One had clearly led the other astray, and he had an

idea which one. He should have known not to trust them to stay in one place.

Yasir burst into the room, torch trailing smoke, and slowed. "Liam?"

"I'm fine," he laughed sheepishly. "Just startled."

"Getting to know the existing residents," Niko said, jerking his head toward the sounds of scurrying from the corner. "Where's Vasili?"

"Right behind me." Yasir's raised torch illuminated some of the gloom he'd emerged from, but there was no sign of Vasili.

"You sure about that?" Niko grabbed Yasir's torch, ignoring the man's grimace, and set off into the dark before he said something he'd regret. Vasili would be fine. The dark didn't bother him. Only confined spaces unsettled Vasili.

He heard Yasir tell Liam to feed the campfire and then jog up behind him. "We were in the library. He insisted."

"Of course he did." Because whatever was so urgent couldn't damn well wait until the morning when they were all *safe*. "You can ignore his orders, you know."

"And risk pissing him off? Have you met your lover? Besides, he found something in the ceiling in the hall— a map of the palace, he said."

"A map?" Niko tried to recall if he'd bothered looking at the ceiling but only remembered the pigeons from their last visit.

"He wanted to go to the library. When Liam... I just... He'll be all right."

Niko was content with assuming the same until the

scent of blood wet the air. His heart thumped its way up his throat. "Vasili?" he called. If elves heard them, so be it.

"Up ahead... That's the library door," Yasir said.

Niko fell into a jog. "Vasili?!"

"He should be right here."

The library, with all its scattered books, was empty. Niko swept the torch back and forth, sending the shadows scurrying. But no Vasili. "Dammit, Yasir." He turned on his heel and almost fell over the pile of books against the wall, then the pile moved. He brought the torch down. "Vasili..." The prince was braced with his back against the wall, his knees drawn to his chest and fingers locked in his hair. He lifted his head and stared through Niko. Wetness gleamed on his cheek.

"Nikolas," he rasped and lowered his left arm. In the dark, the blood against his pale skin looked black.

"Shit." Yasir took the torch, allowing Niko to crouch.

"A cloth, Yasir? Something?" Niko reached back.

"Here." He'd dug a strip of satin from a pocket and handed it over.

Niko met Vasili's vacant gaze. "I'm going to touch your arm."

Vasili rolled his eye, fluttered his lashes down, and thumped his head back against the wall. "Do it," he rasped.

The blood smeared away, revealing a short but deep cut above his wrist. Niko looped the fabric tightly around his forearm. The bandage would stop the bleeding.

"Who did this?" Niko whispered.

"Nobody."

Torchlight gleamed on the bloody dagger at Vasili's side. Niko discreetly scooped it up and handed it back to Yasir. "Can you walk?"

Vasili opened his eye and squared Niko in his sights. Icy blue had chased away the silent plea for help. "I cut my arm, not my leg, Nikolas." He accepted Niko's help to stand all the same and leaned into Niko.

Yasir walked ahead, keeping the path lit, this time careful not to lose them in the dark behind him. Liam had stoked the fire anew, making the grand hall glow. He frowned at their arrival, his frown quickly turning to concern.

"Sit," Niko said, freeing Vasili. "Keep it elevated."

"Yes, thank you, Nikolas." He swung himself into the chair. "I am proficient in treating cuts."

If he was this prickly, then he was fine, but something had clearly happened.

"I'll take watch," Yasir offered, adding, "Liam?"

Liam followed him out of the hall, and a soft quiet settled, disturbed only by the fire's crackling. Niko sat at the fireside and leaned back against the chair's side, careful not to touch Vasili's knee. The words to ask what had happened rested on the tip of his tongue, but he feared the reply. The dark flame had tried to chew its way out of the Cavilles for generations, resulting in madness. Vasili's eventual descent had been written in blood long ago.

Dawn's light crept through the window boards by the time Vasili asked, "My dagger?"

"Yasir has it."

"That's probably wise."

Niko rested his head back against the chair and admired the ugly ceiling. It was, indeed, a map of the palace. He'd drawn much of the same design when he and Julian had studied the muddle of corridors, rooms, chambers, and hallways. The random staircases and strange, nonsensical layout had annoyed him at the time. Clearly, that was deliberate. Whatever lay at the palace's heart didn't want to be found. "Still bleeding?" he asked.

"No."

"Good."

"Hm."

They fell into the quiet again, and sometime during the past hour, Vasili's knee came to rest at Niko's shoulder. Niko wasn't inclined to move when they had warmth and quiet, and clearly neither was Vasili. It reminded him of all the hours they'd spent in silence in the cabin, living in the now.

"There are marks in the library floor," Vasili said, his voice as soft as it had ever been. "If we move the pile of books, I suspect we'll find the family crests and perhaps a void beneath."

Oh, to think like a Caville. "Is that where you'd hide your suspicious texts?"

Vasili snorted a short laugh. "Any fact dangerous enough to cripple the royal bloodline stays firmly in my head."

What a terrible way to live. He would never understand the way Vasili thought. He did, however begrudgingly, respect it. Nikolas would not have survived that long among the Cavilles. He barely survived a few months inside their walls.

"Vasili," he sighed. There was unlikely to be a better time to tell him about Amir than now. Twisting to look up at the prince in the chair, he hesitated, finding the angle between Vasili's knees to be a subservient one, and, given Vasili's arched eyebrow, Niko wasn't the only one distracted. "I, er..." He cleared his throat, but as his gaze roamed the sprawl of prince, it came to rest on the bloody satin bandage, and a new dart of lust stole half his breath. Memories jostled—Amir's needle in his arm, the king's mouth on his, his hand on—

Niko tore his thoughts from the past and quickly stood, taking himself across the floor to the windows. Sunlight shimmered on fresh snowfall, making the world outside soft and white. Folding his arms, he leaned against the wall, half watching the outside and half watching Vasili gingerly rise from the chair.

If he knew Amir was alive, he'd want to go after him, putting himself in Alissand's path again. Niko couldn't allow it. He'd almost lost him too many times. Amir could rot in that carriage, and with any luck he'd die there, flame be damned.

"Have you thought any more on utilizing your gift?" Vasili asked it casually, perhaps because he was used to the dark flame in his veins.

"A gift is freely given, not forced."

He conceded with a dip of his chin. "Poor choice of words."

Niko chewed on a dry laugh and shook his head.

Vasili had wanted this all along, since long before they'd met. He would have found himself a genuine sorcerer, one not indebted to elves. A Yazdan to call his own. "No. Don't ask me again, Vasili."

"It's a part of you, whether you like it or not. Why not learn to control—"

"I'm not Julian."

"No," he said carefully. "You are not him. And it's important you understand that. You are capable of far more. Denying your potential achieves nothing."

Niko ground his teeth and glared outside.

"There are words which help shape it," Vasili continued. "The dark is a power, but also a gateway. The fiends are just one example of its use. As are the beasts. The Yazdan sorcerers could pull entire armies from the shadows—"

"Stop."

"Nikolas, you could end this war and reclaim Loreen. This house, your parents, it's clearly your fate. Denying it is foolish, like forging a sword and refusing to use it."

"Then let me be a fool." He grabbed his coat and left the room, calling back, "I'll send Yasir to the library to help uncover your secrets." He cared for Vasili—the bastard—but at times like this, he couldn't stand to be near him.

After sending Yasir and Liam back to the hall, he checked on the horses, cleared the snow so they could reach the grass beneath, and began walking the tree line, keeping to the tree cover to break up his silhouette. Animal tracks crisscrossed fresh snow, but not elf tracks. The air hung still, not a breath through the trees. Just the sound of his boots crunching through snow.

Bucland Manor loomed like a damn noose around his neck, its facade miserable. Not even a quilt of snow hid its history of neglect.

Niko crouched near the edge of the approach road and considered how Mah had plotted with Lord Bucland. The memory of her was a thin one, more a feeling than anything substantial. He'd written her from the front but never received a reply. Few soldiers did. Did she write him with the truth in those final weeks, sensing events coming to a head, but the letters had gotten lost?

If she'd said a word, a hint, something as he'd kissed her goodbye, he might have been forewarned. But she'd kept her secrets. Just smiled and told him she'd see him soon. No word of the Yazdans, nothing of the flame or how the Cavilles were cursed with a devastating power. Just a smile and a goodbye.

Niko rested his arm on his knee and turned his hand palm up. A thought, an internal twitch, and the dark flame spluttered to life, cupped in his palm. It licked up his fingers, hungry to be free. He'd used it when he'd attacked the wagon, and again when he'd sprung Vasili from Alissand's guards. In the days since Loreen, he'd summoned it to his hand, made it slither over his fingers. It was easier to use it than concentrate on holding it back. It sizzled and spluttered now, like an angry sprite, but this little flame was deceptive. Given a longer leash, it roared to life, and when it did, he'd felt nothing like such power in all his life.

He'd liked it all. Everything Amir had done to him, the power he'd wielded, the empty sensation as he'd cut down elf after elf and had the flame devour them—a feeling that nothing mattered, so why not let the flame consume everything in its path? He'd liked it.

Vasili had fought it all his life. Niko had had it for a few weeks and was fast surrendering to the dark seduction.

He couldn't tell Vasili any of it. Vasili had to stay strong, focused. If Niko told him his secrets, it might undermine what little strength the prince had left.

A twig snapped deeper in the forest behind him. He snuffed out the flame and scanned the shadows for movement. A deer would startle and run. A wolf would crouch and wait, and an elf... He wouldn't see them coming until they were swinging their blades.

Niko slowly rose from his crouch and retraced his steps through the snow, listening hard for any more signs they may not be alone.

The sooner they left Bucland far behind them, the better.

THE LIBRARY LOOKED NO LESS NEGLECTED in daylight. Half the ceiling had fallen in, exposing the second floor. Vegetation had crawled in around the windows and consumed many of the books. Most of the books had been pushed from the center, where Vasili, Yasir, and Liam lifted the wooden floor tiles, exposing a suspicious hole with a single book inside. A book they all poured over now.

"Well?" Niko asked, approaching the crouched group.

"It's in Seranian." Yasir glanced up but was quickly pulled back to the pages.

"I can read it," Liam added. "At least, the pages that aren't faded or glued together."

Niko glanced at Vasili crouched alongside them. Considering the discovery, he didn't appear thrilled. His pale lips pinched in worry. Catching Niko's gaze, he straightened. "Show Nikolas the sketches."

Yasir pinched the pages and carefully turned them over one by one. Dust puffed into the air, settling down again onto the charcoal sketch of a man wrapped in strange, diagonal lines. Yasir turned the book, giving Niko a better angle to view the art. The figure was clearly a man, naked and exposed, with lines running over him. All of it was odd, but considering the detail on the body, the fact the face was missing made the whole piece unsettling.

"What is it?"

"*Alsijnl*," Liam said, the sound like *al-sinj-a-nul*. "The text is faded, but that word suggests it's a prison or—"

"He's a Caville," Vasili interrupted. "A vessel. Faceless because he represents all Cavilles."

"We, er... We don't know that... for certain," Liam added.

Vasili turned away and strode toward the overgrown window.

Gods. No wonder Vasili's expression was grim. If the sketch was of a Caville, then it might as well have been of *him*. But it couldn't all be bad. If they'd found that much already, then the book would prove useful. "Perhaps its other pages will yield information on how to remove the flame from its vessel?"

"Perhaps," Vasili said, making it clear he'd only echoed Niko's word to humor him. Both he and Yasir looked more miserable than they had in days.

"This is progress," Niko added. "Let's focus on that. Are there likely to be further secrets in this gods-awful place?"

Liam gathered the fragile book into his arms. He and Yasir stood, with Yasir saying, "Possibly. But without searching every room, we won't know."

Vasili absently toed through the discarded books, diligently not looking at or engaging with anyone. The contents of the sketch had shaken him.

"Liam, stay here and learn what you can from those pages. Vasili, Yasir, and I will return to the Caville palace and see if we can discover exactly what the map is trying to tell us."

"Won't it be crawling with elves?" Yasir asked.

"When I retrieved Adamo, it appeared abandoned. Elves have no interest in the palace. It's nothing to them but piles of stone and mortar. They just wanted the people inside dead."

Vasili winced and made for the door. "Come, then. Let us find whatever is at the heart of my godsforsaken home."

∼

RUBBLE FALLEN from high above had obscured the tunnel entrance.

Niko tied his horse to a tree and, with Yasir, set to work clearing the rockfall while Vasili kept watch. Unbroken snow confirmed there were no elves nearby, but some could be inside. If they came across any, they'd soon meet with the surprising end of Niko's blade. Yasir had left his long gun with Liam, for protection, but he had his binding talents to fall back on. Nobody seemed inclined to mention how Niko could turn anyone to ash, and he had no desire to remind them.

With the rubble cleared, Yasir lit the torch with a flint and steel he'd found in the Buclands' scullery and handed it to Vasili. The prince artfully mastered his blank expression and headed inside.

The map indicated the corridor they needed to follow led off the south wing kitchens and zigzagged through various servants' chambers before passing right through a hatched marking. Probably a false wall.

A lot had changed since he'd rescued Vasili from the flames. Fire and elves had ripped through the palace, the evidence of both all around as they emerged from the tunnel into the palace. Water, dirt, and debris had flushed down one side of the corridor, probably from heavy rains. Mildew streaks stained the colorfully painted walls.

"You all right?" Yasir whispered to Niko.

"Fine."

The last time he'd been inside the palace, it had

been with Amir, and those memories were still murky. He'd prefer not to think on them at all. But clearly Yasir was concerned.

The palace's confusing corridors switched back, took stairs up, and spiraled down, until coming to the high-ceilinged kitchens. Niko had been led through the same kitchen by Julian after his imprisonment—so long ago it seemed like a whole other lifetime. One in which he'd hated a prince and met Julian, believing every word that left the man's lips, falling for his charm while trying to avoid Vasili's wrath. Those days seemed innocent compared to the last few weeks. And to think he'd do anything for the vicious prince walking ahead now.

The kitchen cupboards had been thrown open, their pots and pans strewn about the floor. A stench of decay hung heavy in the still air. The torch flames flickered. Yasir pulled his collar above his nose and stepped over a small misshapen mound.

In the gloom, Yasir likely hadn't seen how the mound was a body. Niko knew the smell well. In the mornings at the front line, a thick, wet miasma used to hang low in the valleys. Decay from the bodies trampled underfoot.

Vasili had stilled, his torch raised. He looked at the body and then up at Niko. Was there more coldness in his eyes than usual? Niko couldn't be sure.

"*Listen*," Yasir hissed.

The torch's flames licked at the air. Niko's heart thumped behind his ribs. He listened hard and picked up the sound of a fast, rhythmic clicking. The clicking grew louder. Vasili swept the torchlight over the fire-scorched kitchen walls toward the noise, revealing a doorway. The clicking quickened, racing closer.

Niko slid his sword free and moved around the body to Vasili's side. Whatever was coming, it was gathering pace. He tightened his hold and watched the lit doorway. It could be an elf—the smaller ones moved fast, but they rarely made a noise.

A blur shot from the doorway and veered from the light. Its clicking claws skidded on the kitchen floor before it found purchase and fled.

A hunting hound. The palace kennels had been full of them, yapping and yowling. It was a wonder they hadn't been eaten by elves. Maybe that was why it was running?

"*Fuck*," Yasir exhaled, face pale.

Niko started for the doorway. The dog had been terrified, and whatever had it running scared was likely still here. He kept his blade out. "Keep moving." He'd made it a few steps before realizing Vasili wasn't following with the torch.

He stared down at the body.

"Vasili?"

Startled by his name, he looked up. The shifting flames caught his deep grimace. He knew the deceased. Niko looked again at the body. The gown was threadbare but had once been colorful. Her silk scarf covered much of her face, the rest greying and sunken. The decay was advanced, so he couldn't be sure of her identity, but Vasili clearly was.

He said nothing and suddenly moved ahead, striding through the doorway, taking the torch and its light with him. Niko quickly flicked the scarf over the woman's face and pressed his fingers lightly to it. "You will not be forgotten, Maria." Perhaps she'd come seeking the same secrets they did, but her journey had ended in tragedy.

Pushing the guilt aside, Niko continued after Vasili. The old corridors in the lower levels of the palace had long ago been hewn from rock, making the air cold and the slightest noise echo. A draft wafted cobwebs above their heads. The corridor seemed to take them on a meandering trek, interrupted by a door here and there, but with no real destination, until abruptly ending at a wall.

Vasili lifted the torch, illuminating a vast sunflower painted onto the white lime plaster. In the flickering light, the flower towered over them, its head drooping. A sorry-looking thing, cracked and faded with time.

Vasili pressed a hand to the flaking paint. "He said it had to be this wall. Told me it was too dark here, even in daylight."

He had to be speaking of Amir and his brother's love of painting. Had Amir known something lay beyond, even as a boy?

Vasili withdrew his hand and stepped back to appraise the huge flower. "I told him nobody comes this way, so it wouldn't be seen. I didn't know he'd painted it anyway."

Niko sheathed his blade and spread his hands against the wall, feeling for cracks. Yasir rapped his knuckles along the wall's surface, knocking here and there until one knock chimed a hollow sound. A void lay beyond.

"Stand back."

Yasir backed up a step, and Niko thrust his boot through ancient plaster, leaving the sunflower in place. A few more kicks opened a gaping hole. "The torch." Vasili brought the torch close enough to the hole to reveal narrow stone steps spiraling downward into more darkness. The breeze was stronger now, misting their breaths in its sudden coldness.

Niko tore more plaster free, enough for them to climb through easily, and ventured inside. The twisting staircase beckoned.

Yasir climbed through. His shirt got hung up on a splintered piece of wood. With a grunt, he tugged it free. "Life with you, Niko, is ruining my wardrobe."

Niko snorted, waited for Vasili to join them, and followed the prince downward. The deeper they went, the harder the cold air nipped at his fingers and face.

The stairs ended in a narrow section of stone tunnel. Darkness gnawed at the torchlight's fringes. Vasili moved on, keeping the torch high, pushing the dark back.

"Huh."

Niko turned at Yasir's tone and saw him kneel. He pressed his fingers into the dusty, glittering grit.

"What is it?"

Yasir rubbed the substance between his fingers and thumb and brought it to his lips. He grimaced. "Salt."

The whole floor sparkled with it, and the rocky walls shimmered as though coated in frost.

"Your palace was built on a salt mine?" Yasir mused aloud, glancing up at Vasili.

Vasili narrowed his eye. "You know as much as I do."

"An old one," Niko added. But that would explain the rough tunnels running through the palace's foundations and perhaps why Bucland's map was leading them here. Salt was the only thing that seemed to have any impact on defending against the dark flame. If the legend was true and the nasdas had been trapped inside a mountain, what better place than a salt mine?

They moved on, crunching deeper through thick salt and into the cold. Eventually the tunnel walls opened wide into a vast, hungry silence. The torchlight pushed at the dark, but the dark didn't surrender more than a few feet.

A flutter of fear tripped Niko's heart. The cold, the salt, the chasm ahead. It *felt* significant in a way nothing else had. Vasili had raised the torch, but against the yawning space, he suddenly seemed so small.

"Here." Yasir took the torch and found a sconce in the wall with an old lamp inside. Its reservoir of oil glowed green. The flame took to the lamp wick and spluttered to life, throwing a steadier light into the cavern.

"There's more." He lit the next lamp, then the next, and with each new flame, the dark retreated. A domed construction arched over them, so vast it could surely hold several of Yasir's ships. The walls all sparkled. And the air dried Niko's tongue as he dragged it across his lips. With more lamps lit, the dark crept back, exposing a metal frame fixed to a pedestal in the center of the space.

Niko drifted closer to the structure. Salt still

69

crunched underfoot, and when he looked down, he caught a glimpse of decoration etched into stone. Sweeping the salt aside revealed more swirls. Writing, like that in the book. Old Seranian... below the Cavilles' palace. This was what they'd been looking for.

With every lamp lit and the shadows all gone, Yasir approached the strange metal cocoon-like structure. "What is it?"

Its design had been hammered by hand. Hinged arches came together along a central ladder no taller than a man. Niko circled around it, reading the metal. The salt had absorbed any moisture over the years, keeping rust at bay. The metal gleamed, as though constructed just yesterday.

With the next step, Niko came to stand beside Vasili at the front of the structure, and suddenly, horrifyingly, the structure's purpose became apparent.

It wasn't a sculpture but a cage. Its great cage bars lay open like a shell, waiting to enclose its prisoner.

"Walla, this is from the book," Yasir whispered.

It seemed that way. Trapped in iron, surrounded by salt, deep within the old foundations of the Caville palace. "Does this fit your tales, Yasir?" Niko whispered.

"The sorceress Zarqa' trapped the nasdas in flesh, inside a mountain, and the three keys locked the prison."

And that flesh was a Caville, restrained inside this iron cage.

Vasili stared at the cage, lips slightly parted, face blank but for the few small lines at his brow. He didn't look afraid or furious, he just looked like the prince who'd survived the horrible machinations of a historic curse, and nothing could surprise him. But his mask was a well-practiced one.

"The three families were here to see it done," Yasir said, standing at Vasili's side.

Given Bucland's coat of arms appeared to be a hammer and sword, it was likely the Buclands had been metalsmiths in the past. They'd crafted the cage. A Caville was the vessel—destined for the cage, and the Yazdans lured him here, into what was supposed to be the flame's and perhaps the Caville's final moments.

"The Yazdans were meant to keep it here," Yasir said, his thoughts aligning with Niko's.

"A griffin must forever hold the flame," Vasili whispered, continuing to stare at the iron contraption.

The cage was intact, its shackles open, not broken. "Someone let it go, or it never got this far," Niko added, thinking aloud. That someone had likely been a Yazdan.

Vasili swallowed hard enough for Niko to hear. His artfully blank face had gained a few tremors, most notably at the corner of his lips where he fought their tremble.

By the three, Niko wanted to haul him close and turn his face away from that horrible thing. Remind him that he was safe, that he wasn't alone. Remembering the writing on the floor, he swept the salt aside, revealing more of the strange wording. "Vasili, do you recognize the language?" Yasir would know it, but Niko wanted Vasili's attention on the writing and not the prison.

Vasili's lashes fluttered. He looked down at their feet and brushed salt aside. "Seranian."

"Hm..." Yasir knelt again. "It's old, older than I can read. Liam could read it. But I'll never get him down here."

"And he shouldn't have to come," Niko agreed. The less Liam had to do with any of this, the more chance he and Yasir had of eventually escaping it.

Vasili pulled his cloak tighter, and Niko watched as his gaze was drawn back to the cage.

If anyone tried to fix the prince into something so monstrous, Niko would have their skins. He'd cage himself first.

"I've seen enough," Vasili said sharply. He turned on his heel and crunched over the salt back toward the entrance tunnel.

"We should at least clear the salt and see all the words. We can relay them to Liam." Yasir swept more salt back. "This could tell us *everything*. Niko, look at it. It stretches all the way around..."

Clouds of dust rolled into the air as Yasir quickly pushed piles of salt from the hidden words. He was right. They did need everything they could find, but this place and its biting atmosphere were beginning to dig beneath Niko's skin. The cold had sunk into his bones and deeper, as though it ate at his soul.

A high-pitched whistle shattered the quiet.

"Niko—!"

Vasili's shout whirled Niko on the spot.

Elves spilled in from the entrance corridor, loosing their arrows toward Vasili. He miraculously managed to dodge one, but the second slammed into his thigh, tearing a cry from him.

Niko bolted toward him. More elves spilled in, cloaked in patched leather. They moved like the wind, like ghosts, and fanned out. Too many to fight.

Fear lodged his heart in his throat. He reached for the flame but felt only the coldness in his veins. The vast amount of salt held it at bay.

Three elves encircled Vasili, arrows drawn and ready to punch into the prince's skull. Vasili bared his teeth, but with his hands clamped at his thigh, he had no means to defend himself.

They'd all die trying to fight so many.

Four elves closed ranks in front of Vasili, blocking Niko's path. They drew their bows, arrows nocked, and Niko slowed to a halt. Behind him, elves approached Yasir, similarly armed and ready to end his life. He couldn't fight them and win.

One of the elves barked a noise, his grey eyes locked on Niko's.

Niko tossed his sword to the floor, where it rang his surrender. He lifted his hands. Elves grabbed his arms, yanking them down behind his back. They bared their sharp teeth in hideous grins.

An elf grabbed Vasili. He tried to pull himself free but only succeeded in earning two more to grapple with him. He bucked, wildly thrashing. An elf locked his hand around Vasili's throat and hauled him forward as easily as if he were a doll to be toyed with.

"Vasili, stop." Niko's heart thumped, and fear laced his throat. The prince found his gaze. "Don't." The more he fought, the more they'd hold him and the worse it would be. "Don't," Niko said again, softer this time, and the fight drained from Vasili. His face was wracked with fear. He knew what was coming.

Niko held his gaze, trying to convey how he'd do anything to stop this, to save him, but right now, the safest play was to do nothing.

Vasili's gaze begged for help, begged for this not to happen.

The elves swarmed, staying silent, and dragged Yasir by Niko. He looked over, his gaze full of hope. Niko nodded once. They would escape, but not here. They hadn't killed them immediately, which meant they wanted something, and that was their mistake.

Vasili was gone; they'd taken him into the corridor. Panic and fear for the prince tried to sabotage Niko's thoughts. He shoved all feeling aside and played at being the obliging prisoner. Once outside, all that would change.

 asili

WHERE THEIR HANDS TOUCHED, his skin burned. None looked him in the eye. They knew who he was. They might have even been waiting for him.

Nausea pooled saliva in Vasili's mouth and blurred his vision. He barely saw the corridors they dragged him through.

They'd throw him in a cage, they'd tie him down, and they'd cut and cut and cut, and this time, they'd find their prize. They'd bleed him until there was nothing left but his silent ghost. Just like before.

He'd been in this cage before, and there was no way out. He could not survive that again.

Using the flame was always a risk, more so of late now that it sensed freedom. If he unleashed it, he might never wrestle back control. He'd be lost. Lost to the elves or lost to the flame. Those were his choices.

Vasili squinted into daylight. More elves crowded the tunnel exit. So many it seemed like all of them. One held Adamo's reins. The horse snorted and shied, kicking up powdery snow.

An elf grunted and another similarly replied, approaching Vasili with a length of leather strips braided into a rope. Vasili wet his lips. He still had an elf at each arm and one behind him, holding his wrists. If he summoned the flame, they'd know the value of their prize. Right now, they only knew they'd recaptured their scarred prince.

Elves hauled Niko from the tunnel, with Yasir behind him. He squinted into the light too, his dark, soldiering eyes reading the threat, looking for weaknesses. Had he been alone, he'd have already fought and gotten himself killed. He looked determined, as though he might try something in his typical blustering way. If he used the flame, they'd be quick to fire arrows into him.

Nikolas caught his eye. Vasili gave his head a small shake. *Don't.*

Nikolas glanced back at Yasir and shared a conspiring look. They were going to get themselves killed.

Leather ties secured Vasili's wrists behind him. Two of his guards left, leaving just one holding Vasili's arm. Vasili had a second hidden dagger—Yasir still had its twin. But it was hidden within his corset's stitching. He couldn't get to it while his wrists were restrained outside his cloak.

The satin bandage from around his wrist slipped free and cold air touched Vasili's wounded wrist. He twisted, trying to get a look at the elf examining his arm. "Don't!" he snapped. The elf grunted and grabbed Vasili's forearm with both hands. "Stop!"

"Hey!" Nikolas bellowed. "Hey, elf! Leave him be." Nikolas heaved his weight from the three holding him, and as large as they were, Nikolas still had enough muscle to challenge them.

Clammy fingers touched Vasili's wrist, unleashing a torrent of memories, instantly dropping Vasili to his knees. His sudden drop pulled the elf down aside him. Vasili bared his teeth at the creature. *"Don't. Touch. Me."*

Then Nikolas was moving. He'd pulled free of his guards. Shouts rose. He charged like a bull toward Vasili and plowed into the elf behind him. They both tumbled into the snow near Adamo's feet. The horse reared, Niko rolled, and Adamo landed hard. His enormous hooves slammed into the fallen elf's chest. Then the horse came down again, crushing the elf's ribs so that he never moved again. Adamo screamed, eyes rolling. He tore from the elves and bolted straight through their number.

Yasir, wrists bound at his front, grabbed the galloping whirlwind and unceremoniously swung himself into Adamo's saddle. Adamo plunged into the woods and was gone with Yasir. A handful of elves raced after him.

Vasili swung his gaze back to Niko, finding him

pinned in the snow beneath four elves. He grinned bloody lips. Damned fools. Him and Yasir both. An elf bludgeoned Nikolas on the back of the head. He fell limp, eyes closed.

He was lucky to be alive.

Hands hauled Vasili back to his feet. He fought not to heave his insides up as they marched him to a rickety, old, open-top hay cart and roughly shoved him on it. Nikolas's heavy, groaning body was dumped on the cart at Vasili's feet moments later, and, with a guttural shout, the cart lurched into motion.

Yasir and Adamo were free.

As for Nikolas and himself, Vasili wondered if this was how their stories ended. They had always been an unlikely pairing with no chance of survival. Still, he'd have liked to have lain next to him, safe and warm, one last time. Their moments together were too few and far between.

He'd need those good memories for what would surely come next, while elves cut more pieces of him away.

The cold air nipped at the wetness on his face. He hastily wiped his cheek dry on his shoulder and shuffled down in the hay, closer to Nikolas.

By the time the elves stopped to make camp, Vasili had lost all feeling to his toes and fingers. The cart had become stuck shortly after setting off, resulting in their train marching through the snow on foot. They did at least allow him and Nikolas a spot near one of several roaring campfires.

Elves grumbled and growled nearby, their language difficult to decipher. Vasili knew some from listening to their growls for years. They understood some Loreen words. Anything Niko and he said might be understood. They had to be careful.

There hadn't been a chance to mention his dagger to Nikolas, especially with the elves always nearby, but now the camp had spread out some and he and Niko were huddled closer together, seemingly ignored, for the most part, they may be able to snatch a few words.

An elf approached and delivered bowls of thin soup and chunks of bread for them both, then remarkably untied them. The elf mimed the action of eating and left. Vasili eyed the soup warily. Whatever its ingredients, he was starved and needed it. Using the chunk of rough bread to soak up the soup, he devoured it all.

"What are you thinking?" Vasili set his bowl aside.

Nikolas had gained a quiet stillness since their capture. He studied the enemy and had spoken little, preferring to observe. Vasili observed him in return, noting the way he watched the elves, reading their every move. For all his faults, he was a formidable soldier. Having Nikolas at his side made all this bearable.

"They're taking us east," he finally said, keeping his voice low between them.

Vasili had realized the same on seeing the direction of the setting sun. "They keep mentioning a settlement or base of some kind... something they've built."

Nikolas flicked his dark eyes up. "You speak elf?"

"Eight years was a long time to listen. I hear their language. I'd butcher it to speak it."

Nikolas checked no elf was closely observing them and shuffled closer. "How are you holding up?"

An interesting question, and one few people had ever asked him. "I appreciate your company." What else was there to say? If he admitted how close he was to unleashing the flame, Nikolas might kill him himself.

Nikolas's warm smile had power in it, because nothing else soothed Vasili's heart like it. Without him... Well, Vasili would have fought them by now and paid heavily for that mistake.

Nikolas's smile bloomed into a grin. "You *appreciate* my company. Well, prince." He cleared his throat and mimicked Vasili's accent. *"I appreciate your fucking company in these dire circumstances also."*

Vasili smiled and held Nikolas's warm gaze. Nikolas knew him better than anyone. He'd seen all the sides Vasili had crafted over the years, and he still sat beside him, so perhaps there was a part of Vasili who didn't deserve this wretched life after all, and Nikolas recognized it, even when Vasili did not.

Their moment of quiet understanding ended when Nikolas grumbled, "This dinner is far better than the one you ordered I attend alongside your wretched family."

Vasili laughed softly at the memory and its comparison. They were prisoners in an elf camp, about to be hog-tied, beaten, and likely bled, and Nikolas had Vasili laughing. He'd be a puzzle if he weren't so easy to read. And that was why Vasili loved him. There was an elegance in Nikolas Yazdan's brutishness. He had honor, integrity, and strength. Things Vasili had forsaken long ago in order to survive.

He made Vasili see himself *differently*.

Nikolas sobered, his smile quickly dying. "The body in the palace kitchens—"

Vasili sighed and said nothing.

"She did not deserve that fate." Nikolas spoke with feeling. He'd known her, liked her even.

"Fate is cruel." Their fates would likely be no better. What hope was there for them, really? "What if we run?" Vasili whispered. The question was a desperate one and a fool's wish. Desperate fools were the first to die, but Vasili couldn't help himself.

Nikolas briefly scanned the camp before replying. "They have scouts posted some distance from the camp," he said quietly. "If we run and somehow got free of all the elves here, they'd close in on us in a few whistles."

Of course he was right. If running were an option, the elves wouldn't have left them unguarded. Cunning and vicious, elves could not be easily manipulated. They didn't bend to coercion like members of the court. They did not reason or negotiate. Vasili's only weapons were blunt here. "I have a dagger," he mumbled quietly. "Tucked against my back."

"Keep it safe," Nikolas quickly replied, his tone short. "What of the flame?" He leaned closer still and kept his voice so low Vasili barely heard him.

Unleashing the flame had to be their last resort. "Had you accepted my help to hone it, then perhaps, but you did not, and thus any attempt at controlling it would be chaotic. You'd cut down perhaps a handful before they overwhelmed you. It would make you a target."

"And what of you? You used it during the battle in Loreen."

"To control Amir's already infected soldiers." He recalled that gods-awful battle and the way the flame had strained at his hold, desperate for freedom. If it hadn't been for Nikolas's arrival at the hands of Amir, Vasili might have lost control altogether. "Every time I unleash it, the more it fights. Cavilles are not meant to harness it. That is the Yazdan way. The next time I use it, I fear it may go free."

"But... it won't be free." Nikolas downcast his eyes and shifted away, putting cold distance between them. "Amir isn't dead."

Vasili must have misheard. "What?"

"He's not dead." He looked up again, but this time those emotive eyes of his were heavy with guilt. Which was absurd; he wasn't the one who'd deliberately missed his brother's heart, leaving him very much alive on that street.

The guilt on Nikolas's face hardened to grave suspicion. "Wait." He peered closer. *You knew he lived?*"

"This is hardly the place—"

"*Talk*, Your Highness," he growled. "Or elves be damned, I'll make you."

If he didn't tell him now, Nikolas would cause a ruckus and this freedom they'd earned would soon be shut down. "Considering I was the one who plunged the dagger into his chest, yes, I knew I'd missed his heart, thus not killing him."

Nikolas gave no reply, just stared.

Really, he should not have been surprised, yet he always was. There was something naïve and delightful in how he always hoped for the best in people, even when those people repeatedly disappointed. Although, from Nikolas's thunderous expression, he clearly did not believe his naïvety was delightful.

Vasili had feared this conversation. Had hoped it might never come to pass between them. Amir would have crawled off and whatever befell him would be his doing, not Vasili's. Of course, lies always had a way of revealing themselves. But this lie wasn't designed to be malicious. He *had* planned to kill Amir right up until he'd plunged the dagger downward and missed.

Ridiculous sentimentality had steered the dagger away at the final second. His brothers had no such qualms regarding murdering him. Yet, Amir... He'd just wanted to be seen, and everything he'd said on that street had been true. Vasili *had* ignored him when they were boys. Ignored him, shut him out, pushed him aside —to protect him.

But sentimentality hadn't been enough to save Amir. If he'd killed Amir in the street, all of the flame would have funneled into Vasili, and he wasn't strong enough to contain it. Never would be. He'd learned that from keeping Talos subdued with spice and having the flame push at his mind. Missing Amir's heart had enraged the broiling flame, but it remained contained. For now.

A good thing, considering Vasili's current company of elves.

"I planned to kill him." He couldn't stand to face Nikolas's glower any longer and stared at the fire instead. The flames were cool in comparison. "I'm not strong enough to hold all the flame, Nikolas."

"You missed because you were afraid."

"Yes, I'm fucking afraid," he hissed, careful to keep his voice low. "The flame is stronger than me."

"You're stronger than you think."

He laughed at that. "You know who I really am. For all my many faces, I'm still the man who crawled out of an elf-cage weak and broken. That wretched, pathetic man with no voice of his own."

Nikolas's cheek twitched.

"It's in my head. It wanted Amir dead because it knew, once fully restored, it would burn through me and be free. Now it just wants me to cut open a vein and bleed myself dry so..." He trailed off, remembering where they were. Although no elves appeared to be in any way interested in their conversation, it was unwise to speak so freely among them.

"Is that what happened in the library?"

Vasili bowed his head. "How do you know Amir's alive?" he asked after a long silence.

"Alissand had him in a carriage, like he had you. I found him. Left him there."

Then Nikolas hadn't killed Amir either. Vasili closed his eye and breathed out slowly. "It never ends, does it?"

"You should have killed him, Vasili."

Vasili scowled. "This prince appears strong, but the man is not. Do not confuse the two, Nikolas."

Gods, he didn't want to argue with Nikolas, not now, when this could be their last conversation.

He always seemed to push him away. One day, if they survived this, Nikolas would leave, like he'd threatened countless times. He'd walked away before, leaving Vasili with a hollowness no amount of spice could fill. Vasili had found him again, in his half-collapsed cottage and in the Yazdan home, but the next time Nikolas left, Vasili feared it would be the last time. On that day, Nikolas would be gone, just like Alek.

"Why didn't *you* kill him?" Vasili asked, hating how raw he sounded. Nikolas was more than capable of killing Amir. He'd threatened it often enough. The only surprising thing in all of this was that he hadn't.

Nikolas clamped his lips together and shook his head. Whatever the reason, he couldn't or wouldn't speak it.

Everything would have been easier had Vasili made Nikolas a sorcerer when they'd first met, instead of falling in love with the bastard. He'd have *owned* him, might even have won the war with him. Love was clearly a terrible weakness.

He placed his hand next to Nikolas's, his little finger touching Nikolas's. If the elves saw, they'd likely separate them.

Nikolas pulled away.

Well, that was to be expected. Vasili had betrayed and lied to him multiple times, causing him untold suffering. He still wasn't entirely convinced Nikolas cared for him in any meaningful way. They'd had the cabin in the woods and a handful of moments thereafter, but those were fleeting, mostly sexual, and those times had been *before* Vasili had handed him over to Amir.

Everyone had a line, a point at which they shattered, and Vasili had shoved Nikolas across his.

And now he'd succeeded in pushing Nikolas away. Again.

Vasili turned his sour thoughts to the elves. In all the years they'd held him prisoner, he'd watched and listened and concluded them to be part animal, part man, and part something else—something akin to the dark flame. Everything they did, every act, every task, was performed with ruthless efficiency. The same efficiency with which the flame consumed.

"I no longer know what I'm fighting for," Vasili said softly, startling himself by speaking the thought aloud. Nikolas looked over, and Vasili admitted, "The city, my home, my people, everything I've fought for has slipped through my fingers."

Nikolas stayed silent for so long that Vasili assumed he agreed, until he said, "You're fighting for freedom. So *they*,"—he gestured at the camp and the countless elves —"don't bring about chaos. And you're fighting for me."

For all his rage and disgust, for the new lines around his eyes and his haunted expression, Nikolas still believed in hope. How could a man endure so much darkness and still see the light?

"You're fighting for what is right," Nikolas said. "It's all we have left."

iko

THE ELVES MOVED off at first light but driving snow quickly closed in, slowing the pace. Towering pines swayed and groaned, jostled by the wind. Snow dashed Nikolas's face, half-blinding him. The elves relentlessly marched on.

With visibility down to a few strides, Niko could only make out a handful of elves ahead and behind them. There'd be no better time to escape. It was a risk. The storm was just as likely to kill them as the elves.

Vasili trudged ahead, his heavy cloak a blurred smudge in the near whiteout. The bastard had known all this time that Amir still lived, and he hadn't said a fucking word. But now was not the time to dwell on lies. He'd argue with him later. Now might be the only opportunity they had to run.

Vasili had said Nikolas had little control over the flame, and while that might have been true, he'd used it well enough to kill Alissand's men. He *could* control it. That was what made its use so damn terrifying.

He glanced behind. Two elves marched in his tracks. One saw him looking and fixed his glare on Niko.

Five elves were close by, with Vasili and himself between them. They'd be slow to react to an escape, blinded by snow, and the flame wouldn't hesitate to devour them all. Despite Vasili's warning, he could do this. He *had* to do this.

With his hands bound in front of him, Niko bowed his head to the biting wind and calmed his thoughts, finding the place in his mind where the darkness slept. It felt like surrender, like lying down after a hard-fought battle and letting fate take him. That part did not come naturally, but it did come, and once he'd summoned it, there was no going back.

Black flame boiled over his hands. He saw Vasili turn, saw his lips part and his eye burn with indignation, but then the flame was free, turning the snow black, parting and flowing *around* the prince to get to its feast of elves.

A muffled shout disrupted Niko's attention. The flame's path twitched.

"Down!" Vasili yelled.

Niko dropped to his knees, and a blade skimmed his hood.

"No!" A ribbon of black flame unraveled from around Vasili and lashed outward.

Niko twisted, falling sideways in the snow as Vasili

bore down on the elf behind him. Vasili dipped his chin, sent a snarl toward the elf, and the flame—now under Vasili's control—devoured him, scattering his ashes into a whirl of furious snowflakes.

The elves from the rear dashed forward, blades shining. A thought, a flicker, and Niko's flame was on them, pouring over them, drowning and burning them until there was nothing left but their screams in the howling wind.

"Get my dagger!" Vasili ordered, turning his back on Niko.

Niko peeled Vasili's wet cloak away and skimmed his fingers along Vasili's lower back, finding the hidden seam. He plucked a thin butterfly dagger free and hacked at Vasili's ropes. Once free, Vasili took the dagger from Niko's fingers and cut his ties.

Niko grabbed his hand and pulled him into the storm. Didn't matter where. The drifting snow would cover their footprints. To the elves, it would appear as though they'd vanished. Vasili's hand in his became the single most important thing. He focused on that, and on moving forward, pushing through the blizzard one step at a time.

A glance back revealed trees with snowflakes funneling between their wide trunks, but no elves.

They'd done it.

Now they just had to survive the storm. He pulled on Vasili's hand, received a furious glare in return, and reeled the shivering prince into his arms.

"You'll get us b-both killed," Vasili stuttered, suffering from the cold.

Niko couldn't stop the grin, and when Vasili's brow pinched even harder, his smile grew. "At least we'll die free."

Shivers wracked the prince. He hunkered closer, fitting neatly in Niko's arms. They had to get out of the wind, find an old animal den somewhere, some shelter, anything.

Vasili stilled suddenly, his body as rigid as ice. "Niko... They're in the trees," he whispered.

Cold dread seized Niko's heart.

Elves dropped from the branches, landing all around, and, in a matter of seconds, surrounded them.

Damn them to Etara's hell!

Niko summoned the flame to his fingertips, felt the dark creep into his mind and tasted the desire to destroy them all, but in those precious seconds, the elves surged. Niko lashed out. He caught one, washing the dark over him, turning him to ash, but more plowed in, unafraid.

Vasili snapped a warning. His grip vanished from Niko's, and Niko whirled to see elves had their blades pressed to his throat. They wouldn't kill him. They needed him. Blood dribbled down the blade. "Don't."

Vasili's eye turned black, and his lips twitched, and now the raw power inside him was very much alive.

One of the elves struck him on the back of the head, knocking him out cold. *Niko would kill them all!* Pain slashed across his lower back, stealing the strength from his legs. He was on his knees next, staring at the bloody snow, watching the flame snuff from his fingers.

The blow to this head made all the trees spin into silent darkness.

HE WOKE ACHING and hollow on his side, wrists tied behind him to a wide, vertical pole propping up a conical tent. A campfire cast enough light to see a few scattered fur-lined bedrolls and a circle of cut logs making up a seating area.

Thoughts slow and broken, Niko struggled to his knees and pulled on the ties holding his wrists to the pole, not expecting them to give. The effort made his gut roll. He gathered the saliva in his mouth and spat.

The ground was dry, packed hard from use, and scattered with dried leaves. Murmurings from multiple elf voices outside the tent provided a low background rumble.

Then this was their main camp? How had he gotten here? They'd fled, and...

The snow... the flame...

Vasili!

"Hey!" Niko pulled harder at the ties holding his wrists to the pole. Digging his boots in, he leveraged all his strength into uprooting the pole. It didn't give, and the effort left him gasping.

"Hey!" he croaked again.

They'd taken his cloak. As far as he could tell, he wasn't hurt beyond the dull thumping down the back of his neck. They hadn't bled him. Yet. But Vasili... Gods, he needed to know he was all right or, by Etara, he'd unleash the flame and everything he had on the wretched beasts.

He stilled his thoughts and closed his eyes, letting his body go slack and his mind blank, inviting the flame to take hold.

Nothing happened.

Blinking hard, he shifted to his feet and tried again, sighing this time. Usually the power was eager to be free and would rush to his fingertips.

Still nothing.

What...

He kicked at the ground. Salt glittered under the leaf litter. That answered the question as to whether they suspected he had the flame. "Bastards," Niko cursed. "Hey! You savage pricks! Come face me then. Cowards. *Gods-damned creature-cowards.*" He yelled until his voice was hoarse. Nobody came, and his rage dwindled, leaving him cold and spent.

They had Vasili.

They would lock him in a cage. He'd fight, he'd survive, but not without collecting fresh scars to add to those already running deep.

Niko swallowed a useless sob and used it to fuel his hate instead. As soon as an elf came close enough, he'd rip into them. He'd remind them exactly who he was— what he was: The butcher who had turned their own savage methods against them. He'd cut them, bled them, made them beg.

And he'd do it all again to save Vasili.

But the hours passed, and the light seeping in through the tent's seams changed, turning brighter.

Daylight, perhaps. Thirsty and shivering now the fire had burned down to embers, he slumped against the pole and wondered how it had come to this.

There had been no sign of elves at Bucland Manor, and none at the palace, and again during their escape attempt, until suddenly they were everywhere, dropping from boughs and branches, too many to fight.

They'd been in the trees all along, at Bucland too when he'd heard the snapping twigs. That's why he hadn't seen any tracks in the snow. The elves had watched them for days, waiting for Vasili to emerge. Clever bastards. He'd give them that. Too damn clever.

The only thing that mattered now was getting Vasili away from them.

An elf pushed through the tent flap. Female, clad in strips of stitched leather. She avoided his glare and circled behind him.

Niko yanked at his wrists. "Where's Vasili?" Her rough fingers clamped onto his arm, and a hot stinging sizzled his skin where she began to cut. "Hey." He jerked, trying to pull free, but only succeeded in moving an inch. "Where's Vasili? My friend? You have him? What have you done with him?"

Her grey lashes fluttered, but there was no other indication she heard or understood a damn word.

"Where is he? Is he close?"

Her probing fingers delivered a burn inside his wrists, and the tickle of liquid ran down his arm. He gritted his teeth. Raging at her was useless. She was nothing. A grunt. He needed to catch the eye of a senior—a chief. Someone with authority. He'd met the higher elves, killed some at the front. They'd never bargain, but they might gloat and reveal if Vasili was alive and if he was close.

Nikolas's only chance was to get free of the salt and unleash Etara's hell on them all. There would be an opportunity. There always was. He just had to find it, and soon, before they broke Vasili all over again.

The elf left. The cut she'd made in his wrist began to throb, adding to the ache in his head. He needed to piss, but there was little chance of any humane treatment from elves. He was lucky he still had his fingers and ears. Those were usually the first to go.

More hours passed, and he let his bladder go. His capture, being tied, cut, it didn't hurt. He'd been through worse. What hurt was every second he thought of Vasili being held down. They'd cut him with their blades and drink from his veins. Always from his front, so he had nowhere to hide. Making him watch with the one eye they'd left him with.

What if they took his other eye?

Gods, this fucking *waiting* was torture!

The tent flap opened, and a tall, stocky elf entered— armed to the teeth with two recurve short swords at his hips. His green-skinned body was covered in simple scraps of leather knotted together with clumsy, thick stitching. The way he carried himself, head up, back straight, his swagger confident, suggested he was important. Their ages were always difficult to determine. All were rough-skinned and gnarled, but this one had a quick sharpness to his gaze that suggested some youthfulness to him. His type was the most difficult to kill.

He stopped so damn close that Niko could smell the oil from his leathers. The elf studied Niko up close, reading every line in his face.

"Get a good look." Recognition stalled his thoughts. He'd met his elf before, in the Yazdan prison. This elf had fashioned a crude lock pick from a tin can, freed Niko from the cell, and fled.

The elf's lips curved upward into a savage grin. His teeth were sharp, meant for tearing meat from bone. *"Butcher,"* the elf dragged the word out, making it less a word and more a guttural sound. Niko heard its meaning all the same.

Niko grinned back. "You know my name. What's yours?"

He made a sound like *"La-sh-ugah."* The nearest Niko could translate was *Lasher*. *"Ehndnusdus,"* Lasher grunted, making no sense.

"Where's Vasili?" Niko asked. The elf blinked and cocked his head. "Where. The fuck. Is Vasili?!"

Lasher bared his teeth in a grin or a leer and turned on his heel.

"Hey!" Niko bucked against the beam. "Hey! Damn you! Tell me. Do whatever you want to me, but don't hurt him!"

The tent flap fell back behind him, leaving Niko once again alone.

CHAPTER 8

 asili

ROPES BURNED HIS WRISTS. His knees sank in the mud, wetness soaking through his clothes, chilling his skin. Elves growled and snarled all around like the nightmare had never ended. Only, he wasn't dreaming. Escaping had been the dream.

Perhaps it had never ended. He'd escaped in his head, dreamed of another life, another world, a world in which Nikolas had saved him. A dream in which he'd tried to claw at scraps of control, tried to make a difference. He'd lost a brother, killed his father, gained an enemy, and a lover. But none of that had been real. It couldn't have been. Because elves were all around again. Shoving at him. Pushing him down. Leering. Grunting.

He couldn't do this.

A rough hand cruelly grabbed his chin and jerked his

97

head up. Long nails dug into his cheek. The elf holding him sneered, grunted words lost behind the heavy thumping of Vasili's heart. He knew this one from before. Their leader, their chief. He'd been the one to order his torture, the one Talos had planned to return Vasili to as some pathetic peace offering.

Cold, hard steel pressed against Vasili's cheek, the dagger point resting below his unscarred eye. Fear turned his insides to water and his skin to ice. No, not his eye. Anything but his remaining eye. Fingers, ears... his cock, even. *Just not the eye!*

Arguments raged among the elves. Vasili barely heard them. He stared at the chief, stitching every last detail into his memory. If this were to be the last thing he ever saw, he would remember it all. Every line around the elf's thick, snarling mouth. Every scar potting the elf's grey skin. The slate grey of the elf's hollow eyes. The strings of long hair, knotted with stones and twigs.

Vasili stared into the eyes of his enemy and knew... If this were to be his end, he'd take them all down with him. Including their king.

Another elf appeared and tore the chief from Vasili. This new one was bigger, angrier. They shoved and fought and roared.

Vasili choked on fear, gasping for air. He'd fought before. Fought for years. For so long. Forever. He'd fought for hope, for a people who hated him, for a dying kingdom, for a freedom he'd never have. He'd fought because there was no other way. But he could not fight this. *Them.* Again. Not like he had. They would tie him down, they'd take his remaining eye, and they'd drain his body of blood. He'd be hollow again, and he couldn't stand it.

Hands grabbed his arms, hauling him backward through the mud. "No!" His heels dug gouges, leaving tracks in the mud. He couldn't survive this. He knew it as surely as he knew what came next. *"No—don't!"*

The ropes holding his wrists were cut, but not to free him. His coat was torn free. He rocked as they yanked and pulled and shoved him between them. His shirt tore, buttons flying. His wrists were caught again. A shove and he was on his back, blinking at the tent canopy. They spread his arms outward. Fresh ropes bit into his wrists, holding him down. Always on his back... nowhere to hide.

He closed his eye. Every small cut, every kiss of cold metal at his chest, the warm slither of weeping blood, the stroke of warm tongues. No... he'd never been free. This was his life, as it had been forever.

Nikolas was here—in his memory, telling him to fight, to never surrender—but Nikolas was a dream of a broken mind, and dreams weren't real.

He'd fought before, and days had turned to weeks to months to years. He'd fight again, one last time...

This time, he could choose to end it, make these wretched elves pay. They'd brought him back, thinking him their weak and hollow prince—the same boy they'd bled in a cage. The prince with no voice. Oh, but he had a voice now, one full of rage.

All that fighting would cost him this time was control.

Nikolas would call it surrender. He'd blame Vasili for

all the wrongs he could not fix. But fighting his fate had only gotten him closer to it. All he had left was surrender.

Thick, muscular tongues lapped at his wrists. The wet sounds of their feasting filled his ears. Some scuffle was still happening nearby, elves squabbling like carrion birds over scraps of meat.

He'd endured enough.

Salt dried the air he dragged across his lips. He recalled the glitter of it on the ground when they'd dragged him into the tent. The salt would have been enough before, when he'd had only a fraction of the flame burning within him. Now he was half its whole. Now the darkness brimmed and simmered within, desperate for escape.

Surrender, it whispered. *Surrender and kill them all.*

He'd always imagined the flame would take him quickly. But as he sighed and let go of the relentless battle, it crept through him slowly, savoring every given inch of body and mind. Like submerging into a hot bath and sinking beneath the surface. The first to go was sound. He wept in receipt of silence. Next, the physical agony faded—their wretched touch, their horrid invasion—gone behind a shield of numbness.

He was falling; it was already too late to reclaim himself.

He heard in his mind the memory of Nikolas telling him how one day he'd be his assassin. As the flame devoured Vasili's body, that day had come.

CHAPTER 9

iko

THE RUCKUS outside the tent dragged him from a dreamless sleep. Moans and howls filled the night.

Someone ran by the closed tent flap, their shadow there and gone again. A low wail rose, abruptly ending in silence. Other screams were rising too, but not retreating, just ending, brutally cut off sounds Niko knew well from when he'd driven blades through elf bodies. A battle raged outside, but one with no clash of swords or shouts of men. Fighting did not accompany the dying. But how was that possible?

Gooseflesh shivered across his skin.

The big elf, Lasher, burst through the tent flap and dropped to the ground beside Niko. He took a knife from his belt and severed the ties at his wrists with a quick flick.

Niko slumped forward, rubbing his raw wrists. Lasher was letting him go? "What's happening?"

The elf grabbed his shoulder, heaved him onto unsteady feet, and shoved him out the tent. He staggered in the mud. Campfires spluttered, their embers rising into the strange, red-hued dusk's light. And all around, elves knelt in silence. Hundreds of them, their heads bowed and shoulders low. It didn't seem real or possible.

What madness was this?

Lasher shoved him forward again, keeping Niko moving. None of the kneeling elves stood. Some were bloody, some bore wounds so dire they shouldn't have even been upright.

Movement ahead drew Niko's eye. A man emerged from the gloom—his pale body wrapped in a cloak of shadows. Blood wept from countless new scars on his chest and arms. His white hair blazed like icy fire. His eye glistened like black glass.

A half smile lifted the left side of the prince's lips. A smile not his own.

Lasher's fingers dug into Niko's shoulder, holding him out, like a shield.

"Vasili?"

The sounds of the crackling fire and the crunch of his boots through encrusted snow disturbed the heavy silence.

Vasili stopped several strides away. He dipped his chin, lifting his gaze to peer through pale lashes, and swept a hand to encompass his bowed audience. *"See how they kneel."* An echo of a voice overlaid Vasili's, just like it had with Talos when the flame had writhed free of the king's bonds.

After a lifetime fighting his destiny, Vasili had surrendered.

Niko's heart sank. "No." He stumbled forward and received a dagger-like glance, stopping him dead. He could get him back, like he had before. "Vasili, this isn't you."

"Clearly, you have not been paying attention. I am who I was meant to be. The question remains, Nikolas, are you strong enough to stand against me?"

How? He had no weapons and was weak from hunger. What could he say or do that would change what was already done?

"They thought to bind me, to bleed me, to consume me!" The laughter that bubbled from Vasili was nothing like his own. *"They will die for that mistake."*

Niko's only weapon was the flame itself, the same flame burning his Caville from the inside out. He freed it with a thought, letting it drip from his fingertips. Other shadows moved in the night, but whether they'd come to his aid or to kill him, he couldn't be sure.

Vasili saw his hesitation and chuckled. *"The power you wield is mine."*

He turned and walked back, between both flanks of kneeling elves. His blood in their veins, their minds his to control, exactly like the possessed palace soldiers. An army of elves at his disposal. Had the flame always wanted this?

"Vasili, fight it! You must!" Niko freed the hold on the dark within him, lashing it toward Vasili, but Vasili merely laughed as he walked away. His cloak of shadows rippled over the kneeling elves, and when it receded, ash ate at their silent bodies, adding to the campfire embers floating in the air. They died in silence, consumed within by the power they'd stolen. And then Vasili was gone, vanished into the night, falling ash and the absence of elves the only evidence of his vengeance.

Niko dropped to his knees, sending up puffs of ash. He'd failed to protect him from this. He'd promised to save him, he'd promised to stop him, and he'd done none of those things. He'd just... let him go.

The camp lay still. The fires still burned, but Vasili had erased the elves. All but one.

Lasher snarled, tugging on Niko's arm.

Vasili was lost. He should go after him, but to what end?

Gods, Niko wasn't strong enough for this. Maybe he'd never been.

The elf got both hands under Niko's arm and heaved him to his feet.

"Go," the elf snarled, shoving him.

Niko tore free so fast he almost stumbled over. "Fucking touch me, and I'll break every bone you need to stand, elf!"

The elf bared his teeth and lunged. Niko jerked away, but this time his boot slipped in the slushy mud, and the elf had him in his grip again, trying to wrestle him back to his feet. Despair flipped to blinding rage. Niko twisted, yanking the elf down, unbalancing them both. Niko's knee sank in the mud. He grabbed for the elf's neck. Lasher blocked him and slammed the ball of his palm into Niko's gut. The blow landed hard, instantly ripping the air from Niko's lungs. Lasher's elbow struck Niko's jaw, and the next Niko knew, he was facedown, mud seeping between his lips. He spluttered, crawled on his hands and knees, and, wiping his face, he staggered back to his feet. "You want to join your friends?"

The elf stood back, caked in mud, his grey eyes pinched and teeth exposed in warning. But he hadn't reached for the array of blades strapped to him. Did he think Niko not worthy of those blades? That mistake made him a fool.

If Niko could get a grip on one of his blades, this fight would be over.

Lasher pointed into the dark. "*Go.*" His growling voice butchered the word, but its meaning was clear.

Niko staggered forward, thoughts unanchored in the storm of hurt and rage and fear. He lurched, took a swing at Lasher. The elf danced to one side, and Niko grabbed for the exposed blade at his hip. The fist came out of nowhere and struck his jaw like a hammerblow, throwing Niko onto his hands in the mud a second time. He spat blood, dug his fingers into the soupy mire and ash, and levered himself upright again.

The elf still stood and stared, weapons untouched, face hard.

Niko's rage twitched inside. If he could just get a damned weapon... He dabbed at his split lip, spilling blood over his muddy hand. The campfires still burned, and the ash still swirled, and the damned elf stood there, clearly capable of taking one of those blades and running Niko through. Weak, bruised, exhausted, and unarmed... Niko was losing this fight.

He swayed, almost falling again. The short-lived anger had abandoned him, and now everything hurt. He didn't know what to do, where to go, how or who to fight. Vasili was fucking gone, his mind lost to the flame, and Niko had *nothing*. "Kill me then!"

"Go," the elf barked.

Go. Like he could just walk into the night after Vasili and make everything right.

"What do you want from me?!" Niko yelled.

Lasher pulled one of his curved blades free and marched toward Niko. He almost welcomed the death this elf was about to deliver. Wasn't it all he deserved after failing the prince? After failing at everything.

Lasher grabbed Niko's wrist, reversed his grip on the blade, and pressed the blade handle into Niko's palm.

Niko frowned. What was this? Some trick?

Lasher stepped back and pointed into the night. "Butcher, go."

Was he mad? What was to stop Niko from running the blade through him right now?

Lasher made a low warning growl, then ducked back into the tent. He reemerged moments later with a coat, cloak, and traveling bag and dumped it all at Niko's feet.

Then Lasher threw on his own cloak, heaved a bag over his shoulder, and started walking toward the edge of the camp. He was almost at the farthest edges when he turned and barked some mangled word again.

Niko scanned the empty camp. The fires would die and the scavengers would come. Vasili was gone. There was nothing here for him. He was free, with a blade in his hand, and all he had to do was follow an elf into the dark.

He buried the blade into his pack, threw on the coat and cloak, scooped up the bag, and started after the elf.

CHAPTER 10

*Y*asir

THE GLASS GARDENS were his favorite of all the Yazdans' gardens scattered about Seran. The grounds appeared artfully neglected and overgrown, which was perhaps why the elves, after sacking much of the city, had left these grounds largely intact.

Yasir trotted Adamo down the now-familiar pathway. Tropical plants, their great leaves and branches fed by underground springs, offered shade from the sun. In the distance, atop its hill, the red castle-like outline of the Yazdan house was silhouetted by the setting sun. From this distance, it looked abandoned, but he knew from his supply runs that there was activity within.

In the several weeks since escaping the elves at Loreen, he'd thought only of Liam's safety, which meant retreating south, to the only place he called home. In all his years as a seaman, all the ports and bays and exotic faraway lands, he always returned to Seran, and not just because the price of silk was already generous here. Seran had a vibrancy, a beating heart, that touched Yasir's soul. Or perhaps it wasn't so much the city he loved, but its people, Liam among them. The glass gardens were where they'd first met; Liam as a banquet server and Yasir as Roksana's well-known silk merchant. It seemed fitting he and Liam make this place their temporary home while considering their next move.

Adamo trotted by a glass sculpture, one of many throughout the grounds. Some had been smashed, but a few gems remained, glittering in the red-tinged light.

Yasir dismounted Adamo, tied him loosely to a palm, and pushed in through the door of the timber-built gardeners' hut. Liam looked up from the book and grinned but quickly returned to deciphering its pages. "Any news?"

"Nothing of any use." Yasir removed his hat and jacket and set both down, then poured some tea from the warm pot. "But every day I see a new street cleared. The market looks ready to function again. It's remarkable, really."

The city was broken but not beaten. So long as the elves stayed away. *Why* they stayed away was something nobody appeared to know, but nobody questioned it either.

Yasir leaned against the small counter and sipped the drink, eyeing Liam with his nose buried in the Bucland book.

"It says here—it's damaged, but I can put fragments together—the nasdas was a part of this world when it was wild and chaotic, making monsters for Etara's wars, but when Aura and Walla suggested they bring balance to the world instead of chaos, Etara was forced to"—he pressed a finger to the page and squinted—"brush or *sweep* the nasdas aside." He looked up. "The language used... It suggests the nasdas could be Etara's child—she made it, and when it was discarded, its rage grew, and instead of just..." He waved a hand. "...going away like the gods wanted, it lashed out, seeding chaos and binding the *beasts beyond the shadows*, which I think we can safely assume are those creatures you can... er, command." He looked away. The subject of binding had always unsettled him, as did the manner in which Yasir had come to adopt such *yudu*—bad magic, as he called it —by sampling Vasili's blood.

"Then it's a petulant child with a god-like talent for destruction." That didn't bode well. "Anything on how to stop it?"

Liam flicked back to the page featuring the faceless man. "Nothing certain. It was trapped in a man by the sorcerer Zarqa', who used its own power against it somehow, so it can be captured, but..." Liam frowned. "Honestly, I don't know. There are sections missing, torn out, or just so faded I can't read them. It does seem to point to everything being exceedingly bad if it should get free of its vessel."

Liam talked some more about the old legends. Yasir listened, cupping his mug in both hands and breathing in the sweet aroma of mint tea. Through the tiny hut window, he saw Adamo's tail switch, and flies lazily danced in the shafts of sunlight filtering through the plants.

He should be north with Niko and Vasili. He should have stayed with them, fought alongside them, instead of running away. But Liam... The elves had been on his tail for days, and by the time he'd shaken them, he was already halfway to Seran. Vasili had made it clear Liam should return south. Niko too. And so here he was. In a hut. Drinking tea.

Liam folded the book closed, tucked it under the chair's cushion, and joined Yasir at the counter. He looped an arm around his waist and leaned in, nuzzling close to Yasir's jaw in the way he knew he couldn't resist. "The book was hidden for a reason," he said. "I'll find something we can use, I know it."

Yasir tried to smile reassuringly, but Liam's teasing hold hardened some as he scanned Yasir's face.

Vasili and Niko could be dead. He didn't say it, because every time he thought it, he resented Liam for taking him away from his friends, but he loved him too. So what was he supposed to do with that? He and Liam had never really been in an official relationship, at least, they'd never voiced it. But Yasir had always found his way back to him after months at sea, and Liam had always opened his door, even if it was sometimes accompanied by a raging argument.

He couldn't sit and wait and drink tea for much longer. "There will be Yazdans in Seran." Yasir set his cup down, and, sensing his change in mood, Liam withdrew. "Not Alissand. We need to stay away from his sorcerers. But someone useful."

"Roksana?" Liam guessed, taking himself across the small hut to perch on the edge of his chair.

Roksana was resourceful and intelligent. If she were alive, she'd still be nearby. "She's the most reasonable of them all."

"Didn't she help *capture* Vasili?"

"Yes." Yasir squeezed his eyes closed and pinched the bridge of his nose. "I just... If I can talk with her, maybe I can convince her Vasili is more than the flame. That he's worth fighting for, not fighting against. Frankly, it's all I can think of."

"Or maybe she'll kill you," Liam said, adding a dash of heated Seranian sass to his voice.

"She won't."

Liam crossed his legs at the knee and planted both hands on top. "Why not?"

"Because she has a weakness for fine silk, and I know where her last shipment is."

"At the bottom of the harbor?"

The air had chilled some at Liam's icy tone. Yasir knelt at his feet and placed his hands on his warm thigh, gently stroking higher. "*Walla's Heart* isn't in the harbor. She's in Bahrakan Bay, a few miles up the coast. I sent some crew to haul her anchor before the elves scuttled all the ships. There's no reason to believe she's moved."

"I'm not going to sea with you, precious."

"I would never ask you to." He raised Liam's fingers to his lips and lightly kissed them. "I must do something, Liam. I can't stand by. If I find Roksana and just... speak with her, I know I can help. For Vasili."

Liam uncrossed his legs and, leaning forward, stroked Yasir's cheek, his face suddenly sympathetic. "You care for him?"

Did he care for Vasili? Care wasn't the right word. The prince had intrigued him since he'd sauntered over in a northern tavern and offered to buy Yasir lunch. "Ah... it's complicated."

Liam bowed his head, closed his eyes, and sighed. "Do you love him?" he asked, looking up and straight into Yasir's gaze.

"No." He tipped Liam's chin up. "I love only one man."

Liam's smile had turned sly now he was on surer ground. "But Vasili is a prince."

"You're my prince."

"He's very pretty."

"So are you."

"Flatterer." A blush tinted Liam's face.

Yasir kissed him softly, a small brush of the lips, a tease more than a kiss, and Liam sighed closer. Liam loved him. He'd loved him since they met in the garden outside when Yasir had spent the night sweet-talking him. It was an honest love, and he gave it freely.

"Don't hate me for bringing you home," Liam said quietly, the tip of his tongue wetting his lips.

"I don't—" He looked away.

Liam caught his chin and turned his face toward him. "*Walla's Heart* is more than your ship, she's your soul. You were never meant to be anchored. I know it,

I've always known it. I'm grateful for any time I have with you before you're gone again. I won't keep you here. I'd never forgive myself if you thought me an anchor."

"Liam, I don't think that."

Liam let go but bent closer. "We're going to save them. Both of them." His stern expression lightened. "We're going to get through this. I feel it." He took Yasir's hand and placed it over his heart. "You feel it too, don't you? Aura's grace shines on us."

He did not deserve this man. He wasn't sure if anyone did. He was too precious, and if anything happened to him, the world would be a darker place. "I do," he said quietly. Any louder and Liam might hear the tremor in his voice.

Liam grinned. "Good." He let his hand drop. "So how do we find Roksana?"

iko

EVERY DAY and every mile they walked brought a new horror. It began with the smell of ash in the air, then the taste of it on his tongue, and it ended in a landscape scarred by flame. Charred earth, pine trees stripped of their needles and scorched where they stood. Grass turned to ash underfoot and mixed with snow. A world of color and life turned grey and empty.

When he'd left the elf camp a week ago, following Lasher down a path he didn't know, he'd wondered a great many things. Would Vasili survive the cold, would he go south, did he have a plan, or was there nothing of the prince now the flame controlled him?

Vasili would have stopped it by now, if he had the means. Any hope that he could wrestle it back under control was fast fading. The path of devastation meant it was getting stronger.

This was what Talos had almost surrendered to. This was what Vasili had been fighting his whole life against. This was the same desire burning in Niko's veins, itching to be set free.

He and Lasher trudged on, clothes streaked with ash and wet from melting snow. The elf rarely spoke and when he did, it was usually in two-word grunts. Niko still expected a trick, but the farther they marched from the east and out of elf territory, the less Lasher seemed likely to attack. So what did an elf want with Niko? Niko had repeatedly asked him over their evening campfires but received only a dry look in reply.

On the ninth day, the grey-walled city of Loreen with its many spires loomed in the distance. Vasili's path had led him home.

Niko wordlessly walked through the ash and might have walked right up to the city gates if the path hadn't veered south in front of them.

He stood where the ash ceased and the city began and stared up at the huge city gates.

"Follow," Lasher grunted, urging Niko south.

The gates lay open, held in place by mounds of snow. Nobody was left to lock them. Vasili had fought for Loreen, and now it lay in ruin. He'd fought against the elves, against the flame, for the people, and nobody had cared or listened. They'd wanted the curse inside the prince, not the man himself. The only surprise in all of this was that Vasili hadn't surrendered sooner. "I can't stop him," he said.

"Butcher stop nasdas," Lasher grunted—the same words he'd grunted a hundred times.

"*How?*" Vasili,or the nasdas—whatever it was now controlled the same power Niko had in his veins. It had *laughed* when he'd tried to stand against it. "How, elf?! When it can do this?" He gestured at the dead scar in the landscape. "I have nothing to fight him with!"

Lasher marched up to eye Niko. "Butcher mend. Or all die."

"You're the ones who want to free the damn thing." This was absurd. He should kill this elf, take his blades and his provisions, and continue after Vasili alone. He wasn't sure why he hadn't. Maybe because Lasher had hunted and cooked the rabbit and grouse they'd found, lit and managed the campfires, found water to drink. This elf almost seemed *reasonable*. But they all killed ruthlessly and mercilessly. So this nonsense had to be a trick, but to what end? To use him perhaps, like the others of his kind had used Julian?

"Why are you here?" Niko asked, his voice carrying far through the city gates and into abandoned streets. "Is this what you want?" He gestured at the dead earth again. "You want the nasdas free? You want its power?"

The big elf's flinty eyes seemed to say he was getting impatient. Well, so was Niko. "End prince," Lasher said.

Kill Vasili. Of course. And set the flame free.

Niko shook his head. "No." He looked at the palace and how it clung to ancient rocks. Its empty towers clawed at the grey sky. The cage was still beneath its maze-like tunnels. A cage to hold a Caville.

He'd had plenty of time to think since the elves had

dragged them from those tunnels. That cage was where it had begun seven hundred years ago. A Caville must forever hold the flame. "There has to be another way," he whispered.

Lasher glowered then pointed over Niko's shoulder at the abandoned palace. "Nasdas keys. Elves kill keys."

Gods, he was so tired of this elf-bastard's cryptic shit. "The keys are the families," he growled back. "Kill them all and the nasdas goes free. Just like you've killed tens of thousands of people for. Your kind *wants* it free. You want power and chaos. We've been trying to stop you for hundreds of years! Gods, I don't know why I'm talking to a fucking elf." He started down the road, stirring ash about his boots, lifting its taste into the air. He'd grown sick of tasting death and of talking to an elf.

"Not all families, just keys," Lasher called.

Niko turned. *"What does that mean?"*

"Not all elves want." He thumped his chest. "Chief bleed prince for blood. Chief dead. Nasdas kill him." He pointed to himself. "Not want blood." He waved a hand at the sky. "Many elves not want blood, just *end*."

Niko eyed him again, this warrior elf. As tall as Niko and muscled from a life honed to kill. He didn't wear human tokens, severed fingers or ears, like some of the rest of his kin and hadn't shown any of their grotesque desires. His grey eyes were shrewd, always watching, never distant. "Then why attack the Yazdan house? Remember? You were there. You freed me from that cell. Why?"

Lasher nodded, sensing a moment of understanding. "End keys. End nasdas. End fight."

End the nasdas and the elves would stop fighting? Who *was* this elf? Did he have authority, or was he just a grunt, like Niko? "Kings make truces, not soldiers." Niko turned away again and trudged on. This elf could say anything, but without any authority, it meant nothing. "The world won't listen to us, elf." Besides, ending the nasdas would see Vasili dead, and that wasn't happening. He'd watch the world burn to see his prince safe.

Niko chuckled at his madness. Etara, listen to him. He'd sacrifice countless lives and lands for the love of a man. And not even a good man. But there were few men in this world more worthy of saving than Vasili Caville. Besides, Niko had already made an oath: *The good man.* The man he'd take away and carve out a life with. Vasili had made him swear it, not knowing Niko already knew that good man; that man he was destined to save just happened to be wrapped up in layers of lies and deceit. The good man was the part of Vasili that Vasili seemed so desperate to hate. The man with no voice of his own. Nothing in this world was going to stop Niko from saving him, or the wretched, vicious, wonderful bastard he was at all other times.

"Kill," Lasher urged, quickly catching up.

"Gods, elf. I'll kill you if you don't quit the orders."

"Nasdas must—"

"The nasdas can fuck off, and if you continue to push me on this, this little truce will be as dead as you once I'm done."

Lasher narrowed his eyes. He understood the sentiment, if not the words.

"I'll find him," Niko sighed, "and I'm saving him, no matter what the world, the elves, the fucking Yazdans, or anyone wants." He pushed the dread of the iron cage and its possible meaning from his mind, adjusted the traveling pack, and glared at the fog-choked dead forest they were about to plunge into.

Yasir and Liam would be together somewhere, and Yasir would be working on something to help. And gods, Niko needed him, because if his gut was right, then Vasili was heading south to find the Yazdans, to slaughter them all, and while there, he'd find Amir and kill him, like he'd been unable to in Loreen. He'd reunite the flame with all the pieces of itself.

Gods help them if he succeeded.

 asir

ADAMO SHIED as Yasir had him approach the cliff edge. A hot wind gusted, spooking the horse some more, bringing with it the occasional bubble of laughter from the crew aboard the ship anchored in the bay below.

Walla's Heart. Yasir's ship. But *not* his crew.

"Thieving wretched pirates." He leaned forward in the saddle and studied the flag fluttering on the ship's pole, colors unfurled. A black flame on gold. The Yazdan crest. With no luck finding Roksana in Seran, he'd come to the bay in the hopes his crew would have news. Instead, he'd found the very woman he'd been looking for.

Whirling Adamo, he cantered the horse back into the shelter of the heathland and to Liam waiting on his own mount. "Not good," he said. "The Yazdans have her."

"What are you going to do?" Liam asked.

"A parley, I suppose."

"And if it's Alissand aboard?" Liam's tone wobbled some, probably at the memory of his capture under the shah.

Yasir didn't relish the thought of meeting Alissand again either. "Then we find somewhere safe to wait all this out." He turned his face away, casting a glance toward the road that would take them down into the bay, and hoped Liam didn't hear the lie. It was only a small lie. Liam *would* be safe, he'd make sure of that, but if the Yazdans weren't friendly, then Yasir was returning north. He'd let Niko down in not telling him about Alissand capturing Liam. He couldn't let him down again.

"Wait at the crossroads by the brook," he told Liam. "If I'm not back by dusk, return to the gardeners' hut. Don't wait forever." The line was the same he tossed out like a joke every time they parted, but this time it was real. Walla's ocean hadn't taken him in all the years he'd ridden her waves; the Yazdans weren't going to take him now.

Liam gathered his reins and turned his horse, reining alongside Adamo. "Be careful, Yasir. They have dark *yudu*."

He trotted his horse away, and, when Yasir was sure Liam was out of earshot, Yasir added, "So do I."

When this was all over, if it ever ended, and Seran had risen from its rubble once more, he'd offer Liam more of himself. Perhaps ask him to be wedded. Yasir turned Adamo toward the bay and smiled at the thought. Although, if Liam knew what was good for him, he'd decline.

The sun was riding high in Aura's blue skies by the time he walked Adamo onto the beach. *Walla's Heart* had never looked so fine as she did anchored in the sheltered waters. She'd survived the elves unscathed, even if she was sailing under the wrong captain.

He plodded Adamo to the gentle surf's edge. Moments passed before shouts rose and the crew launched the skiff. He couldn't make out the occupants, just four cloaked figures. If they were Alissand's men, at least while at sea their stolen power would be less, like Vasili's and his had been during their time on the waves.

It seemed an odd place for the Yazdans to find sanctuary.

The skiff approached, oars hard at work. Yasir backed Adamo from the boat as it rode the gentle waves. The woman at the front cut a striking figure with the red sash at her hips and multiple golden earrings jangling in one ear. Roksana.

Well, then. Tired of waiting for his silks, she'd taken his ship instead.

Her crewman lifted their oars and rode the skiff onto the beach. Roksana jumped into the shallow surf and waded up the sand. Two gem-encrusted pistols adorned her hips, accompanied by a recurved Yazdan blade.

Her tanned face wore only the slightest wrinkles of age. Her dark hair was bound in multiple braids and those in turn bound into one thick tail that lay over her shoulder. She hadn't changed at all.

"Ah, Yasir. I thought it was you."

"Did you?"

She tapped her head, indicating his hat.

He promptly frowned at the woman who was sometimes his spice and silk buyer, sometimes advisor, and regrettably once a bedfellow among two others, long ago now. "You appear to have helped yourself to my ship, Roksana."

She glanced behind her, as though forgetting where she'd come from. "That old thing? I found it here with barely a single crewman aboard."

"You know very well she's mine."

"Well, needs-must and all that. We did have something of an elf problem, of which this ship miraculously escaped. How convenient. Almost as if her captain knew of the attack before it happened."

He did not appreciate such an accusation. "I was in Seran, Roksana. At the harbor, in fact, when the elves came. We were woefully unprepared, thanks to your brother. Alissand abandoned everyone for his own selfish reasons, leaving you to protect the city. He abandoned us all." He watched her closely and caught her wince before she hid it behind her typically broad and very convincing smile. He gave her his own fake smile as Adamo shifted restlessly beneath him. "The Yazdans were supposed to protect Seran. Your family failed us."

She tucked her thumbs into her belt. "You can blame that on your Prince Vasili. Had he not swept through us at the funeral, decimating—"

"Amir killed your father, not Vasili."

"Amir, Vasili, Cavilles are all the same."

"They're not, and you know it. You just don't want to see Vasili because he stands against everything you've been told." He paused, assessing her mood. She didn't rush to argue, and her dark eyes looked on, so he took that as his cue to continue. "We are not our families, we're not the past, and if we don't change things, we won't have a future to look forward to. Your lover—you've never told me her name, but I know she exists—you protected her fiercely from all this. Did she survive?"

Roksana turned her face toward the sea. "She did."

"And what future do you see with her now?"

She bowed her head, and when looking up again, her smile had vanished. "I agree, this was not how things should have happened. But Yazdans do not conspire with Cavilles. That is what you came here for? To convince me your prince is good?"

"If I were to try and convince you of that, we'd both know it to be a lie. He's not good, but he is all we have left to fight a greater war."

"Hmm. I'd agree with you, but Alissand brought a gift back from the north."

Did she mean Vasili? Had Alissand recaptured him? Surely not. Yasir's heart pounded as he tried to keep his face blank. "What gift?"

"The *other* prince. Younger, stockier, more spiteful. *That* one."

"Impossible." Yasir laughed in relief. "Amir is dead. I

saw the body myself. You will have to try harder, Roksana."

Her frown tipped. "He's certainly not well, but he is most definitely alive. Alissand has him."

"But I saw Amir's body."

"I don't know what to tell you, other than he's alive."

He'd seen the body, as real as day. Vasili had plunged the dagger into his brother's chest and the flame had erupted around them both. But if Amir was alive, then Vasili's fatal blow had missed. And Vasili had *lied*.

Yasir spat a curse under his breath. "Gods-damn him!"

"Your prince isn't worth your devotion, captain." Roksana chuckled. "He's a snake. They've always been that way."

If Amir was alive, it only changed one thing. Vasili did not hold all the flame. "A liar or not, whatever Vasili is, he did not abandon Seran. He came to warn you of the elves—"

"Too late a warning."

"Because you caught him, tied him up, and bled him like an animal!" Adamo stamped and shied. Yasir took a few moments to tighten the reins on the horse and his own frustration. "For years, he sought your counsel. He trusted you." She winced, and, sensing weakness there, he pushed on. "You threw his trust back at him." Another wince. "Alissand abandoned everything for greed and power. Seran fell because of your uncle, not because of Vasili. The prince has never abandoned his duty. He has always fought for his people, for yours, for all of us. He is cursed, nobody denies that, least of all him, but even with that curse, he strives to protect those who cannot protect themselves."

"Vasili Caville is a monster."

"Because nobody gave him a choice," he snapped. Weeks aboard his ship with Vasili, evenings in which spice had weakened the prince's formidable barriers, and Yasir knew the man better than almost anyone, besides Niko. There was no doubt Vasili was in many ways horrible, but he was also the strongest man Yasir had ever met.

"What good has it done him, Yasir?" Roksana's glare sharpened. "His city is lost. His court abandoned. His people flocked to our streets, draining our coffers, and then the elves came and... For all your talk of duty, what good has Vasili done?"

Killed his own father to stop the flame. Kept the curse controlled at great mental cost. Tried to stop the elves from gaining a foothold beyond the front line. "No man can fight a battle alone. He sought your help, knowing his chances were slim. In return, you betrayed him, and your brother bled—"

"I know what Alissand did!" she lashed, suddenly breathless. "Gods, I know it!"

He gave her a moment to settle. "You must see how wrong everything is?"

"And what of you, Yasir? For all your righteous talk, have you not done the same? Have you not bled the prince for power?"

"It was a mistake. But I do not regret it. Those events brought me here and made me a part of this so that I might ask you to reconsider his plea for help.

You're on the wrong side of this war, and I think you know it."

Closing her eyes, she gave her head a shake. "Do you even know where Vasili is?"

"No." He wouldn't tell her if he did.

"Then what use is this conversation?"

"He will return. He'll fight, and when he does, he will not be alone."

She laughed softly. "Always the romantic. The fact remains, we have Amir. Alissand is readying our guards to hold Seran against any and all outside forces, including Vasili."

"Alissand is blinded by his desire for the flame. He cares for nothing else."

She held his gaze. "As long as the flame exists, it must be controlled. This is the Yazdan legacy."

"*A legacy written by Yazdans.* You're better than this, Roksana."

"I can't help you, Yasir." She turned, about to leave, but hesitated and looked up. "Is Niko alive?"

"As far as I know, yes."

"Then he's likely with Vasili. I had hoped he'd see sense."

Adamo whinnied softly and shied, urging Yasir to tug on his reins gently. "Nikolas is by far a greater shah than Alissand will ever be. Even your father knew it to be true. He gave him his ring."

Roksana stared, her face like iron. She cared for Nikolas, that much she failed to hide. The Yazdans always looked out for their own. And perhaps somewhere inside all of those Yazdan lies they'd been telling themselves for centuries, she saw the truth. Yasir could only hope she'd realize that soon.

She dug into her jacket pocket. "Give this to him."

Yasir leaned down and she dropped an item into his hand. The very Yazdan ring he'd seen on Niko's finger. "He won't take it." He folded his fingers around it nonetheless. "He despises the Yazdans." Her eyes showed the pain of an old ache. "He'll only take this ring if you work with him and Vasili, Roksana, not against."

She smiled sadly. "I did think Vasili different. Alissand's ways were not mine. But Yasir, there is no way out for Vasili. The flame will consume him as surely as night consumes day. It must be controlled, or there will be nothing left of our homes, our lands, and our lives. Your prince is a vessel. All vessels eventually break."

"You don't know Vasili."

"On the contrary, I fear I do." She turned on her heel and headed back to the skiff.

"And I want my ship back!" Yasir called after her, startling Adamo.

Roksana tossed him a grin and climbed into the boat, throwing him a wave.

He watched her crew row her back to his ship and peered down at the Yazdan ring in his palm. Whether he'd done any good, he couldn't be sure. Roksana did care, more than her brother. But generations of Yazdans had woven their self-fulfilling prophecy, and having her break from that was asking for a miracle. It would take more than his words. Only a Yazdan could change her course now.

 asili

HE'D BELIEVED SURRENDERING A WEAKNESS, but he'd never felt stronger. No fear, no doubt, just moving forward. He wanted the world to burn like he'd burned all his life.

With every step, the flame fed. With every day, its influence beat inside him like a second heart, one far louder and stronger than his. It was undeniable. And glorious.

There was music in his head, and with every rise and fall of its melody, more power spilled through his veins. Beasts were torn from shadows, summoned to his side, protection against any force that might try and stand in his way. But nothing dared to. Towns turned to ash as he passed through their streets, bringing with him a symphony of darkness, and he was its maestro.

His soul had never felt so unencumbered.

The flame did not covet revenge, but Vasili did. Revenge on a world that had endlessly tortured him. Revenge on a people who had stolen his blood and the blood of so many before him. Cavilles. Used. Bled. Tortured. Driven mad and tossed aside.

That legacy was over. It ended with him, with his every step toward Seran.

The Yazdans would pay with their lives.

All but one. His griffin.

Vasili's stride faltered. He fell to a knee, thrusting a hand against the ground to steady himself. Ash puffed into the air and swirled, dancing. So beautiful. Vasili watched it fall and then saw a dead landscape of grey beyond. Used. Bled. Tortured. Wrongness twisted his heart. *He* had done this. He lifted his ash-coated hand, but instead of seeing blood, he saw only the flame burning cold against his pale skin.

This had to end. He had to end it now.

Where was Nikolas? He'd vowed to stop him, knowing what was at stake. Vasili looked for his assassin, seeing only raining ash. Nikolas wasn't here. He'd seen him, hadn't he? Or had that been a dream?

Laughter bubbled up his throat. The same laughter he'd heard on his father's lips. Madness and power.

Pushing to his feet, he walked on, and behind him, the world burned cold.

 asir

"She didn't kill you then," Liam commented, keeping his eyes glued on the book in his lap.

"Sorry to disappoint." Yasir closed the hut door and made his way to the little stove to warm his hands. Night had descended faster than he'd expected, leaving him trying to find his way back from the bay and the ill-fated discussion with Roksana in the dark. Adamo had startled at every owl hoot and scurry of some small beastie.

"Look." Liam turned the book, showing a section of terribly worn text. "I've been struggling to make any sense of it, but it mentions the *alsijnl* over and over. The prison."

"The cage we found." He'd hated the thing and

dreamed of it regularly, imagining himself trapped inside its iron brackets. Gods only knew what Vasili thought of it.

"I think it was used to funnel the nasdas into the vessel, the first faceless man."

"The first cursed Caville."

"If it was used to force the nasdas inside the man, maybe it can be used to extract it."

The salt, the chamber, the cage. It did all point to a connection between a man and the nasdas. The fact the Caville palace had been built on top of it also matched with the many legends and myths surrounding the old tales.

"Without killing the man?" Yasir asked.

Liam sighed and leaned back in the chair. "It doesn't say."

Yasir rubbed his hands together and splayed them in front of the stove. He'd seen the look on Vasili's face in that chamber, despite the prince trying to hide it. He knew that cage was his fate.

"Does it say how it works?" he asked.

"There are spell words, but they're too faded to read."

"May I see?" He took the book from Liam and scanned the page. Very little made any sense, the language beyond him, but some of the faded words resembled parts of the writing uncovered beneath the salt inside the chamber. Sighing, he handed it back.

Liam watched him remove his coat and hat and place both on the chair by the door.

"There's only one cage," Yasir said. He knelt against

Liam's leg and laid an arm over his knee. "So whatever happens, whoever goes in the cage, that person must hold *all* the flame."

"Vasili does. Doesn't he?"

"No. Alissand has Amir. He's alive."

"But Vasili said Amir died. You saw—"

"I didn't stop to check the body. Nobody did. And... Vasili has been known to bend the truth somewhat."

"Ah."

"So, according to the book," he continued, "we somehow return both princes to Loreen palace, kill one of them, then trap the other—who would then hold all the flame and its formidable power—in a centuries-old cage, say the words, and hope it works." It sounded flimsy, at best.

"Or?"

"Or we do nothing, the Yazdans get bloated on Amir's power, they war with the elves, probably winning, but at the expense of our city and home. The flame still exists and will eventually break free, and if it does so while away from the palace, where it's tradition-ally been contained, then winning the war won't matter once the flame consumes everything."

"The book agrees that if the nasdas is freed, the best we can hope for is to die quickly."

"And all because a goddess swept her naughty creation under the rug to please her sisters."

"Maybe she was a Yazdan," Liam quipped. He laid his hand over Yasir's and gave it a squeeze. "Was it awful?"

"No, Roksana was reasonable, but she usually is until

she stabs you in the back. I hope my words got through. Until they do, she's with her brother and against us. I suspect Niko is the only one who can change her mind."

"And he's not here." Liam sighed.

"No. He is not," he said sadly. Niko's presence made anything seem possible. For all his rough gruffness, he had an innate strength most people lacked, Yasir included.

"You want to go back, don't you?" Liam asked.

"I do and don't." He smiled warmly. "I don't want to leave you."

"Pfft." He waved a hand. "That's never stopped you before." Yasir felt a little unexpected heat warm his cheeks. Before he could admit to caring, Liam asked, "Did you fuck him?"

"What?" Yasir spluttered.

"Niko. Did you two—"

"No!"

"But you thought it," Liam teased.

"A little," he admitted.

"A lot," Liam countered with a gleam in his eye.

Yasir grinned wider. "Have you seen his ass? Gods, he's a feast for the eyes."

Liam laughed. "A feast for the mouth too, no doubt!" He tapped Yasir playfully on the hand. "He turned you down for Vasili?"

"Not in so many words." Liam gave him the disbelieving face, full of dipped chin and fluttering lashes, and Yasir's denial fell apart. "Fine, yes. He's smitten with Vasili. It's always been Vasili, even when they pretended they hated each other for weeks in the

138

wagon. I've never seen two men so thoroughly in love and so ridiculously blind to it."

Liam sighed. "So much sexual tension. How *did* you survive?"

"With my hand." Yasir grinned and mimed a pumping motion. He rose to his knees and stroked his hands up Liam's thighs. "And thoughts of you, my dear."

"You and Vasili didn't...," he said suggestively.

His relationship with Liam had never been exclusive, not least because it had never really been called a relationship. Until Alissand had taken him. It was only then that Yasir feared he'd lose Liam before understanding the gift he'd been given in him.

"Only Niko is foolish or brave enough to get close to Vasili," Yasir said.

"Hm... good," Liam purred. "Then you're all mine."

"I've always been all yours."

Liam draped his arms over Yasir's shoulders and pulled him close. "I'll pretend that's true for the sake of my heart." Liam's mouth on his was a demand, this time, not an ask, and Yasir hungrily answered it with his own while feeling his way under Liam's shirt to stroke warm, smooth skin. He'd truly missed the uncomplicated comfort of Liam. This hut wasn't their home, and they were a long way from safe, but having nearly lost him to Alissand, he really didn't want to let him go.

Liam withdrew from the kiss and stroked his cheek. "It's different, isn't it? Us, I mean."

A painful knot choked him. "When I saw you bound by Alissand, I feared I'd lost you, and I hadn't told you all the things I should have."

"Tell me now," he whispered.

"You're my harbor. I'll always come back to you. I love you, Liam."

Liam's smile slowly grew. "Make love to me like we have all the time in the world, because soon I know you'll be gone."

iko

THEY'D FOUND two horses wandering the roads. One, a piebald mare, carried half its tack trailing in the ash alongside it. Given how the land was scorched dry, the fate of their riders was all around them.

Lasher rode bareback on the chestnut while Niko salvaged the tack he could and mounted the piebald. For the next day and night, they narrowed the gap to Vasili.

Loreen's cold, snowy lands gradually gave way to the flat plains of desert, the ash more obvious now as it fluttered over stone and sand.

Niko spotted the lone figure walking toward the horizon, cast in shadow by the setting winter sun. There was no mistaking him. Even at a distance, the prince's creeping shadow stained the landscape. He'd traveled all this way on foot. He can't have stopped, not to rest, to eat. The flame would drive Vasili into the ground.

Niko kicked his horse into a gallop. What could he possibly plan that Vasili wouldn't see coming? He had Lasher's blade, but the flame would cut him down before he'd have a chance to draw it. The only other weapon he had was the hope that Vasili was still in there somewhere, able to listen, to rein the flame back under control somehow.

The shadow around the prince swelled, like a blot of ink soaking into paper, and the fine hairs on Niko's arms rose.

He glanced behind for Lasher, but the elf and his ride had vanished somewhere in the heat haze. He was alone. Good. Vasili *would* kill an elf with a click of his fingers. But not Niko. If he'd wanted him dead, he'd have killed him at the elf camp.

Niko hunkered down, galloping his ride hard. The hot wind dried his face and cracked his lips. As the distance shortened, the more distinct the figure became. His clothes were stained with ash, his choppy pale-blond hair turned grey with it. His slim frame appeared skeletal inside the dark.

Emotion swirled in Niko's head. He blocked it. The rage, the fear, that could all come later. He summoned the hardened calm and numbness that had seen him through a hundred battles.

Blackness surged from Vasili, blotting out the pale blue sky, turning it to night. A wave of it washed across the rocky ground. Niko's horse squealed, stumbled, and threw its head, desperately trying to break free and flee. Niko gripped the reins as the horse danced and reared.

The wave of dark struck.

It appeared to happen slowly, between one heartbeat and the next. The flame lapped over the horse's head, down its neck, consuming fur and mane. Terrible, crystal clear fear iced Niko's heart. He'd been wrong. He'd die here, turned to ash like the thousands of souls the flame had already consumed.

No. No!

The horse whirled and danced and screamed, and all around the flame swirled like a storm, with Niko its eye. The weight of its touch pushed at his mind and burned beneath his skin.

"No!" Niko drove the denial through his mind, his soul, his heart, through all of him. He would *never* let the flame win. "No," he yelled into the swirling darkness again.

The torrent collapsed, suddenly splashing to the ground and vanishing like fog under the sun.

His horse snorted and panted, shaking its head, trembling beneath Niko.

With his vision a blur, sweat stinging his eyes, he scanned the suddenly bright land, and there knelt Vasili. He'd fallen to a knee with his head bowed.

"Vasili!" Niko dismounted, stumbled, and lurched toward him. "Vasili... listen... it's not over. You can push it back, you can beat it..." The words came in a rush, one after the other. He staggered on. Vasili's narrow shoulders heaved. He'd survive. He always survived. He was Vasili. He'd fight the whole damn world if he had to. "Vasili?"

The prince slowly lifted his head. His eye shone a glassy black. The smile on his lips was not his own. He flung out his left hand and a gods-awful scream erupted from the horse.

The animal reared again, but shadows born from the air snaked up its legs, consuming the beast inch by terrible inch. "Stop!"

The whites of its eyes conveyed true terror, and then it was gone, just like the elves, turned to scattered ashes.

Niko swung his gaze back to Vasili. He'd imagined what he might say on finding him, words of hope and strength, so he knew he wasn't alone, but as Vasili rose to stand and returned Niko's glare, any words seemed meaningless against such a force. Words couldn't harm it. It didn't care for Niko, it didn't care for life, just for more chaos, more power. It didn't care for Vasili either. His torn shirt gaped; bloodstains, dust, and ash marred his chest. Ash greyed his face and crusted the blood on his lips. The flame was slowly consuming him too.

Niko wet his lips, trying to soften and take away the taste of ash. "Vasili, please..." His voice cracked. "You can stop this."

Vasili's wooden smile twitched. He turned on his heel and continued his march toward the rippling horizon.

Niko dropped his hand to the elf's blade at his hip. He knew what had to be done. Take up the blade, plunge it into Vasili's back, and end this. For Vasili. He pulled the blade free. His blood raced, thumping through his ears. He was the prince's assassin, was he not?

Gravel crunched under his boots with each new step toward the prince.

Niko raised the heavy blade.

This had to happen, to free Vasili from the curse, the real Vasili—the man in Niko's memory, the quiet prince from the river pool, who'd allowed Niko to touch him. Niko remembered the weight of each kiss on Niko's skin—each one a truth. He felt them all again, relived them in his mind, and knew this feeling for what it was. He loved Vasili Caville, the cursed prince, the voiceless man, all of him. *There is nothing else in this world that frees me like you do.* Vasili knew how this ended. *You will kill a man.*

Niko lengthened his stride, gaining on the prince. It had to be quick. Precise. Painless. He'd suffered enough.

Niko's heart quickened. His mind narrowed to one single purpose, one thought. *Free Vasili.*

Through the back.

Into the heart.

He'd killed countless men. He'd kill one more now.

But none had hurt like this.

He swung the blade *down.* A twitch, a step and a turn, the prince's snarling mouth, the flash of his dark eye. Vasili dodged, and the punch of a cold dagger slammed into Niko's shoulder and jerked free, jolting him to an abrupt stop. Vasili's cold fingers clamped around Niko's throat, lifting him off his feet.

"I cannot be stopped!"

His icy fingers squeezed. Vasili's snarling rage-filled face blurred.

"Not by you, Yazdan."

Niko's chest was ablaze, his heart a thrashing, starved thing pounding against his ribs. His feet dangled in the air, his body and heart burned, and the sword slipped from his fingers.

Vasili yanked him eye-to-eye. *"I. Am. Eternal."*

Niko dug his fingers into Vasili's, trying to pry them free of his neck, but his stone-like grip crushed harder. There was no air to speak, no sound to make, he'd die without telling Vasili he was loved. If he could just reach him, somehow, in these final moments, he could bring him back. He knew it. He just had to hear those little words.

Sharp lines etched Vasili's pretty face, making him a cruel mask. This wasn't him, but the voiceless man was in there. Buried. Hidden. Afraid.

Tears squeezed from Niko's eyes. If he died here, he'd do so with the truth on his lips, spoken in his last gasps. *"I... love... you."*

Vasili's brow pinched and the savage lines smoothed from his face. His horrible, cruel, ugliness crumbled, replaced by open-mouthed horror.

His grip vanished. Niko barely felt the ground as he rushed to meet it. His jaw hit stone. He gasped, choking on sand and ash. Air dragged down his throat like broken glass. But he breathed, gods he breathed!

Vasili... where was he? Through streaming tears, he saw only sand and stone in the rippling heat. Coughs barreled through him, burning him up. He just had to remember how to breathe again... Just breathe. Slowly, painfully, the spasms in his chest subsided and his heart calmed.

He got his knees under him and searched for a figure in the haze, heart leaping at the sight of Vasili, but then plummeting again when he recognized Lasher's broad outline, leading his horse beside him.

Vasili was gone.

Niko folded around the hollow ache inside. His shoulder throbbed and wept blood, but he couldn't bring himself to care. Vasili had heard Niko, he'd seen him, he was still alive inside the flame. Vasili *had* let him go. But the flame was too strong and would only get stronger. Niko wrapped his arms around himself, holding his trembling body together. He could not save Vasili alone.

The weight of a touch settled on Niko's shoulder. He looked up and blinked through grit and tears at the elf staring down at him, his grey skin pinched into an expression something like determination.

Lasher offered his other hand, and Niko gripped it tight, accepting his aid to heave him to his feet.

Niko pressed a hand to his shoulder and winced as more pain bloomed. Vasili may not have killed him, but he was capable of stopping him at every step. "We need help." They needed Yasir. And Yasir would be in Seran.

Lasher nodded, either understanding or just agreeing with his tone.

"How do you feel about a trip to Seran?"

CHAPTER 16

iko

AFTER DAYS GALLOPING AHEAD of Vasili, Niko parted
ways with Lasher at Seran's outskirts and watched the
elf disappear into verdant undergrowth, wondering if
that would be the last he saw of him. Given the elf's
persistence, he'd likely reappear at some point, hopefully not to stab a dagger in Niko's back.

Niko trotted Lasher's horse into Seran's hot, rubble-
strewn streets. The narrowly packed, terraced houses
bore the scars of battle. Broken windows, cracked
doors, crumbled walls. But scaffolding clad their facades
too. Elves had brought Seran to her knees, but she was
already finding her feet.

An elf force was the least of the city's concerns. The
dark flame would not be deterred by pistols and swords.
These people busily rebuilding their homes had no

defense against it. He contemplated telling every man and woman he passed by that they should prepare to defend themselves from the shadows. But they'd think him mad. Vasili was their only hope, and he was...

Niko pushed on. Dwelling on what was done wouldn't help the future. He needed allies.

He plodded the horse to Liam's house, finding it in ruins. The harbor, too, was choked with sunken vessels, *Walla's Heart* likely among them. The Whispering Pearl's windows were boarded, the inn closed. With no other avenue to pursue, he had only one recourse. The Yazdans.

Alissand was too lost to the flame to be reasoned with. Roksana had helped capture Vasili and left Niko in the cells. Had it not been for Lasher, she might have kept Niko there indefinitely. But Roksana was Mah's sister, his aunt. There had been something there, some caring remnants in Roksana toward him, for Leila's sake.

He passed through the bustle of the docks. Cranes loomed at the water's edge like vast wooden tripods. Orders bellowed on the wind to the sounds of clanging hammers. Asking after Roksana bought him several scowls. One man spat in the dirt, but one young sailor spoke of her ship moored in a bay northwest of the city.

Saddle-sore and weary, Niko finally found the bay and Roksana's ship as dusk stole the daylight.

He tied his horse where the brush gave way to sand and approached the six-man crew readying a skiff at the lapping surf edge. "Ho there." They'd noticed him approaching across the sand, and while they hadn't immediately freed their blades, they didn't look pleased to see him either. Clearly a hardened crew, they were all older than Niko, their faces weathered by long years at sea.

The biggest of the lot stepped forward. He looped a rope around his elbow and hand, around and around. "Stop there, stranger."

Best to keep his hands free of the sword at his hip. Outnumbered and outmuscled, these men had the steely-eyed look of people who made their enemies disappear. "Roksana aboard?"

"Who's askin'?" He still looped the rope, so it wasn't likely he'd be able to reach the twin blades at his hips quicker than Niko could reach his own blade, but the men in the skiff behind him would.

Pulling a confident smile into his lips, Niko spread his empty hands. "Her nephew." Best avoid using his name. His Yazdan looks would confirm his lineage. "Maybe I can join you?" The crewman looked him over from head to toe, his assessment clearly one of indifference. "I've ridden days to reach her." Hopefully, that would explain the sand and ash staining him and his filthy clothes. "She'll want to see me." If this man said no, he just might have to draw his blade and make him change his mind. The others would have to scrabble out of the boat to save their friend, and in those precious seconds, Niko would have the blade's edge at his throat. They eyed each other carefully, the rope still looping.

"You with that cunt Alissand?" the sailor finally asked.

The others in the skiff behind him stared on, eyes hard.

"That cunt tried to cut my throat, so I reckon not."

"Aye," the crewman finally agreed with a nod. "Grab an oar."

Aboard and rowing among them, the hard stares didn't ease up. As the skiff cut through the surf, a shiver cooled his spine, lifting a nameless weight off his soul. Instincts told him the lightness came from the flame's retreat. Vasili had spoken of the flame being quieter at sea. He'd barely had time to consider the strange sensation before they were pulling alongside the ship's huge, barnacle-clad hull.

Climbing the rope ladder brought him abroad a deck he recognized. The same cargo hatches and ladders down into the hold, the same slightly bent cabin door. This ship was *Walla's Heart*. It was busier now, with Roksana's crew numbering twice that of Yasir's.

"Wait 'ere."

Niko leaned against the rail and eyed the crew, careful to keep his elf-blade within reach. All the Yazdans to date had sought to imprison him or turn him. His aunt included. Despite the ship being familiar, this was enemy territory.

Roksana emerged from the cabin wearing a red, flared coat and black-linen trousers. Hoop earrings dangled from her ears. Her grin stretched, lighting up her tanned face. "Gods, Niko, you look like something the ship's cat threw up!" She summoned a crewman and ordered him to fetch a bucket of fresh water and soap and a change of clothes. And all before she'd said hello.

Her grin and easy body language seemed to suggest they were friends, but that wasn't how Niko remembered things. "The last time we spoke, it was between bars, aunt," he drawled.

"The last time we spoke, you knocked me out cold." She stopped out of sword's reach and eyed the elf-blade at his hip. "Interesting weapon. Rum?"

"And have you poison me?"

She scoffed. "What's a little betrayal between family?"

"Where's Alissand?"

Mention of her brother straightened her back. "At the house, I imagine."

The crewmate returned with news of the water and clothes waiting in her cabin.

"Shall we?" she gestured toward the cabin door.

Escape was just a jump away. If he stayed and entered the cabin, her crew could easily overpower him, but none seemed interested in their conversation. If they'd been ordered to watch him, they hid it well. "Let's be clear, because I'm on my last thread of patience with fucking liars and cheats. If you so much as glance at me wrong, I'll finish what was begun, and this time, you won't get up."

Roksana chuckled. "A man after my own heart." She ducked inside the cabin. "You sound more like Vasili every day, you know," she called back. "Come in, Nikolas. I give you my word as the captain of this ship, you're safe among us."

Niko ground his teeth and eyed the bustling crew. He needed Roksana, but he also needed her to be on his side, not the side of the Yazdans. And that was a lot to ask.

The cabin hadn't changed since Yasir's ownership, besides Roksana standing behind the huge desk, instead of the colorful Lajani. He'd have preferred Yasir were here and not his aunt, and a pang of regret soured his mood even further. "How is it you have Yasir's ship?"

She poured herself a cup of rum and gestured toward the bucket and clothes on the cot at the side of the cabin. And a plate of fruit and bread. "Clean up, if you like."

He eyed the gifts like he would any other gift from a family he'd come to despise as much as Vasili must have despised the Cavilles.

"In the absence of her captain, I decided to adopt her," Roksana said.

"Piracy." He crossed the cabin and picked up an apple.

"Privateer, please." Roksana dropped into the chair and kicked her boots onto the table. "Please, Niko. Just eat the apple. It's not poisoned."

She could smile and offer him gifts all she liked; it didn't change the past. "It's like you don't remember how thoroughly you lied to me."

Looking away, she sipped her rum and sighed. The flutter of her lashes gave away the doubt on her face. "The Yazdan way has always been to control the flame," she whispered. "For the good of us all."

He snorted and shrugged off his filthy coat. Only once it was off did he see the thick creases clogged with ash and sand. The thing really was a mess. "You control it for greed. I didn't know my grandfather, but I'll take a guess and assume he was exactly the same as the rest of you bloodsucking bastards, all the way back to when our ancestors were tasked with keeping the flame contained and stole it instead, making slaves of the Cavilles." He stopped and glanced at Roksana. She'd raised a brow. He hadn't come to reignite the fires of war between them. Tearing off his filthy shirt, he picked up a wet cloth and quickly washed the grime from his arms and chest.

"Father *was* the same, you're right," she continued. "Until Leila left. Her leaving broke something in him. He'd have liked to have known you, I think, once he got past the Caville standing beside you."

His grandfather had given him the Yazdan ring in his dying moments. The old man's eyes had been filled with regret. Was the gift of his mah's ring a demand he continue to control the flame, or a plea to break it? He'd never know. Besides, he'd lost the ring—tossed it at Roksana. It was probably for the best.

He ran wet hands through his hair and tugged out the knots and sand, then dressed in the fresh clothes, relieved to be in the lighter linens of Seran attire again. Roksana stayed quiet, staring at her closed cabin door as though she could see through it. Something had changed in her. Change had happened to them all.

"Pour some of that rum." He approached the desk. "We're both going to need it."

Lifting an eyebrow, she shoved a cup across the desk for Niko to pour his own.

The hot, sweet liquid went down smoothly. Niko leaned a hip against the desk, letting the quiet hang between them. An array of subtle expressions crossed his aunt's face. Her smile had long gone, and in its absence the lines at her eyes had gotten deeper. "Why are you on Yasir's ship, Roksana?"

"I like it," she said brightly. "I've always liked it."

Niko waited a beat. "Now tell me the truth."

Her delicate throat moved as she swallowed. "I've always preferred the sea. It's... wild and free. She can't be tamed. Walla demands respect, and those that give it to her, she treats well." Niko arched an eyebrow. "I don't consume their blood, Niko. I never have, but being at sea takes that temptation away. Alissand... He's always desired power."

"You're afraid of him."

She pinched her lips together. "He was different before. Father kept the Cavilles at bay, so we didn't think much on the old tales. But then things changed when Leila left, and Alissand began to argue with father. He wanted to march north and take Loreen. I... I didn't listen. I wasn't here. I didn't *want* to be here. And Alissand changed."

"The flame corrupts."

"It's not just Alissand. It's all of it." When she met his gaze now, her dark Yazdan eyes shimmered, glassy with emotion. "I fear we've made a terrible mistake." She picked up the bottle of rum, sloshing more into her cup.

"A mistake generations of Yazdans have made." Niko drank the rum, finding it warm and soft against parched lips.

"Yes," she admitted. "It's difficult to go against your own blood when it's all you've ever known."

"And it's about to get worse." He went on to explain as much as he dared regarding Vasili. Could he trust a woman who had so viciously betrayed him? He didn't have time to find out. Vasili was coming. He needed allies, and Roksana could be one. Not all of her had been lies, and the more he spoke, the more he hoped the emotion on her face was real and not some ploy to maneuver him into a Yazdan trap. Trust began with hope.

He told her of the elves and his recapture, but not of the iron cage beneath the palace. He recounted the events of Vasili's escape and Vasili's fall to the flame, but not of the elf Lasher.

She listened grimly, and when he'd finished, she reached for the rum once more, fingers trembling. "You're sure Vasili is coming?"

"The flame is. To wipe out the Yazdans. And to kill Amir, reuniting the two halves of itself. If it succeeds, we're all lost."

She wrapped her fingers around her cup. "Alissand will stand against him."

Alissand would fling his sorcerers at Vasili and fuel the flame with every death. "Alissand is blinded by the same power that runs through Vasili's veins. He may be able to slow Vasili down, but he won't be able to stop him. Sorcery against sorcery is fire against fire."

"Then how do we stop this?" she asked quietly.

If only he knew. "Yasir was working on a solution, but I lost him in the north."

Her face brightened. "That rake?" she chuckled. "He's in Seran. We spoke some days ago. Actually, he came asking for help on Vasili's behalf. He was none too pleased about the ship situation."

Yasir was close. Finally, a twist of luck! "Where is he now?"

"I don't know, but he won't have gone far." Her face fell. "Niko, he doesn't know the flame has Vasili."

And telling him would hurt like a blow to the heart. "We have to find him."

"I'll send some men into Seran to track him down. The fool is too loud to hide."

Roksana briefly left the cabin to issue orders. Niko waited at the desk, sipping rum and rubbing an ache from his forehead. Would Yasir, Niko, and Roksana be enough to bring Vasili back from the edge of darkness? There was only one way of knowing, and that was to face Vasili for a third time. And hope it wasn't the last for them all.

"At least Vasili doesn't know Alissand has Amir," Roksana said, returning to the cabin.

"He does," Niko replied grimly. "I told him."

Her stride faltered and stopped. "Then we must remove Amir from Alissand's clutches and hide him somewhere to buy time." She scanned the cabin until her gaze flicked back to Niko. "The water... If we bring Amir here, it might hide him from Vasili."

If the water truly did neutralize the flame, then there was no better place to hide Amir.

"Alissand has him under heavy guard at the house." Roksana paced. "They're bleeding him... It's foul, wrong, Niko. By Walla, I wish I'd seen my brother's thirst sooner. It might have saved lives." Rubbing her arms, she sighed. "Alissand will never let us inside. Since I've ignored his summons and taken up residence here, he suspects I may have strayed from the Yazdan creed."

"Then go to him. Obey his summons, make him believe you're a Yazdan, and get to Amir."

"It's not that simple, Niko. The blood, it's turned them..."

"I know what it does to men," he said quietly, recalling Julian's final moments beneath his hands and his own lapses in judgment. The flame made puppets of them all.

"What's to stop it doing the same to me?" she asked.

"You've resisted it this long. And you're stubborn."

She snorted. "Ha, a stubborn Yazdan." She crossed the floor and downed the remaining rum. "Alissand has made himself an army of the cursed. The air in the Yazdan house smells like blood and ash. Like death. The staff are all dead-eyed and cold as stone. Seeing it... what the flame has done, it's what drove me out here, Niko. We have lost our way, but the city needs someone to stand against all this. It needs someone to fight for all the good that's left in the world. I can't do it alone, but we could." Her gaze settled on him.

Her hope was misplaced in him. "I am not immune to the flame's call." How easily the flame spread, burning from one mortal soul to another. So eager to feed, helped by those too naïve to know they were surrendering their fate to a darkness. First Amir had unleashed its curse on Loreen's palace guards, and now

Alissand continued Amir's will, infecting others. Perhaps wherever Amir was, he had some control left. Perhaps he steered Alissand.

He fell silent and swallowed at the sudden dryness in his throat. He knew the blood's call, having licked it from his fingers, and from his time under Amir's thrall. It was a good thing Roksana would go because Niko couldn't trust himself not to succumb to the same siren call Roksana feared would take her.

His aunt watched him quietly, and it seemed like in this silence, they shared the depth of fear and a knowledge of their fates having been written long ago.

"I'll go to Alissand and find Amir," she finally said. "I owe you more, but I'll start there."

"The odds are against us," Niko said.

Roksana tipped her cup and grinned. "When has that ever stopped a Yazdan?"

 asili

THE RED, mismatched houses of Seran baked against the distant turquoise of Walla's ocean and Aura's cyan sky.

Vasili drifted between carts and people, observing them as they bustled, like hollow dolls placed in a fantasy world. Stone cobbles dug into his bare heels. He'd lost his boots somewhere, but such trivial things were of no concern. The people were far more interesting. They looked back at him like he was a ghost they only now believed in. Each person glowed, full of color, like stars in a night sky. Stars that could be snuffed out. Children clutched their parents' hands, their innocence a sweet allure to the hunger inside. Life bloomed everywhere, in the noises and lights and smells of the people. In their delightful chaos.

"I can sell you some boots, if you like, sir?"

The voice stood out from the rest. Vasili stopped his meander and stepped back, drawn to the trader and his stall. He had kind eyes, the soft kind. Silvering hair and beard betrayed his middle years.

"You look like you've had a hard time," he went on. "I can do you a deal..."

The trader twittered, lips moving, mouth forming meaningless words. Why would Vasili pay when he could just—

He flicked his hand, and the man behind the stall stopped twittering, stopped breathing, stopped *living*.

Vasili scanned the selection of shoes, settled on a pair of boots with tarnished buckles, and slipped them on. Yes, that was much better.

"By the gods," someone passing gasped out. Her gaze caught the ash fluttering in the air and fell to Vasili before she recoiled in horror. "What are you?"

He turned away. Others stood and stared. Their ebb and flow and background chatter shattered, becoming broken screams. Vasili silenced each one until there was no noise at all, just the hiss of ash over stone.

He walked on, deeper into the city, heeled boots striking the stone with every step.

CHAPTER 18

iko

"NIKO, there's a rider on the beach."

He jolted awake, startled to find he'd dosed in the captain's chair while waiting for Roksana to prepare to meet with Alissand.

"Come!" she barked, grabbing her tailed jacket and dashing back out the cabin.

He climbed into the skiff alongside her. The sun had set long ago, the rider only visible by the light of his torch flame. "Any ideas who he is?"

"We'll soon find out." As soon as the skiff's hull skidded up the sand, she was out and marching toward the lone figure. "Who sent you? My brother?"

"Yes," he said. His narrow face was drawn, made more hollow by shifting shadows beneath his eyes and cheeks. "There's a disturbance in the city. Alissand has summoned you." The man's flighty gaze skipped over Niko and Roksana's crew of six behind them.

"What kind of disturbance?"

"An attack, it seems. I wasn't told."

Roksana glanced back. "You have a horse, Niko?"

"I do."

She nodded at her men, and three separated, disappearing into the dark.

"Where is the disturbance?" she demanded of the messenger. "Of what nature? Talk, man."

"The m-markets. People... people dying."

"Is it elves?"

"Not elves," he said, assuredly, but that was all he was sure of. His gaze skipped again to Niko.

"Then what?" she asked.

"Talk of... a monster. I don't know. I didn't see it, but the guard who did said the creature was of shadow and turned people to dust."

Vasili.

Niko stepped forward to demand more when Roksana hastily pulled him aside toward the noise of the surf so they wouldn't be overheard. "Before you go charging off and Vasili chokes you again—"

"He won't—"

She frowned. "Niko, Alissand's forces will be in the city, responding to the attack. He won't have Amir with him. This is our chance to get to the house and get that princely prick away from my brother. We'll bring him here, just like we said."

"But Vasili—"

"Niko! Vasili is here to find Amir so the flame will be whole again. We have to get to Amir first."

That would mean trusting her, but wasn't that exactly what he'd come here for? She was right, they did need to secure Amir, but if Vasili was close, he had to try and talk him back. "I might be able to talk him around—"

"Because that went so well last time? He choked and stabbed you. Next time, he'll kill you, and I can't do this alone. You can't go to him. Not yet. We will, when we're ready."

Her three crewmates reappeared, horses in tow. All substantial men, all armed with blades and pistols. With them and Roksana, they could likely storm the Yazdan house and bring Amir to the ship.

"We get Amir out," she said, looking him in the eyes. "And we bring him to the water, where the flame can't reach its other half. *That* will save your prince."

It was the only damn option he had. He nodded, but as she turned, he caught her arm instead and pulled her close. "Betray my trust again and not even Etara herself can protect you."

"You have my honor as a captain. We both know my honor as a Yazdan is worthless."

asir

SOMETHING WAS VERY wrong in Seran. He threw out a hand to stop Liam in the street beside him and listened. A bitterness touched his tongue and a coolness ran through his blood, making the fine hairs on his arms rise. The city had rung with the sounds of hammering for days now, but the hammering had ceased, and the streets were silent. "Get inside."

"Wait—"

Yasir yanked open a random door. The owner surely wouldn't mind a sudden guest, given the circumstances. He shoved Liam over the threshold. "Stay inside and stay down." He'd brought Liam to salvage items from his collapsed house but hadn't gotten that far.

Liam grabbed Yasir's hand. "What is it? What's happening?"

Yasir gripped his lover's shoulders and held firm. "Bad *yudu*." He kissed him quickly on the forehead and dashed out the door.

"Yasir, wait!"

Yasir threw a smile over his shoulder to Liam on the step. Liam's hair was wild, his freckles dark against his pale face.

"Come back?"

Yasir tipped his hat as his heart swelled. "Always." People darted around the street corners, shoving Yasir aside, their faces white and hair streaked with ash.

Screams echoed somewhere far off.

Yasir glanced behind him again to find Liam had gone inside and closed the door. He'd be safe there.

Breaking into a jog, he dashed through Seran's narrow side streets toward the markets. He knew what this was, of course. Ash dallied in the air, dancing around Seran's electric string-lights. And in his veins, the flame simmered.

He freed the salt-loaded pistol he'd salvaged from the rubble of Liam's house and dashed around a corner. A blast of hot, ash-filled wind slammed into him. Shielding his eyes, he blinked through the storm. A blur of a man loomed at its center. Then, suddenly, the wind vanished, the ash settled, and the man in the market square was visible. His white hair hung in tails about his sand-caked face. His ripped and frayed shirt hung open. Ash painted him white, like a ghost.

"Vasili?"

Dread almost dropped Yasir to his knees. He reached for the wall to steady himself.

The flame had taken Vasili. Or he'd surrendered. Either way, the outcome was the same.

Where was Niko? He'd never let Vasili come to this...

Yasir readied the pistol in his hand with a click, and that single, small sound shot like an arrow through the hiss of ash and drew Vasili's single-eyed glare to Yasir. The icy touch of the flame spilled down Yasir's back, stealing a gasp from his lips.

Think... he had to think... Vasili couldn't be lost, could he? There had to be some part of him inside there. "Vasili..."

The prince's eye narrowed.

Salt.

Salt would bring him back. It had worked with Niko in Loreen. A blast of salt to shock him out of his nightmare. He kept the pistol behind his back and pushed through the layer of ash. Vasili watched, head slightly cocked, body unmoving. A silver snake in the grass. He wore the strangest lopsided smile, the kind seen stitched into dolls.

Yasir swallowed hard. "Vasili... You know me."

He didn't blink, didn't move, might not have breathed either, Yasir couldn't see. The thing looking back at him was not the man who'd spent months at sea with him, who'd laughed and confessed all the little things that had seemed so inconsequential at the time. "Do you remember our time at sea... on *Walla's Heart?*

Do you remember how free you were?" His palm sweated on the pistol's grip.

He'd only get one shot.

If he missed, he'd not get a second chance.

Closer. He had to be closer.

Vasili watched on.

"You told me you once hid in Alek's stables to avoid the palace guards. Afterward, you both fell about laughing in the hay... You told me what happened in the hay. Do you remember, Vasili?"

C'mon, Vasili... fight.

Vasili's smile twitched, the doll coming to life.

Gods, Yasir couldn't stand this. It wasn't right. Vasili had fought so long to prevent this. Something had happened, something terrible. Was it Niko... was Niko dead? He wasn't here. Nothing could stop Niko from saving his prince. Vasili, high on spice and drunk on ale on the ship, had confessed how Nikolas made him a freer man, made him better in all ways. The prince had loved him the moment he'd seen him, though he'd never admit it.

Yasir raised his left hand, and the prince's gaze followed. "Listen, Vasili, it's not too late to end this."

The stitched smile frayed and fell away. *"No,"* the prince said, his voice twisted and rough, the words not his own. *"It begins."* Vasili flung out a hand, unleashing a whip-like tendril of dark flame toward Yasir.

Yasir lifted the pistol and aimed at Vasili.

"No!" a voice cried out behind Yasir. A voice that shouldn't be here.

The tendril of flame veered *around* Yasir. Too slow,

Yasir was too slow! He turned. Saw Liam at the end of the street, a second pistol in his hand, his wobbling aim angled toward Vasili. *"Run!"* Yasir screamed.

Liam fired. His gun kicked, and then the tendril of flame was on him, ripping out a silent scream. Liam threw his head back, his back arched, and then between one blink and the next, there was only ash.

Liam's gun clattered to the ground, quickly buried by falling ash.

"Liam?"

Cold fingers clamped around Yasir's neck. He froze. Suddenly... caught.

"Ah," Vasili said, the word pressed against Yasir's ear. *"Here come my acolytes."*

Cloaked figures loomed in the nearby streets, filling every exit, their eyes as black as Vasili's. Thirty, maybe more; Yasir couldn't turn to see. One of them stepped forward. His black cloak with its gold lining marked him as the leader.

"Your reign has ended, prince. Surrender or die," Alissand demanded.

Vasili's dark chuckle poured liquid honey through Yasir's soul, soothing the hate and fear and shock. The fingers digging into Yasir's neck tightened suddenly, and Vasili shoved Yasir away, tossing him aside like forgotten trash. Yasir stumbled toward the wall where Liam's gun had fallen, where he'd been standing moments before. He knelt, thrust a hand through the ash, and found the gun. Ash dried his lips, his tongue. He raked trembling fingers through the ash coating the ground. "Liam?" he whispered. He couldn't be gone. He'd been right here.

Yasir had told him to wait. He was supposed to wait! He always waited for Yasir.

A sob choked Yasir now and brought him to his hands and knees.

"Surrender?" Vasili's voice filled the streets.

Yasir looked—the command in his voice demanded it.

Vasili threw his arms wide and Seran's string-lights all flickered. *"There is no surrender."* He took a single step toward Alissand and spoke a single word: *"Kneel."*

It was more than speech, more than a word. *Kneel.* A command driven into blood and through the veins of everyone gathered. The circle of people dropped, one by one, falling dominoes to the power they'd all consumed.

"No, you can't do this!" Alissand wailed. "Cavilles are vessels. You are weak! You belong to me!"

Vasili's lips curled in a snarl. Another step. *"Kneel, Yazdan."*

Alissand's face contorted, his body warring with itself. "No! Damn you, no!" He fell to his knees as though Etara pulled him down herself and bowed his head, just like all the rest.

With the others subdued, Vasili slowly met Yasir's empty gaze.

Yasir took off his hat and laid it over the ash where Liam had fallen. "For you, my harbor," he whispered.

Looking up again, he glared back at Vasili. "Kill me then. Be done with it."

Vasili strode forward, boots gliding through ash. He stopped to tower over Yasir. His brow pinched, lines appearing in the creases of his ash-stained face. Maybe he regretted what he'd done; maybe he only now recognized the light he'd taken from this world.

"I always believed in you," Yasir told the prince.

"You believed in the vessel, and the vessel is weak."

"I hope you rot in Etara's hell." Yasir jerked the pistol from beneath the ash to his hip and fired. Salt blasted Vasili's scarred chest. He roared and flung himself away. The acolytes stirred, rising from their knelt positions, reaching for their weapons.

Yasir scrambled through the ash and darted out of sight, running anywhere until his legs could no longer hold him. He fell against a wall, coughing and choking on ash. Inhuman howls rose from the city. He couldn't tell if they were Vasili's wails, the flame's, or Alissand's. It didn't matter. *Nothing* mattered.

"You were supposed to wait for me!"

He dragged a hand down his face, drying his tears, and pushed from the wall, away from the sounds of a battle that would surely end with only one winner.

CHAPTER 20

iko

ROKSANA LED her crew into the sprawling Yazdan house through a broken window in one of the many empty guest bedchambers. Niko climbed in behind them. They moved silently, following Roksana's gestures without a word. Her men were efficient and trained for subterfuge. She was clearly no stranger to stealth.

She caught Niko's eye. He nodded his readiness. Considering how he trusted Lasher—an elf—more than his own family, what followed should be interesting.

Torches flickered in their sconces, illuminating empty corridors. The majority of the sprawling house was open to the huge, central courtyard garden. Almost every room looked inward over it. The garden had been warm and inviting for the brief months Niko had lived here, but whether it was the darkness or the chilling

winter air, the garden felt cold and hollow. That emptiness followed Niko deeper into the corridors.

He didn't smell blood, or ash, like his aunt had
mentioned, but it would surely come.

Footfalls warned of approaching guards. Roksana's
men sprang forward, ambushing the two guards, dragging them both into a dark side room in a matter of
seconds. They efficiently hog-tied and gagged their
subjects, leaving Niko to reassess his chances of fending
them off should they turn on him.

Roksana grabbed one of the prisoners, pulled his gag
down, and pressed a knife to his throat. "Where are
they keeping the Caville king?"

The guard's gaze skipped over them, reading the
chances of his escaping or even surviving the encounter.

Roksana dug her blade deeper. The guard squealed,
"Don't!"

"Tell me! The king. Where is he?"

The man's watery eyes widened. "He'll kill me."

She bared her teeth and leaned in. "He's going to kill
us all. Help me end his madness."

The guard glanced at Niko. Out of the five of them,
Niko probably appeared the most intimidating, despite
standing well back and letting his aunt take the lead.
For emphasis, he dropped his hand to the elf-blade at
his hip, and the guard's eyes widened. Maybe he'd heard
of Niko.

"Alissand's antechambers," he puffed, deflating now
the truth was out. "It's heavily guarded—"

Roksana brutally slammed the man's head back
against the wall and stepped over his limp body. "Move."

Two more guard details were dealt with as efficiently as the first, their gagged or unconscious bodies hidden in empty chambers. Yasir had once warned Niko not to call Roksana a pirate, but he was beginning to believe that was exactly what she was. If she was as formidable at sea as she was on land, then it wasn't any wonder why she was so revered on the waves too.

Approaching Alissand's wing of the house, their group hung back while Roksana and Niko crouched against a wall and peeked around the corner to assess the contingent of guards outside Alissand's bedchamber. Four guards. Each wearing the red sash of the Yazdans and all with eyes as black as the night.

Guards were one thing, but taking on sorcerers was something else entirely.

Roksana held Niko's gaze, her eyes questioning.

Roksana and her men weren't possessed by the flame like Niko.

He freed the elf-blade and summoned a touch of flame to his fingers, spilling it down the recurved steel, turning the blade into black flame.

Roksana arched an eyebrow, and Niko shrugged, prompting his aunt to muster a smile.

Roksana held a hand up to her men, readying them. Swords gleamed in their hands, mirroring the wicked gleam in their eyes.

She freed her twin pistols and quickly loaded their powder and balls, then raised both guns and drew in a breath.

Niko stepped from around the corridor and summoned the flame. It rushed to fulfill his will, spilling through his mind, turning his thoughts cold. He flung out his free hand, tossing a line of flame at the farthest guard. The flame washed over him before he had a chance to raise his sword.

A bolt of cold struck at Niko's chest. He twisted away from the second guard's sorcery, dropped to a knee, and launched the elf-blade through the air. The sword slammed into the guard's unprotected face, lodging in his skull via the eye, and toppled him backward, dead before hitting the floor.

Roksana's pistol fired, taking another possessed guard down. Her men charged in, overwhelming the remaining sorcerer. Her dagger cut off his muttered words at the throat, but those words Niko knew all too well.

A sudden weight slammed into Niko's shoulders, knocking him to the floor. His jaw struck stone, pain blinding his vision. Gunfire boomed, but it wouldn't do them any good. Niko twisted onto his back. The beast's eyes blazed red. Its jagged teeth snapped together inches from his face. Between the seconds, Niko stared into the eyes of a creature torn from its world and thrown into a battle it did not want nor understand.

Instinct had him toss the flame at the beast, not to fight, but to free it. Fear and rage flooded through his thoughts—the creature's. Words fell from his lips, severing the summons, and the beast wisped away, turning to smoke and disappearing back to the realm it had come from.

Roksana offered her hand and hauled Niko back to

his feet. She slapped him on the back. "Nicely done, nephew!"

He grumbled, retrieved his bloody sword from the dead man's skull, and stood beside his aunt as she swung open the double doors. Another set of doors greeted them, these hanging open, framing a display Niko had seen too many times before.

Alissand had strung Amir vertical to the end of a four-poster bed frame, spread his arms at right angles to his body, and left him there to bleed.

A waft of blood-tainted air slammed into Niko, rooting him in the doorway. Roksana and her men poured into the room. His aunt hacked at Amir's ropes. One of her crew moved in to support Amir's limp body. And all Niko could see was blood. Dried in Amir's hair, smeared across his pale face. He'd been bled from the neck and wrists, the wounds left ragged in their haste.

Good.

Yet something bitter and sharp twisted inside Niko, trying to writhe free. Disgust warred with need. Because this bastard's blood fueled the power singing in Niko's veins. He could take the elf-blade in his hand to Amir's throat, cut him open, make him bleed, and Niko would gorge on his blood, his power.

"Niko!" Roksana hissed.

He blinked out of numbness, surprised to find himself standing in front of Amir with no recollection of having moved. "I..."

"Help hold him."

He couldn't. He couldn't touch him, because he *wanted* to. No, it was more visceral than that. He *needed*

179

to touch Amir. He backed up, stumbling over his feet. "No."

Roksana scowled like he'd lost his mind. But then Amir's ties gave, and he slumped into the arms of her crew. They dragged Amir between them, out the door.

Roksana shoved Niko toward the door hard enough to snap him back into the moment. "Niko, hold yourself together. We need—"

Guards suddenly flooded the corridor. Roksana and her crew plunged among them, sword swinging.

They'd left Amir slumped against a wall.

The sound of clashing swords faded beneath the thump of Niko's hungry heart. He should help Roksana, but he couldn't seem to look away from the slumped middle prince with his matted white hair and pale lips. So vulnerable. He could plunge a blade through his heart and end it now. Or reopen the wounds at his wrist and drink deeply.

"Niko! Get Amir out!"

He frowned at his aunt, at the chaos all around, at more guards rushing down the corridor toward them. All of this was unnecessary; he just had to reach for the flame and—

"Dammit! Niko! Go!" Roksana kicked her attacker in the gut, sending him sprawling into two others. Shadows mingled and swirled, taking form and shape, becoming beasts. *"Get him out of here for Vasili!"*

He scooped Amir into his arms and threw his light body over his shoulder. It was the easiest thing to do, to take him, to run. Guards appeared ahead. Niko cut them down with a hollow thought, driven by the flame's desire to consume anything that dared stand against it. He climbed out the broken window and carried Amir to where they'd left the horses. Tearing the saddle free from his steed, Niko folded Amir's body over the animal's bare back and mounted behind him.

Moonlight lit the road back to the bay. He transferred Amir's body into the skiff and rowed to *Walla's Heart*. The ship's crew obligingly took Amir's limp body below deck into one of the silk storage bays. "Take the boat back to the beach," Niko ordered. "Roksana and the others will return soon. I'll watch Amir."

The crew obeyed. Niko descended into the cargo hold and latched the door to the storage bay closed.

He slowly dragged his gaze toward the wrong prince sprawled on a bed of Yasir's fine silks. Despite the obvious cuts and raw wrists, he didn't look to be malnourished or beaten. His chest rose and fell, and his heart thudded its stubborn beat—Niko could damn well hear the wretched thing.

He unlaced Amir's shirt at the neck and flicked it open, looking for any wounds that might need attention. No scars, besides the deep one his brother had given him by missing his heart. He'd been spared the elf way. His chest rose and fell with each breath, soft and calming, like the ebb of the tide.

Niko skimmed his fingers along Amir's thin collarbone, near the hollow of his neck.

"Yes, just like that, dog. Take it all." The memory hit hard, like a bullet to the skull. Amir on him, his blood on Niko's lips, his cock...

Niko's fingers clamped around Amir's throat and *squeezed*.

Amir's lashes fluttered open, revealing glassy blue eyes. Unfocused, he fixed his gaze on Niko's face and *smiled*.

Kill me, he mouthed, the words unspoken but loud in their silence.

By the three, Niko wanted to. He'd never wanted to end someone more in his entire life. Kill him and maybe fuck his corpse.

Niko tore himself free and fell against the opposite wall. The little storage bay chamber was only a stride across, not enough room to escape Amir.

Amir coughed and wheezed, his shaking hand going to his throat. His eyes rolled, and a gods-awful groan pealed from his lips. "Still... a failure, butcher boy," he rasped, then the bastard chuckled.

"I should rip your fucking cock off and make you eat it, you piece of shit."

Amir coughed again. "All bark. No bite."

Niko's hands trembled to wrap around Amir's throat and choke the fucking life out of him. Vasili was the only reason he hadn't killed Amir yet.

Amir let his head roll to the side, resting his cheek on a pillow of purple silk. "You *want* me."

Niko slid down the wall and pressed the balls of his palms to his eyes. He didn't *want* Amir. He *needed* him. He hadn't chosen Amir, despite his terrible thirst and achingly hard cock. That was all Amir's doing.

"You want me so badly, you can't think straight. You

want to crawl inside my skin, fuck me, drink me. You can't think around me. I'm in your veins."

"Stop," Niko growled, his gut flipping over.

"Does my brother know what we did? Does he know how I fucked your mouth as your eyes swam black for me? How you wept and begged for more? How you called me master?"

Niko bolted from the room and slammed the door closed, padlocking it behind him. But the locked door didn't hold back the prince's chilling laughter. Not possessed, not with the ocean beneath them. This was Amir's natural wretchedness.

"It's too late!" Amir yelled. "I'm inside you forever now, dog. You'll die tasting my cum on your lips."

He climbed the ladder to the deck and stumbled to the rail, dragging cool, salty air across his lips. He had half a mind to toss the padlock key into the bay waters but instead looped it on a strip of leather and tied it around his neck. Amir could fucking rot in the hold.

"Ho!" the lookout called, raising the alarm.

Roksana's party spilled onto the beach, torches haloing light among them.

Niko slumped, resting his forearms on the rail, and bowed his head between his arms. Saving Amir felt like the wrong thing, when the only person he really wanted to save was still out there, suffering.

He couldn't do this. He couldn't carry on while barely holding the pieces of himself together. He *was* going to break. "Not yet," he growled low. "Hold it together."

The crew busied themselves on deck, tossing the ladder overboard for the returning party.

Niko sank his fingers into his hair and locked them there, holding himself down. Disgust still made him sick inside and wet his mouth with saliva. Because Amir was right. He was a twitch away from turning around, unlocking the door, and fucking the prince into that bed of silk while drinking all the blood in his veins.

Gods, if only he and Vasili had stayed in the cabin in the woods, all this shit would have happened without them.

The slosh of boat oars hitting the water pulled him back from his thoughts. He wiped a hand down his face and watched the skiff thump against the hull. Roksana climbed aboard.

"Is he here?" she asked, tone rushed.

"Below deck."

"Haul anchor! Make it fast!" she boomed. "We're being pursued!"

Her crew burst into motion. The rattle of the anchor-chain strummed through the ship's hull, *Walla's Heart* shivering beneath them.

Niko turned his gaze back toward the beach. More torches bobbed toward the water's edge, illuminating figure after figure, until hundreds stood in silence on the sand. They couldn't all be Alissand's guards.

Bellowed orders and the fall of sails signaled their leaving.

Niko gripped the rail and stared across the water at the ring of torchbearers circling a lone man on the sand.

"Wait..."

"We can't," Roksana approached from behind him, her voice soft. "If we go back, we're all dead."

At the distance, he could make out his tousled white hair and ragged clothes. Vasili. It had to be. He couldn't leave him. There had to be a way to reach him...

His gaze skimmed the dark rippling waters between them.

"Drop the anchor."

"Niko—"

Pity softened his aunt's eyes.

"The flame is weaker at sea," Niko said. "But it wants Amir, it wants to complete itself. If we can get Vasili aboard, its control over him will weaken. It might be enough."

"And if it doesn't work, he'll kill us all in a blink. It's too risky. We must get Amir away from him."

"Roksana, Vasili asked you for help and you threw it in his face. Had the Yazdans helped when they had the chance, all of this could have been avoided. Your family screwed his for centuries. Make it right. You owe me this."

She stepped up to him. "I understand love, Niko. The woman I love, I sent far away from all this to save her. Your love for Vasili blinds you to the truth. Your prince is already lost."

He would *never* believe that. "He could have killed me and didn't. He's still Vasili, but he needs our help. He's always needed help. Everyone turns away or betrays him. Please, give him the chance you should have given him before. One chance and Vasili *will* do the right thing. You have my word."

"You're asking me to hang my life and the lives of my crew on love?"

"There's no greater cause worth dying for."

She rolled her lips together and sighed. When she turned toward the beach, the distant torchlight reflected in her Yazdan eyes. "I had better not regret this. Drop the anchor! Haul the sails! Did I misspeak? *Get to it!*" She gripped the rail beside Niko and stared across the dark bay waters. "Now we'll see if the flame is fool enough to take the bait."

CHAPTER 21

 asili

A SINGLE FIGURE rowed toward the beach. A sacrificial lamb. This would be interesting.

Vasili stepped closer to the water. Soft waves lapped toward the toes of his boots. His heels sank in wet sand, water pooling around them. A cool, thin touch traced down his spine. The first real shiver of feeling in... weeks.

The figure in the boat ceased rowing beyond where the small waves crested, bobbing out of reach. Alone, backed by moonlight, he could be anyone.

"We have Amir."

Nikolas Yazdan. An interesting choice. Had they sent him to talk, thinking some part of his old self lingered to take pity on them?

Vasili had brought his own puppet Yazdans with him. They were all weak, dangling on the end of his strings. Alissand's mind was the strongest, twitching and jerking against his hold like an animal caught in a trap. But easily subdued. Alissand knelt behind him in the sand now.

With the moonlight behind Nikolas, he couldn't see his face, but it didn't matter. Nikolas was an open book. Deceit was not in his nature.

"I'll take you to him," he continued.

More small waves lapped about Vasili's boots. He looked down, thoughts oddly distracted by their gentle kiss. He'd come for Amir... so why then was he hesitating?

"Vasili?"

Lifting his gaze, he tried to see the ex-soldier's face. Nikolas didn't lie. He was terrible at it. He *could* trust him.

"I want him dead, Vasili. You know only half the things he did to me. He must die, but I can't do it myself. Whenever I go near him, I lose my mind."

The fragment of flame was potent in Nikolas, given to him by Amir. Vasili could merely reach out and have him kneel. He lifted a hand, probing for the new mind to join those he'd already recruited, but his reach spluttered over the water.

Ah, there was the trap. The water. He saw it now, the yawning absence of power in front of him. A weakness.

But Amir was close. Onboard that boat. He felt that

much too. If he united the two halves of the flame, he'd be without weakness and free.

"It must be you."

"All right."

Nikolas rowed the boat through the low surf, keeping its stern angled toward the beach so as not to capsize.

Vasili clicked his fingers, summoning Alissand to his side.

"Alone," Nikolas growled, and now Vasili saw his dark face, full of shadows.

"Very well." He turned to Alissand. The shah cowered. Good. *"Stay."*

Vasili climbed into the boat and gripped the sides as Nikolas dug an oar into the sand and heaved the small vessel back into the surf again. Salt water splashed against the hull, dashing Vasili's skin, tingling his face and lips. It was nothing. A minor distraction. Worth it to complete himself finally.

Nikolas rowed hard, his arms heaving the oars through the water.

"Would you betray me, Nikolas?"

"Never." His gaze fixed on Vasili's. Behind him, the ship loomed larger.

A thick shiver rolled through Vasili, chilling him. This... there was something wrong with all of this. Dark waters shimmered under moonlight. The water. They'd hoped it would weaken him. They were wrong.

"My griffin," Vasili whispered, watching Nikolas's face harden with determination. *"Did you truly believe I'd step aboard if I were at risk?"*

His eyes narrowed by an almost imperceptible amount. He had believed it. Or hoped it, at least. Poor, naïve Nikolas, always hoping for the best.

He stopped rowing and nocked the oars in their brackets. The boat bobbed halfway between the shore and the ship.

A smile lifted Vasili's lips. *"Finish rowing, Nikolas."*

"She was right," Nikolas said, cheek twitching. "This won't work."

"She?"

Nikolas slammed into Vasili. He tilted and flung out a hand to stop himself from toppling over the side, but his fingers sailed through air. The boat tipped, Vasili teetered, and Nikolas pushed, spilling them both into cold, hungry waters. Shock robbed his thoughts and tore the flame's icy grip from his mind. He gasped. Water surged down his throat. Bubbles raced toward the surface. He reached for them and the inky shadow of the boat above.

Nikolas's grip slammed down on his shoulders, *pushing* downward. Vasili bucked, wildly kicking, lungs burning for air, but Nikolas's steely grip hardened. His dark eyes stayed fixed on his, his dark hair drifting, his face blank, and his eyes fierce.

No, the fool! He'd kill them both!

Vasili wedged his hands between them and tried to lever him off. Nikolas didn't move, didn't let go, just stared.

The thumping burn scorched from his chest to his head, spilling throbbing light into his vision.

His assassin.

The drum-like beat was everywhere now, but fading too, muffled behind a suffocating quiet. He was glad, in the end, that he hadn't died alone.

CHAPTER 22

iko

He had seconds to act.

The moment Vasili's thrashing ceased, he scooped him into his arms and kicked for the surface, breaching it with a gasp. Gods, this had to work. He slammed Vasili against the skiff's hull, pinning him above the bobbing waterline. Vasili's head struck the hull and lolled to the side.

He'd tried to time it right, when he was unconscious but not drowned. Too long and the flame would think him dead, escaping its bonds. Had it been too long?

"You wretched, bedeviled man." Niko manhandled Vasili against the skiff and landed a slap across his face. "Don't you dare fucking drown." With a fist in his ripped shirt, he shook him hard and slammed him against the boat again.

"Niko!" Roksana called from high above.

The enormous *Walla's Heart* hull creaked and groaned closer. Two ropes spilled over her rail, down to the water, then a platform slung between them.

He kicked from the skiff and hauled Vasili onto the platform, then climbed on himself. "Hurry!" Niko braced over Vasili. With his wet hair plastered to his milk-white face, he looked dead. "Come back, you vicious prick. Come back and hate me for this, hate me for everything." He had his hands in his shirt again and rattled him like a doll. No, he hadn't just killed him, he couldn't have. Niko bowed over him, forehead-to-forehead. "Vasili, you hear me and you hear me good. You do not die here. Understand? I vowed to save you... you cannot,"—his voice caught—"you cannot die."

Vasili convulsed, spluttered water, rolled to one side, almost damn near tipping them both off the platform, and vomited up half the bay. His groan was entirely Vasili-like, not some horrible corruption by the flame. But Niko had to be sure. Using his thumb, he peeled back Vasili's eyelid, revealing a startling blue eye, one full of indignation that Niko dare touch him.

Hands grabbed them both, hauling them aboard.

"The flame?" Roksana demanded as the crew manhandled Vasili and carried him away. Niko tried to go after him, but his aunt blocked his way. "Niko?"

"He's himself, for now." He almost sobbed.

"Get him inside the cabin," she ordered her men, suddenly the voice of authority Niko sorely needed. "Warm blankets. Hurry! Haul anchor! Out to sea!"

They escorted Vasili out of sight into the cabin as

the ship's sails snapped full above his head, the wind grabbing hold.

He hadn't been sure it would work. But seeing him in the boat, the flame riding him hard, using him, like he'd been used his entire life, there had been no going back and no other choice.

And now Vasili was here... *alive*. But how badly wounded? The first sight of him on that beach, so thin, his face drawn and black eye hollow... He hadn't been sure there was any Vasili left to save. Niko had fought not to row to him and shake the flame from his bones.

He grabbed the rail now and breathed deeply, steadying his legs. Across the waters, on the beach, the torches retreated back into the night. This wasn't over. But with both Cavilles free from the influence of the flame, perhaps they'd bought themselves some time. Now he just had to figure out what to do with it.

SUNLIGHT SEEPED through the narrow cabin windows. Niko hadn't slept, too concerned for Vasili asleep on the cot. His eye being blue was a damn good sign the flame had withdrawn its control, but they'd only know for sure when he woke.

He looked weak enough to snap in two, but his breathing was steady. Through the night, Niko had checked his frail wrist, feeling for his heartbeat. It was there, fluttering against Niko's fingertips.

Niko watched the door too, half expecting

Roksana's crew to bundle Vasili below deck with his brother.

Roksana arrived sometime after dawn. She studied the sleeping prince, under Niko's watchful glare, and then nodded for Niko to join her outside.

Niko emerged, shielding his eyes against the glaringly bright sun. All around lay endless ocean and sky. He'd never left the land behind before. It was isolating. But freeing too. The flame couldn't reach them here.

"Here." Roksana handed him a bread roll stuffed with fish meat. "Eat."

His stomach growled in reply. He took the roll and quickly devoured it in a few bites.

Roksana leaned a hip against the mast. "I suppose I should officially welcome you aboard *Walla's Heart.*"

"Yasir's ship."

She waved his observation away. "He'll be safe in the city, I'm sure of that much. Lajani has more lives than a shiproach."

Yasir would hopefully have gotten Liam to safety too. Niko would find them again, once he'd figured out what their next move was. But he wasn't thinking on any of that until Vasili woke and he knew what was left of the prince. His gaze tracked back toward the cabin door, thoughts drifting.

"How is he?" Roksana asked.

"Alive. Any more than that, I can't say until he wakes."

There was no knowing what was left of Vasili's mind. Whatever the elves had done to trigger this, it seemed unlikely he'd be the same Vasili that had teased him at the northward inn. If it was like the cabin in the woods again, he could perhaps manage it, depending on how long Roksana let them stay. Niko would prefer to ship Vasili and himself off to some faraway land where none of this could reach either of them, but as Vasili had told him many times, running away wouldn't solve anything.

"There are fresh clothes and soap, for when he's ready," Roksana said. "You can have the captain's cabin as long as you need it. I'm rather enjoying bunking with the crew. The swines play a mean game o' jacks."

"Thank you. For all of it." And he meant it. He couldn't have gotten Vasili back without her. She'd done everything she'd said she would, and more.

"Let's hope it helps."

Niko untied the key to Amir's lock and handed it over. "He'll be as angry as a rat in a barrel by now."

She slipped the key into her pocket. "Oh, I know. He wasn't quiet about his treatment. Says he wants a cabin with a view. I'm afraid we're not used to accommodating spoiled prince-brats."

Roksana appeared to have gotten the measure of Amir quickly enough. "Just keep him away from Vasili. And me. I can't handle his bullshit with everything else..."

"What happened, Niko?" she quietly asked. "At the house, when we broke Amir out, you were only half with us."

She must have already suspected. Niko sent his gaze out toward the sparkling horizon and thrust his hands deep into his trousers pockets. "I'm tied to the bastard in the worst way."

"I assumed Vasili—"

"No. He drew that line and didn't cross it, but Amir..." He cleared the quake in his throat and slid his gaze sideways toward Roksana. "I'll kill him if I get my hands on him. Or worse... The need is less out here, but it's not entirely vanished. I'm still fucked."

His aunt's sympathetic half smile hit him hard in the heart, reminding him he'd been fighting all this for too long. "I'll deal with Amir," she said. "You focus on Vasili. Everything else can wait."

She left him standing in the sun, staring after her, as her crew bustled and the ship creaked on the soft ocean swell. This moment felt like a pause, but breaks in the battle were dangerous because he might never want to fight again, and this war was a long way from over.

NIKO WOKE to the thump of a boot hitting the cabin floor. The other boot sailed by next, hit the floor, and skidded to join its partner against the far wall.

Vasili sat hunched on the edge of the cot bed, hands buried in his knotted hair. His shoulders heaved, breaths coming too fast. The creased, salt-encrusted trousers dangled loose black threads over his bare feet.

Niko slowly rose from the chair. If he could just get a look at his face, he'd know if they were all safe or about to be slain in a blink. A board creaked under his foot.

Vasili's thin shoulders curled in, making himself small.

Just a few more steps. "Vasili?" His voice was suddenly loud between them.

Vasili dragged his hands down his face and blinked at the cabin door. His eye was blue, his pale lashes crusted with salt. Stains on his face marked the tracks of his tears. Gods, he wanted to go to him, wrap him in his arms and never let him go. This was all so fucking wrong.

Vasili shot from the bed and sprinted for the door.

"Wait!"

Too late. He was out and gone. Niko dashed outside but stopped dead at the sight of Vasili standing on deck barefoot. The wind tugged at his matted hair and trousers as he lifted his pale face to the sky. He blinked quickly, lashes fluttering. And laughed. The sound made Niko's heart ache. It wasn't manic, as he'd feared, just gentle, peals of laughter.

"It's so quiet."

The crew had stopped work to stare. Vasili noticed, and the joy quickly fell from his face, surrendering to a more typical Caville mask of indifference. He caught Niko watching too, and his brow furrowed. Wordlessly, he marched back inside the cabin.

Roksana arched an eyebrow and relaxed the hand she'd held above her pistol.

He couldn't blame them for being nervous. Niko wasn't entirely sure who or what they were dealing with either. He hadn't expected laughter.

He entered the cabin and latched the door behind

him. Vasili stood at the washbasin, pouring water into the bowl. He plunged his hands in and splashed his face, gasping. Taking up a cloth, he slowly dragged it across his face, down his arms and chest.

The silence seemed to demand Niko speak, but he wasn't sure what to say. Anything he could think of seemed trite, so he crossed his arms and waited.

"If you're going to hover like a nervous nanny, can you pass me a shirt?" Vasili half turned his head, avoiding meeting Niko's gaze but at least acknowledging him.

He was coherent, talking, *fine*. He even sounded like his old self, his voice sharp with the Caville lilt.

Niko retrieved a shirt from a clean pile and approached, handing it out for him. Vasili snatched it from his fingers and tossed it over his head, shrugging it on. Sleeves billowed, hiding his thin frame. He teased the laces, trying to tie them with trembling fingers. When the laces vexed him, he cursed and swayed, suddenly grabbing for the washstand, knuckles whitening. "I'm all right," he said softly, still not looking behind him at Niko.

"Bullshit."

Vasili's shoulders stiffened. He shoved from the basin, crossed the room—still avoiding Niko's glare—and grabbed the trousers. Then stopped, staring at the garment in his hands. The hesitation only lasted a few seconds before he was in motion again, stripping out of his trousers to tug on the fresh pair. Gods, he was thin. His thighs lean. And Niko only now noticed how cut up his feet were.

Niko grabbed the boots, pretending to inspect them so he didn't stare at Vasili like a fucking idiot. The boots looked new, while the rest of his clothes had been reduced to rags.

Vasili tugged on his shirt cuffs, making sure they hid the silvery scars at his wrists. Then he noticed Niko holding his boots. "Put them down."

A tone in his voice had Niko immediately setting them down. "Vasili—"

"Better yet, toss them overboard."

That seemed... excessive. They were perfectly good boots. He filled his lungs instead. "Vasili, we need to talk."

"And say what?" He padded barefoot across the cabin and looked Niko directly in the eye, as though issuing a challenge. He'd looked at Niko like this when they'd first met, as though Vasili were spoiling for a fight. But Niko knew him now, and the mask he wore was made of glass. Fragile *and* transparent, at least to Niko.

Vasili suddenly grabbed the boots and, in a swirl of white hair, was out of the cabin again, moving like the wind. Niko caught up with him in time to see the boots go sailing over the side of the ship. They landed in the water with twin splashes.

The crew went about their business, studiously *not* watching the slightly unhinged Caville throw his boots overboard for no apparent reason. Niko loitered behind by a few steps, at a loss as to how to help him. Vasili was still dangerous, but in the typical Caville way and less of a world-ending nasdas way. When afraid, he lashed out. This was his way.

Roksana started forward. Niko subtly lifted his hand to stop her. She'd been a large part of the reason why Vasili had broken down before. He *looked* fine now, he was even behaving like a Caville, but it wouldn't last. It couldn't.

When it became clear Vasili wasn't about to follow the boots into the sea, Niko leaned against the rail beside him. They'd stood together like this in almost exactly the same place on the deck, looking back at Seran's docks. Now there was nothing to look at but miles of shimmering ocean.

"The deck is full of splinters. You need shoes," Niko said.

Vasili snorted and stared at the horizon. The breeze teased his ragged hair over his scarred eye.

"Are you hungry?" Niko asked.

Vasili tilted his head. "Starved, actually."

"I'll find you something to eat. Will you be all right here?"

"I'm not about to fling myself overboard, if that's what you fear."

He had. "Vasili—"

"I'm not going to shatter, Nikolas." A small smile found the corner of his lips. "I don't recall the last time I ate. Some food would be kind and will stop you looming over my shoulder."

Niko crossed the deck to Roksana and passed on the request for something to eat. "Where's Amir?" he asked, following his aunt as she rounded up some fresh fish and bread.

"The same place you left him, but gagged. The crew got tired of his whining."

"Good." He took the plate of food and glanced back at the prince appearing to relish the wind in his wet hair. "I just... He's not right."

"You think the flame still has him?"

"No. It's what it's left behind that has me concerned."

His aunt smiled fondly. "A good meal goes a long way to feeding the heart too."

CHAPTER 23

iko

VASILI REFUSED to return to the cabin, so they ate the
fish, bread, and rice on the upper deck—a smaller,
raised area above the cabin at the ship's aft, mostly out
of sight from the crew below. Vasili sat cross-legged and
chewed slowly as he watched the sun begin its descent
into the sea, taking the warmth of the day with it.

Niko soaked up his silence, listening to the rigging
clang, the sails strain, and the men jibe and guffaw
below. He knew from experience that Vasili would talk
when he was ready.

As the night's chill thickened, the crew lit basket
fires on deck.

"We should go in." Niko moved to stand.

"Go ahead."

The answer came too fast, and his accompanying

smile was too thin to carry any real meaning. Niko settled again. He wasn't about to leave him alone, not until he could trust him and trust Roksana's crew not to hurt him. She'd helped them, but he'd been burned too many times.

Vasili shivered. "It's so quiet."

It was. The wind had dropped, and the crew were settling for the night. The occasional thump of boots on deck or sudden laugh were the only sounds accompanying the clanging rigging. The vast space all around them was quiet. Niko's gaze fell to Vasili's hand where he spread his fingers against the deck. He ached to touch him. To hold him, like he had at the cabin in the woods, but this Vasili was different again. Even more fragile than the last. How many times could a man break before he shattered forever?

"What's your plan?" Vasili suddenly asked. "Because the last played out *so* well."

Niko couldn't even recall what plan he referred to—perhaps visiting the salt mine under his palace—but considering his note of dry sarcasm, it was clear where the blame lay. "To breathe," Niko said, and it was the damn truth.

Vasili's brow pinched. "Amir's aboard?"

How had he known? "Yes."

"Two of the flame's last sources on one small ship, with a pirate crew of questionable loyalty." Clearly, he'd been paying attention since leaving the cabin. "Who knows we're here?"

"Just the crew and your... the men you had with you

on the beach." Niko said the last quietly, not sure if reminding Vasili of the beach would hurt him.

He shivered again, forcibly this time.

"Come inside." Niko stood and held out his hand.

"I like it here," he snubbed, turning his face away.

"Fine. Freeze your royal ass off." Niko stomped down the few steps and back into the cabin. He lit the small stove and arranged a bedroll and blankets in front of it. By the time he was done, Vasili entered, teeth clamped against his shivering. He knelt at the stove and rubbed his hands for warmth. "I can hear you gloating."

"I said it was cold."

"And I said I liked it."

"Yet here you fucking are."

The argument felt familiar, like old well-trodden territory.

Niko joined him, soaking up the heated glow. The fire, the quiet, the both of them side by side, it reminded him of the cabin in the woods, and when Vasili looked over, his soft smile warmed by the stove's light, he clearly thought the same. Niko blinked at the man beside him. Because there he was. His hidden Vasili. The man he loved.

Vasili needlessly fiddled with his bedroll and blankets. When satisfied, he settled.

Niko tried not to think too much on how Vasili's knee rested against his thigh or how Vasili had moved his bedroll tight against Niko's. He also tried not to focus on how comfortable they'd been lying side by side inside the cabin in the woods and how much he desperately ached for that closeness again. But those times were before. These times were after, and different.

The cabin was dark now, lit only by stove light and a swinging oil lamp. Vasili briefly met Niko's lingering gaze, catching Niko admiring him before Niko could look away.

"Really, Nikolas." Vasili propped himself up on an arm, leaning closer. "Treating me like glass is tiresome." His fingers skimmed Niko's jaw, and Niko found himself unable to resist his pull. The light touch sparked low in Niko's belly, instantly waking the savage desire to have Vasili close. Suddenly, Vasili's cool, slightly cracked lips met Niko's. Niko's thoughts unspooled, caught between ravaging Vasili and holding him at arm's length for his own good. Then Vasili's tongue thrust in, sliding against Niko's. Vasili's hands pressed against Niko's chest, urging him to lay back, and in the heady rush of lust, he almost damn well went.

"Wait." He got a hand between them and eased Vasili back.

Vasili's hand clamped the back of his neck and hauled Niko into a fierce kiss, the kind that detached reason and thought and had Niko's entire body burning for more. The same kind of kiss they'd once shared in a starlit field—so fucking mixed with hate and need and anger that it was as dangerous as it was fucking amazing.

He shoved at Vasili, rocking him back. "Stop, gods-damn it."

Vasili gave only an inch and leaned into Niko's touch. His gaze searched Niko's, his expression questioning. Somewhere on Niko's face he must have found his answer. "I see." He sat back and tugged a knee to his chest.

"You don't want to fuck."

Vasili tilted his head. "Don't tell me what I want."

"You want this." Niko finally laid his hand over Vasili's. So simple a thing, to hold his hand.

Vasili looked at their hands, and, for a second, the shock on his face had Niko almost snatching his hand back. He'd clearly gotten it all wrong, but when he lifted his gaze, tears shimmered in Vasili's eye.

"Everything I did, I wanted to happen," Vasili whispered. "It wasn't the flame, Niko, it was all me." He looked up from their hands, fighting with himself and the hurt, and when Niko reached for him, Vasili clamped his arms around himself—hugging himself closed, making himself small again, and shutting everyone out, including Niko.

Fuck that. Niko wrapped an arm around his shoulders and hauled him against his chest, absorbing his trembling. "I know you, and *that* wasn't you." He didn't have clever or pretty words to tell Vasili he was wrong, tell him that the fact he hurt was all the proof he needed that those things he'd done weren't all him. He didn't know how to heal what had been done to Vasili, and he couldn't take away the horrors of the past few weeks, but he could hold him. He could *love* him. And maybe that was all they both needed.

 asili

HE WOKE on his side to the sounds of gulls and creaking of timber. A heavy weight pinned one leg down while a second lay over his arm. *Trapped*. Vasili's heart fluttered. The metallic taste of panic touched his tongue. His heart, now lodged in his throat, choked any effort to cry out. The timber groaned some more, voices mumbled, prompting a laugh in reply somewhere far off.

A ship. He was on the ship. Not among elves. Not tied down.

His thoughts calmed some, becoming his own again. The panic subsided and fear thawed from his bones. The heavy weight pinning him wasn't ropes or ties, it was Nikolas.

Vasili willed his body to move. The last thing he

recalled was crawling into Nikolas's lap like an emotionally stunted fool. Gods, what a display. He'd clearly fallen asleep there. Nikolas slept too, indicated by the soft breaths tickling the back of Vasili's neck. He'd wrapped Vasili in his limbs sometime in the night.

Vasili was grateful for the warmth, especially as the stove had burned down to embers, but being pinned was not how he'd have preferred to wake. Of course, Nikolas wasn't a threat—well, not like this. He was a threat at other times. But in these quiet moments, he was everything Vasili needed him to be and so much more.

There would always be that small part of him who wanted to shove Nikolas off and clamber away. Not so long ago, he would have. But now the fear had subsided, Vasili found he rather liked the firmness pressed against his back and the leg possessively hooked over his. In fact, now the fear had thawed, a different kind of warmth had begun to sizzle his skin, the kind that had his cock noticeably warming too.

The dark flame and its incessant *need* had, for the most part, vanished. He'd woken blessedly free of madness. As for the rest of the horrors and their implications from the past few weeks... he didn't want to think on it. What he wanted was to take Nikolas's hand and place it over his cock, leaving the man in no doubt what Vasili wanted. But Nikolas still dozed. And on waking, he'd probably tear himself away, as he was so thoroughly conditioned not to touch.

His breaths still fluttered at Vasili's neck, making Vasili's heart race for a very different reason now.

Something heavy thumped below deck, and Nikolas twitched, stirring.

Gods, he didn't want this to end. Nikolas would rouse, tear himself away, and look at Vasili like he was broken again. Any more of that nannying and he really would go insane.

Quickly, before Nikolas gathered his wits, he laid his arm over Nikolas's and fixed his fingers in his. Now Vasili held *him* trapped. Better. He'd have preferred to be the one holding him down, but given the circumstances, this would have to do.

Nikolas stiffened. He swallowed with a loud click, mumbled an apology, and attempted to pull away. Vasili tightened his hold on his hand, keeping his arm trapped, preventing him from retreating.

"Good morning, prince."

The words, spoken roughly, brushed Vasili's ear, spilling lust down his spine, making him ache and hardening his cock some more.

He readied a reply, but Nikolas planted the softest, most delicate kiss on the curve of his neck, turning the words on Vasili's lips into a small, involuntary gasp. Well then, there was nothing to be done but follow where this led.

He pulled Nikolas's hand lower, pressing it hard against the bulge in his trousers. Nikolas's hand opened, his fingers molding around the straining length. Vasili fluttered his eye closed. Yes, that would do nicely. "More."

"Hm," Nikolas purred, his voice gravelly from sleep.

His warm, soft mouth skimmed Vasili's neck again, drifting closer to his shoulder.

If Nikolas insisted Vasili didn't want to fuck, like he had last night, Vasili would happily pin him down and demonstrate how very wrong he was.

"You made a promise." Vasili's own voice had gained a ragged edge, and not from sleep.

"I've made several." The delicious way his deep voice rumbled coupled with his rough hand firmly rubbing Vasili's cock might just be enough to distract him.

With Nikolas spooned against Vasili, there was no missing the hard nudge of cock against Vasili's hip.

Soft lips gave way to blunt teeth nipping Vasili's shoulder, and, almost involuntarily, he tilted his hips, seeking to drive his cock deeper against Nikolas's tight fingers. The motion gave Nikolas room to shift his waist, and a little adjustment saw him seat his restrained cock snugly between the valley of Vasili's ass.

"You promised to *milk me until I cry your name*."

The puff of air against Vasili's back was the gasp he longed to hear. Having Nikolas on his knees or having him on his back, his wrists tied, having him in all ways, was its own kind of torture. Vasili never wanted those moments to end. Having him suck him off had been his own personal fantasy since he'd threatened it aboard this very ship, so long ago now that life felt like a dream.

Nikolas's hand vanished from Vasili's cock but quickly found a new place at his shoulder, where Nikolas pulled roughly on Vasili's shirt collar, dragging it down to expose more of Vasili's shoulder. His tongue swirled and his teeth nipped, and if he kept this up, Vasili really would have to take matters into his own hands.

"Beg for it," Nikolas grumbled.

The idea almost made Vasili recoil, but it did something else too, made his insides throb in the most pleasantly hot and heavy way.

Nikolas's bristled jaw scratched over Vasili's shoulder, and when he next spoke, it was directly into his ear. "Beg me to suck you off or you get nothing at all."

Damn him. This was supposed to be Vasili's game. Vasili's chest heaved, breaths already betraying him. Part of him wanted to resist such a demand. He was a prince, albeit a prince of nothing. He did not beg a blacksmith for anything. But this was Nikolas, the man who thankfully had no idea how debilitating his presence was for Vasili.

"Too much of an ask?" Nikolas withdrew, taking his heat with him. "That's probably for the best." He was rising to his knees, moving *away*.

Anger spurred lust higher. The fucking tease.

Vasili rolled over, got to his knees, acutely aware of his very obvious need tenting his trousers, and grabbed for Nikolas's arm, roughly pulling him around. Both now kneeling, with Nikolas eye-to-eye, chest-to-chest, breathing like the air was too thin, Vasili had him. His dark, sultry eyes had turned sly, and his knowing little quirk of the lips already told how thoroughly he'd caught his prey.

Vasili grabbed his jaw, dug his fingers in, and leaned

close, as though to kiss him, but stopped, their rushed breaths mingling. This man who challenged him, defied him, and so thoroughly understood him that he had no choice but to love him in return. "Make good on your promise and suck me off, now."

Nikolas jerked his chin free and grinned. "That's an order, prince. I'm not surprised you don't know the difference between an order and an ask." His hand fell between them. His rough fingers captured Vasili's cock in his fist, tearing another gasp from between Vasili's lips. "Beg me to run my tongue down this." His grip eased, turned, and his fingers kneaded Vasili's balls while the ball of his palm rubbed the base of Vasili's cock, driving delicious friction.

It was a good thing Vasili was already on his knees. He flung an arm over Nikolas's shoulder and buried his face in his neck. Nikolas's pulse fluttered, inviting Vasili's tongue, and when he sealed his mouth over its heated beat, he similarly assaulted Nikolas's arousal. The trousers between them were proving frustrating, but shoving two fingers lower, between Nikolas's muscular thighs and behind his balls, had the desired effect of making Nikolas's jerk to attention. "I do not beg."

Nikolas's hand plunged into Vasili's hair. His fingers knotted, twisting, his confidence to take Vasili in his hand such a wonderfully unexpected surprise. "You do for me." With his free hand, he tore Vasili's trousers ties open, his movements so rough they jerked Vasili's hips. And then his thick fingers were on Vasili's free cock, skin-to-skin, and the exquisite pleasure at being held firm and having his cock serviced had Vasili throwing his head back and almost giving himself over to Nikolas. Nobody had ever dared hold him so rigidly, not even Alek—retribution from the palace never far from his mind.

"You want my lips on your cock, prince? My tongue licking your slit? Then fucking beg me for it, and I'll make good on my promise."

His heart was a drum, his thoughts a free mess. Nikolas's expert hand slowly stroked, just enough to tease so much more, and Vasili was already halfway to surrendering. Nikolas had no idea how long he'd wanted to fuck his mouth and spill inside him. He'd have preferred to have him tied in some manner, to stop his wandering hands, but even the fear barely registered now. He needed this to forget and to remember. He needed this so he knew he wasn't alone. He needed this to *feel* again. "Do it."

"Beg."

"Bastard!"

His dark chuckle undid more of Vasili's restraint.

"I've never denied it, *prince*."

"Fucking *please*," Vasili relented.

"Gladly." Nikolas's fuckable mouth twitched. "Your Highness."

Nikolas switched his grip from Vasili's hair to his hip. He knelt low and sealed his rough fingers around the base of Vasili's cock, holding him steady. That confident touch alone had need pulsing through Vasili, lighting him up from the inside. The warm seal of Nikolas's wet lips ringed the crown, and a devastating shudder robbed Vasili of all thought. Just need remained. The tight seal of Nikolas's lips swallowed him deeper. His tongue spread, the thick, wet muscle rolling to cup his shaft, and Vasili distantly heard himself curse. He'd wanted Nikolas on his knees for too damn long.

He glanced down to the exquisite picture of Nikolas looking up, his lips sealed around Vasili's cock, his fingers working Vasili's veined shaft, his tongue sliding over the slit, just as he'd promised.

Then he pulled free, licking his lips. Vasili expelled all the air in his lungs. "Don't stop," he breathed. Or had he begged? Gods, only Nikolas could reduce him to this. "More." He sounded desperate and no longer cared.

Nikolas pressed the flat of his tongue under Vasili's cockhead and rolled his tongue's edges, applying delicious pressure. He flicked the tip, and Vasili's knees almost buckled out from under him.

Vasili clutched at Nikolas's hair, flung his head back, and moaned like a whore as Nikolas welcomed Vasili's cock into the tight, warm channel of his throat. Vasili had him caught, on his knees now and under his control, and maybe before he might have been able to restrain the desire, but not now. Nikolas smiled around his shaft. And Vasili was lost to the mindless rush of savage need. Nikolas was so damn accepting, taking it all, faster and harder. A low tingling chased Vasili down, threatening to crest. Like the bastard knew he was close, Nikolas stroked behind Vasili's balls, sliding a finger back toward Vasili's hole as Nikolas's mouth took a pounding.

"Niko." Vasili's back arched. Nikolas's tongue and lips

tightened in cruel synchronicity, and Vasili came amidst the mindless thrusting, shattering him apart until the slow lap of Nikolas's tongue fixed the pieces of him together.

Nikolas rose, wiped his thumb across his smug smile, and fell into a long, salacious kiss, tasting of salt and Vasili's own seed. He was heat and fire, rock and iron, and after everything they'd survived, after every hurt and obstacle, impossibly, Nikolas Yazdan was Vasili's.

Vasili shuddered and fell heavily into him, listening to their heavy breaths. He pressed a hand to Nikolas's chest, over his shirt, and felt the rapid thud of his heart against his palm. His griffin was a wonder. A man like none other Vasili had met. His only regret was that none of this could last. But he wasn't thinking on that. On any of it.

He lazily dropped his hand to Nikolas's prominent erection. Nikolas gently swept his touch away and planted a small kiss at the corner of Vasili's mouth. "This was all for you."

To go from making demands to offering gifts. If Nikolas knew how thoroughly he wrecked Vasili's carefully prepared barriers every time they were together, he'd surely laugh. "Later then?"

"I'll hold you to that."

The cabin door rattled, someone trying to enter, and then a quick succession of knocks abruptly brought an end to Vasili's wonderful morning.

"Nikolas?" Roksana called.

Vasili breathed in, filling his lungs and shoring up his

defenses. For all the miles upon miles of ocean, he was still surrounded by enemies, Roksana being one of them. Nikolas gave him a questioning look, checking he was well. Vasili nodded, hastily tucked himself away, and realigned his clothes into some semblance of composure.

Nikolas opened the door.

"Ah," his aunt said, greeting him with a smile. Her smile faded some when she caught sight of Vasili's scowl. "We have a situation with, er... our other guest. He's becoming a problem."

Nikolas's growl at the news was decidedly beastly. "Then gag him tighter."

Roksana's side-eye in Vasili's direction was full of unasked questions.

With a heavy sigh, Vasili approached. "What is it?"

"He put up such a racket we feared he might kick a hole in the hull. He's demanding to speak with you, Vasili," she said. Her tone was flat. She spoke as the captain of this ship, a ship that wasn't hers—but captain nonetheless. "He wasn't told you were aboard."

"The flame knows." Its pull had become a niggling afterthought, but it was still a shadow in Vasili's mind, and it was acutely aware of the prize below deck.

"You don't have to see him," Niko said.

He ran a hand through his hair, but knots snagged his fingers, reminding him of his general state of disarray. Looking down, he grimaced at the sight of his bare toes. "Some boots?" he inquired. A particularly unpleasant memory tried to swallow him. The same memory that made him toss the boots overboard. If only that memory were so easily discarded.

"I'm sure we can find something," Roksana said.

He waited on deck in the sun, with Nikolas simmering beside him. When Roksana returned with a fresh pair of boots and socks, he thanked her and tugged them on, aware both Yazdans watched him like hungry hawks. Or perhaps hungry wolves. At least these two weren't trying to open his veins. Yet. At sea, Nikolas wouldn't succumb again to the dark flame, but Roksana likely had her own reasons for being helpful.

She led the way toward the hatch in the deck and the ladder down, into the hold. He climbed down the first few rungs and looked up, finding Nikolas's stricken face. He wasn't following.

"I can't," he said, stalking off.

The hold was made up of storage bays, a corridor between them, and a bunk area beyond, where the crew slept and ate. The storage chambers hadn't been designed to hold prisoners, and one look at the buckled timber door confirmed it wouldn't hold Amir for much longer.

Roksana stopped outside the door but didn't reach for the handle. She clearly had something she wanted to say. Vasili waited for the excuses to come. Apologies full of Yazdan air. He'd trusted her, and he shouldn't have. It always came down to that mistake, a mistake he still made after so many years.

"The flame has used you both," she finally said. "I understand that. But I'm in two minds as to whether to dump you both overboard and be done with you, consequences be damned."

No limp apology. Just honesty. He respected that. She was a Yazdan, after all. "If I believed our deaths would result in a victory against the flame, I'd have killed my entire bloodline, and myself, long ago. Unfortunately for all, if the Caville line ends outside the palace, the flame goes free."

She blinked—any further comment apparently stuck in her throat—and opened the door into the small storage bay.

Amir lay on a bed of silk scraps with his hands clasped over his chest and his head propped on a pillow of silk. His mouth pressed into a thin line. "How is it you're permitted to walk free and I'm locked in here like some stowaway?"

Vasili arched an eyebrow. "Probably because Nikolas holds much of the authority here, and he's not particularly enamored with you."

Amir snorted. "He should be fucking grateful."

Roksana bowed out at that. "I won't be far. Holler if he gets rowdy."

Vasili leaned against the doorframe and folded his arms. Considering Amir's ordeal with Alissand, he didn't appear to be severely wounded. He'd been bled. The clothes were filthy, his hair sticking out at odd angles. His wrists were hidden beneath his sleeves, but a bitter smell of blood hung in the air.

Amir huffed through his nose and pouted, like a petulant middle brother. A brother who would do almost anything to be seen. Guilt gnawed on Vasili's resolve. "What do you want?"

Amir cocked his head. "Have you noticed how it's so quiet here?"

"Yes."

"The storm in my head..." He flitted his fingers near his face. "It's all clear now."

Vasili swallowed and briefly looked down. "The flame detests the ocean. Here, for now at least, we're free of it."

Sobs suddenly burst from Amir. He flung his hands, covered his face, and rocked, weeping into his palms. Vasili closed his eye to keep from witnessing his brother coming undone and bumped his head back against the doorframe.

"I can't do this," Amir moaned. He pulled his knees up, making himself small, like the time Vasili had found him hidden in a closet, terrified the shadows were talking to him. "You left me with this *thing in my head, Vasili!*" he screeched, face turning red and eyes streaming.

Vasili sighed. "I tried to keep you from it."

"I won't fucking go back to that wretched hell!" He kicked at the air and pressed his forehead to his folded arms, sobbing some more.

Watching his brother cry after everything Amir had done, everything that had happened, there was a sense of satisfaction in hearing his sobs. But it didn't last. Vasili's frustrations simmered too.

"You stabbed me in the heart," he whined.

"I *missed* your heart," Vasili said dryly.

"Oh, fucking wonderful! Thank you, dear brother, for your restraint!"

Vasili had Amir's neck clamped in his grip before he could draw breath to scream. "Elves took me, and you sent *the guards away*!" Shoving hard, he drove Amir into the bed of silk. His face turned red, then purple. His fingernails clawed at Vasili's hand, and it felt *good*. Felt real. *"You defiled Nikolas, poisoning the only damn thing I've ever cared about besides Mother, because I fucking ignored you?! You're not a victim, Amir. You're a vile, worthless, pathetic excuse of a man and everything I despise about our godsforsaken family."*

Someone dared touch Vasili's arm. He twitched, but the stranger's grip slammed in, grabbing him by the arms, hauling him off Amir. More bodies piled between them. Amir let out a shout, then, "He's half elf! FUCKING LOCK *HIM* UP!"

"Unhand me!" Vasili bucked, almost managing to twist free, but more hands landed on him, wrestling him out of the storage bay. The door slammed, sealing Amir inside.

The crew's hold eased up, and Vasili tore free. He fled up the ladder, needing air, needing the wind on his face and the sense of freedom stretching forever into the distance, and needing their fucking hands off him.

Nikolas was moving fast to intercept. Vasili wrapped his fingers around the ship's rail and breathed salty sea air into his lungs. His heart raced too fast, his skin burned, and the memories flashed again, trying to dig in like a hundred barbed hooks.

He wanted to kill Amir for countless reasons, but mostly for what he did to Nikolas.

Nikolas loomed again. He'd say something full of honesty and reason, and it would crack Vasili wide open.

"Don't."

Nikolas backed off and was gone from his peripheral vision, but he wouldn't be far.

Vasili tipped his face to the sun and just *breathed*. Like Nikolas had said. He just needed to stop and breathe, just for a little while.

He knew what had to be done. He'd always known, in one way or another. But he hadn't been strong enough. Still wasn't. He'd been weak before, because he'd been alone. That had changed.

This peace—this island of calm inside an ocean of agony—wouldn't last, but he'd needed it to refocus, to see the path ahead. The legacy, the flame, the curse: he'd see to it that everything ended with him. All he needed was his assassin to follow one final order.

 asir

THE BURLAP SACK over his head blurred his sight with shades of brown. The air tasted of ash, and his empty gut heaved. He could smell blood. Maybe his own. The men who'd grabbed him on the street hadn't been gentle in dragging him here.

With nowhere else to go, he'd retrieved Adamo from the glass gardens and trotted aimlessly through Seran's streets until dawn. The possessed guards had descended like vultures. He should probably have put up more of a fight, but there seemed little point when everything he'd fought for was ash. Besides, this had been inevitable. Niko had warned him, hadn't he? The flame burned everything it touched. He hadn't believed him.

Vasili had given him magic and power. The exotic, mysterious, beautiful prince with his smooth lies.

He should have listened to Niko.

He should have walked away when Niko gave him the chance. Instead, he'd doubled down, like a fool.

He'd never meant for any of it to touch Liam.

He'd never meant for it to go this far.

He bit his lip to keep from sobbing. There were others in the room. Big men who breathed like horses, but none spoke. More guards. They'd likely brought him to the Yazdan house. To Alissand—the shah who had knelt to Vasili. Did Vasili control all of Seran now? Perhaps Vasili had killed Niko. He didn't want to believe that, but Vasili was certainly capable. But not as cruel as the world made him out to be. Vasili had laughed easily on spice and drink. He even said all the wrong things, becoming quite the likable sort when he wasn't so stiff. Somewhere inside the madness, the man remained. He had to, or all was lost.

But Vasili *had* killed Liam. Yasir saw his murder in his mind again in horrible clarity. Vasili had targeted him, knowing who he was, and he'd smiled as Liam took his final, silent gasp.

The sack vanished from his head, scratching his chin and forehead as it was torn away. Light flooded his eyes. Dust or ash tickled his throat. He coughed and staggered on his feet, wheezing around the ache in his chest.

Shah Yazdan tossed the sack to the floor, folded his arms, and stared. "Captain Lajani."

"Shah Yazdan." He coughed again. "No longer kneeling, I see. Has Vasili let you off your leash—"

He didn't see the backhand coming, just felt its vicious burn and stumbled about on his feet, tasting blood pooling in his mouth. Tears streamed. He spat at the shah's feet. "I take it I'm not here to sell silk." His tongue felt fat and rough. He wet his lips, tasting more ash.

"I'm disappointed, captain." Alissand paced three steps right, and then three steps back, and turned on his heel again. Back and forth. "You were always good to my family. Roksana spoke highly of you. Colorful but trustworthy, she said. You've sold us silk for years."

"Silk on the books, spice under the table," he smiled, cracking the split in his lip. Roksana had his silks and spices now, all in his ship's hold.

"To find you in league with that *creature*."

He glanced at the guards. Seven of them, all bigger than Yasir. Fear fluttered the pulse in Yasir's throat. The shah was delusional, virtually mad, driven that way by his lust for blood. Niko's warning came back to him again. Yasir hadn't known the Julian both he and Vasili had spoken of, but it seemed the shah might be heading the same way as that unfortunate soldier. "I'm not in league with anyone. Just trying to survive."

"No? I saw you at the market square."

"Then you saw me shoot Vasili in the chest."

Alissand's dark eyebrows inched together.

He hadn't seen a damn thing. He'd been in Vasili's thrall by then. "Wait, you think Vasili let me go?" Yasir chuckled. "I ran!"

Alissand stopped pacing and looked into Yasir's eyes. His eyes weren't black now. He just looked like a slightly younger version of his dead father, less wrinkled, skin baked brown by years in the sun, lashes dark and alluring. "You were close to him?"

"With the man, yes. Not with whatever he is now."

"Something happened?"

Yasir turned his face away.

"He did something? Hurt you." Alissand's voice softened on the last two words. "Your delicate lover, what was his name?"

He should damn well know it. He'd kept Liam for weeks, dangling his safety over Yasir, making him betray Niko's trust to keep Liam safe. "His name was Liam," Yasir pushed through gritted teeth. Hearing it made his heart ache.

Alissand sighed. "You have my sympathies, captain."

Yasir flashed him a warning glance. He wasn't buying the bullshit Alissand was trying to sell. "You don't care. You're a lick away from losing your damn mind to the flame."

The shah's smile ticked. He straightened. "Know much of the flame, do you, Yasir?"

"Enough."

"It's remarkable you're still functioning, considering you've consumed it and aren't a Yazdan. It'll drive most men mad within weeks."

He'd heard of such things. Prince Amir had driven his whores insane, and the elves had poisoned Julian. The flame corrupted everything it touched, but Yasir had so far escaped that same fate, perhaps because he'd

230

only taken a little. Unlike the man standing in front of him now. The shah brimmed with the dark. It made Yasir's skin crawl just to look at him.

"It seems to me," Yasir began, "the blood in your veins is just an extension of the flame, making you and your men Vasili's tools. He was able to control his brother's army in Loreen, and clearly he controls yours now too. That must be unsettling."

The shah's face darkened. "Cavilles don't control the flame, the flame controls them. A vessel can't consume its contents. It'll burn him up, if it hasn't already."

Yasir shrugged. "Then I'd wager your hollow Yazdan army are next. We're all dead unless he returns home..." Alissand's brow rose, and Yasir trailed off, instantly regretting those last words.

"Why is Loreen significant?"

Shit. He had to run his mouth off... He licked his lips. "I just meant... If he went home, he'd be... away from Seran..."

"No, that's not what you were saying." The shah lifted his chin. "Hold him still."

The guards rushed in again, grabbing his arms. Yasir put up a pathetic attempt at struggling.

Alissand peered down his nose. "Never could keep your mouth shut. Roksana said that about you too."

"What could I know?" He laughed nervously. "As you said, I'm not even a Yazdan."

"No... but you have spent a considerable amount of time with one. Did Nikolas tell you something? His mother was always keeping secrets—" His hand shot out and grabbed Yasir's throat, choking off his air. "What did he tell you?"

Before he had a chance to even consider a reply, Alissand's fist slammed into Yasir's middle. All the air in his lungs tried to rush out at once, but the hand at his throat choked it off. Yasir folded like a snapped board, and pain exploded in his head.

Alissand released his throat, and, for a few seconds, he sucked on air, only for the next blow to rip pain across his jaw. He'd have fallen if not for the guards holding him up. Blood swilled in his mouth again and bubbled between his lips.

"Tell me!"

He couldn't. Whatever that chamber was beneath the Caville palace, it was too important for Alissand to meddle with. It wasn't meant for him. Yasir knew it in his heaving gut. Niko was the only one who could be trusted with that place. Everyone else could go hang.

A knife flashed. Where it had come from, Yasir didn't see. Hot hands grabbed the fingers of his right hand, and cold steel sank beneath the nail of his middle finger. A scream burst out of him. He kicked, tried to get his feet wedged enough for leverage, but just twitched and writhed in the guards' grips. The pain broke him open, making his thoughts and any attempt at summoning the flame flee from his weak control.

"You found something. You're going to tell me what that something was... and then you and I, Captain Lajani, are going to have a long discussion about your missing ship."

CHAPTER 26

iko

VASILI STAYED at the edge of the deck for hours after trying to choke Amir.

Niko kept an eye on him as he helped the crew with their chores.

When the late afternoon turned into early evening, some of the crew picked up a few instruments and began to sing the day to a close.

Niko found Vasili on the upper deck, leaning against the aft rail, staring into the vast nothingness of ocean and sky, where the sun bled all over the water. Windswept and untethered, wrapped in plain clothes, kissed by the fading light, Vasili looked like he belonged at that rail at the edge of the world. He could never go unnoticed. Too many angles conspired with his soft lips and sharp glances to make him anything other than extraordinary.

In the quiet moments, and the moments when he'd stripped all his layers back, Vasili was spellbinding. Vulnerable *and* fierce. Niko's Vasili.

Soft sounds of humming drifted on the breeze, and it took a moment for Niko to realize the sound came from Vasili humming along to the crew's music. Lady Maria's words came sailing back to him of how Vasili had sung as a boy. And he'd been quite something, according to Vasili's aunt. She'd told him to save Vasili, to take him away, and while *Walla's Heart* didn't really count as safe, he wondered if she would approve of his efforts anyway. Her end had been unfair, but she'd live on in his desire to keep Vasili safe.

Yasir would have appreciated the moment filled with Vasili and the sea and song. He'd have said something romantic. Niko didn't have the same imagination as the captain, so he stared instead.

The humming abruptly ended. Vasili half glanced behind him, not quite meeting Niko's gaze. "Are you done brooding?"

That earned a smile. "I don't brood."

Vasili snorted and smiled softly as Niko settled beside him. The prince reached over, and Niko happily laced his fingers with Vasili's. They were alone, out of sight from the crew, their own private space.

"Nikolas."

The gravitas with which he said Niko's name sent a chill through his blood. Whatever he said next was unlikely to be good. "Before you fuck it all up with whatever scheme or lie you're about to say, know that I would never have stopped trying to save you. If the ocean hadn't worked, I'd have found another way."

Vasili's fingers tightened around Niko's. "What if there was no other way?"

"I'd still have found one."

Vasili smiled softly, and in the fading light, it almost looked as though a slight pink flush touched his face. "Have you noticed the ballast bags?" Vasili asked.

"Ballast bags?" That had not been a question he'd expected, but he recalled seeing sandbags in the hold. "Used to help balance the ship? There are some below deck," Niko guessed, unsure where this was going.

Light reflected sharply in his keen blue eye. "Yes. Yasir ran trade in less legal items and those bags helped camouflage it."

That was hardly a surprise given Yasir's penchant for flirting with everything, including the law. But what did Yasir's underhanded trade have to do with them now? "I feel like I should see where this is leading..."

"There's a substantial cargo of spice among those bags."

There was spice aboard. "And you know this how?"

"What did you think we did at sea?" Sly delight had ahold of his smile now.

Niko snorted. "Not illegal spice-running, Your Highness." He recalled the note Vasili had written him and its whimsical tone. "Were you sober at all during those months?"

The prince chuckled. Vasili had taken to Seran, its people, its life, like he'd always belonged. If a northern prince wanted to run spice with a colorful captain, who in Seran was going to stop him? He'd been tied down most of his life, both figuratively and literally. Niko could hardly blame him for living while he had the chance. And he positively glowed now, recalling the memory.

"Why bring this up now?" he asked.

Vasili closed his eye. The breeze teased his locks of hair across his forehead. When he opened his eye, he continued to stare at the red-stained sea, but his smile had turned wooden. "The second I step foot on land, the flame will consume me. It will kill Amir, by my hand, and control you. I stopped it before, but I have neither the strength nor the will to do so again. Any man or woman who has consumed mine or Amir's blood will be forced to kneel. After that, I will take Seran, raze her to the ground, and that will just be the beginning." He said it all so matter-a-factly, like he was just reciting a list. But when he spoke next, it was quieter, filled with regret. "There is a rage in me, Nikolas. You've seen it. You saw it the moment we met. The flame feeds on it. The things I've done—"

"You were possessed."

He took his hand from Niko's and looked down at it. His lashes fluttered. "Here, now, with you, I wish it were so, but the flame and I were one. It will wash across this land, feeding, growing, until it's so powerful not even Walla's vast ocean will be able to hold it at bay."

Niko's pulse began to thud. Denying what they all knew would happen was pointless, as was offering false hope. He'd always known Vasili was capable of terrible things. *Feared* it, even. Every man was a product of his past, and Vasili's scars ran deep.

"Do you recall how I kept my father controlled with spice?" Vasili asked.

"I do," Niko replied quietly, fearing where this was headed.

Vasili straightened, breathed in, and finally looked Niko in the eyes. "A high dose of spice will render me unconscious. A continually administered dose will keep me out for days."

"No."

"Do the same to Amir, then return us both to the salt chamber beneath the palace."

"No, Vasili." His heart thudded harder.

"Once there, cut Amir's throat. Out cold, he won't feel it. Honestly, it'll be a blessing. The flame will funnel into me. And then—"

"I'm not putting you in that fucking cage." A tremor rocked his voice. *"Do not ask."*

Vasili's cool hand touched Niko's hot cheek, his soft palm pressing in against rough whiskers. "Once I am inside the cage, seal the salt chamber. For good. Nothing can ever get in or out again."

Niko caught his hand and lowered it, meaning to push him away. But now their fingers were entwined again, he couldn't bring himself to let go. "No."

"I'm not asking you. This is an order, from a prince to his soldier. My last order."

"No."

"Niko," Vasili's tone begged again, but not in a way Niko wanted to hear. "It was always going to end this way."

"There's another way."

"There is no other way."

"There's always another way," he whispered. "Yasir will know one. He and Liam had the book—"

Vasili yanked free and braced against the rail, bowing his head. "You must do this!" he hissed. "You made an oath. You gave your word! Kill a man—"

"I killed the man you ordered me to. I killed Julian—"

"It was never about Julian!" He grabbed Niko's hand again and applied it to his chest, the ripple of scars prominent beneath his shirt. "I ordered you to *kill me*, and don't pretend you didn't know it. You're not that naïve."

Vasili's heart beat against Niko's palm. So fragile a thing. He felt his own heart crumble, the pieces slip through his soul. "Don't ask me to do this," he whispered.

Vasili was so close now every line on his face stood out, every horrible scar marking the loss of his eye and a past he'd fought so hard to survive. "I told you this life is not for us."

This wasn't fair. Every good thing in Niko's life had been taken too, and now Vasili was asking him to give him up, to sacrifice him, like what they had together didn't matter. "You also told me it was real. All of it.

The cabin. The kiss. I can't do this thing you ask of me because I love you, you wretched son of a bitch. I dragged you out of that palace fire. I killed Alissand's possessed to get to you. I'd go to the fucking ends of Etara's earth for you, but I will *never* put you in that cage."

Vasili's palm settled against Niko's cheek. "Do this *because* you love me."

Niko leaned into the touch, relishing so rare a gift.

It was impossible, not least because Niko could never hurt him that way. Even if they returned to Loreen, if Vasili was trapped in the metal cage, Niko could never leave him there, knowing the spice would eventually wear off, and then Vasili would wake, only to die alone in the dark and the cold. Fuck that. No. Never. Vasili Caville had only ever tried to do the right thing, albeit a twisted version of it. He did not deserve to be damned because three ancient families couldn't quit squabbling over a power they should never have gotten their hands on anyway.

Niko pulled his hand free from Vasili's grip at his chest and grabbed onto the rail. "No. You'll die there, and I won't let that happen."

"So will the flame. Or at least be trapped, as it should have been before."

"I said no, Vasili."

He shrugged nonchalantly. "Then I'll ask Roksana."

Gods-damn him. "She won't help you."

"To stop the slaughter? To save lives?" Every question was clipped, his anger rising. "The flame ravaged her family. She already believes me lost. She's stubborn and has a righteous streak a mile wide. You're very alike. Of course she will aid me in this." He said the last with conviction, then softly added, "But I wanted it to be you." With that parting blow, Vasili left. The sound of his boots clipped the upper deck and hammered down the steps, taking him toward Roksana as his last words burned through Niko's heart like an open wound. How could Vasili ask such a thing?

He was right though. Of course he was fucking right. Roksana would help him. Which left Niko with no choice at all. That bastard prince. He always got his way.

Niko hurried onto the deck and spotted Vasili already speaking with Roksana. Her gaze flicked over the prince's shoulder and found Niko. Vasili glanced behind him, following her attention. The prick had the nerve to smile.

"Fucking fine," Niko grunted, then clasped Vasili by the back of the neck, reeled him in close, and slammed a savage kiss onto his smiling lips. Vasili's hard mouth surrendered, allowing Niko's tongue to slide in. Vasili soon fought back, kissing with the fervor of a man who knew the sands in his hourglass had run down to dust. They stood on deck, in full view of the crew and his aunt, and Niko didn't give a shit what any of them thought. Vasili was better than them all, and if any of them cared to look beyond the ice, they'd see the real man too, and they'd damn well understand why Niko kissed him like this might be the last time he could.

Breathless, he broke the kiss and pressed his forehead against Vasili's, lost to the man's shining blue-eyed gaze. "I hate you."

"I know."

"Well." Roksana cleared her throat. "That settles that."

Niko glared his aunt away. With a chuckle, she lifted her hands and sauntered off. Vasili still peered at him, nose-to-nose. They stood on *Walla's Heart's* deck, an island in a storm, and with the way Vasili looked at him now, Niko never wanted to let him go. "I promised to suck you off this morning. Is now good for you?"

Vasili's bright laughter burst from him. Their fingertips were the last to part. He tossed a sultry look over his shoulder and headed toward the cabin.

"Ho!" Roksana called. "Ship westward! Turn her about!"

The crew burst into motion. Ropes and rigging spun, sails that had been full moments before fell slack as others were hoisted into place, catching the wind.

Niko joined Roksana on the upper deck. She handed over an eyeglass. He'd never used such a thing before, but raising it to his eye, he eventually spotted the dark smudge blurred in front of the setting sun. It didn't look like much until a splash of a colored flag caught his eye. "Can you tell whose it is?"

His aunt took the eyeglass back and raised it to her eye again. "The colors she's flying are Captain Lajani's."

"Yasir?" Niko's heart leaped. Vasili would be pleased. "Yasir was working on solutions. He'll have something." Something that meant he wouldn't have to drag Vasili to the salt mine and leave him there to die. He'd take any course of action over that.

Roksana seemed less pleased by their distant shadow. She lowered her glass and squinted at the darkening skies. "There's an ill wind, Niko. Best keep your sword close."

asir

YASIR TUGGED AGAIN on the ties at his wrists. Alissand's crew stomped on the ship's deck above. Dust, salt, and grit filtered between the boards and rained into his hair. All around, the ship moaned at being forced through the waves.

The gag in his mouth had soaked through and dried hard, cutting into his lips. If he could just loosen his hands, he might be able to get some feeling back into his fingers. He'd been working the ropes for hours now, fighting nausea so he didn't vomit and suffocate himself. It was fair to say he'd had better days.

To make it worse, the bastards were flying his colors. They meant to ambush *Walla's Heart*, Roksana, and Niko, in the hope of finding Amir, and it was all Yasir's fault.

His fingers fumbled the ropes again. He barked a cry into the rag at his own stupidity. If he hadn't been wandering the city like an idiot, if he hadn't run his mouth off, if he'd just been able to withstand the torture... At least his fingers were numb anyway, so he no longer felt the ache of his missing nails.

Two sailors slid down the deck ladders and approached. At sea, the flame within them was dormant, but there were at least thirty of the gnarly bastards, and Yasir had nothing but his wits, and those weren't particularly sharp.

One of the sailors applied the cold muzzle of a pistol to Yasir's forehead. "Try anything and your corpse goes in the drink."

What he was supposed *to try* surrounded by knuckle-draggers? He nodded his compliance. The other man—wearing a red necktie, of all things—cut the ropes and tugged the gag free.

"Thank you," Yasir mumbled around fat lips, bringing his arms around and rubbing his wrists. His jaw ached. His chest ached. His heart ached. *Everything* ached.

"Get cleaned up. You've got a job to do." They tossed a pile of clothes at his feet and backed up, pistol still armed and aimed at his head.

Yasir regarded the drab-looking grey slacks and tattered waistcoat. Linen was so rough against his skin. He much preferred satin. "You want me to wear that?"

"Does it not meet your high expectations, captain?"

Necktie leered. He had an unhealthy keenness in his eye that suggested he might have more of a personal interest in getting a man naked.

With a heavy sigh, Yasir stripped of his blood-stained garments and applied the horrible (probably lice-infested) clothes provided for him. "I might have preferred death, honestly."

"Doubt you'll 'ave to wait long for that."

They marched him onto the deck. Night had fallen. The crew all looked like animals, as though they spent more time than was healthy in Seran's fighting pits. From the orange glow thrown from the fire baskets, each man looked a twitch away from feral. But no Alissand. He'd stayed behind, perhaps to avoid the water. *Coward*.

"You know what you have to do," Necktie grumbled.

Walla's Heart bobbed expectantly less than fifty meters away, her deck lit by torches and basket fires. Even in these dire circumstances, his heart soared to see her. She awaited his return.

He gulped the knot in his throat. The last time he'd been aboard her, Liam had been alive.

A pistol jabbed him in the back, lurching him toward the rail. "I'm moving!" he snapped, tugging the frayed sleeves down to hide the rope burns at his wrists. High on the mast above, his flag fluttered. It was too dark to see it now, but Roksana would have spotted it earlier. She'd hauled her sails and slowed her pace, allowing them to catch up, because she believed Yasir commanded this crew. She'd think he wanted his ship back. Or maybe she'd come around to the idea that Vasili was worthy of redemption.

That last thought had a brittle laugh bubbling up his throat. He couldn't lose his shit now. Yasir grabbed the rail and breathed sea air into his lungs. If he died here, would that be so bad a thing? Liam would be waiting for him with Aura, like he always waited, and they'd be together again. They'd have an ending worthy of the best tales.

The hard nudge of the pistol pressed into his lower back. "Remember, *captain*. Just play along and save lives."

He somehow forced a smile onto his lips as the two ships came within shouting distance. Roksana's figure was unmistakable, her braided hair thrown over one shoulder. Nikolas's big, brooding outline loomed alongside her. Yasir couldn't see Amir, but Alissand believed he was onboard.

"A-hoy!" Yasir called. His voice cracked, but with the sounds of waves splashing against two hulls, nobody noticed. *"Captain Yazdan."* Would she sense something was amiss? Roksana was a shrewd seawoman. She'd taken more ships than she'd bought. She knew the tricks. She knew Yasir too. Knew *his* tricks.

"Captain Lajani," she called back. "I suppose you want your ship back?"

Why was she not raising the alarm? Couldn't she see his filthy clothing was all wrong? They were still some distance, but the signs were obvious. He wasn't even wearing his hat, for gods' sakes. "Just an audience, Roksana."

"Throw your hooks then."

Panic had his heart fluttering like an injured bird. The crew began flinging grappling hooks across the gap.

Once they were tied on, Alissand's brutes would attack. It would be quick. An ambush. Roksana's might be able to fight them off, but not if she couldn't see what was coming.

The hooks clunked against *Walla's Heart's* deck. The lines pulled tight, and the two ships began to heave closer. The sight of Niko on deck, illuminated by firelight, had Yasir lifting his chin. Niko was alive. He'd survived. Which meant there was still hope left in the world.

The gun dug into his back. One wrong twitch and it would be over. Sweat cooled at his hairline. His heart thumped so loud it was a wonder Niko couldn't hear it.

He'd betrayed Niko before, to save the man he loved. Now that man was dead, and Yasir's life didn't seem to matter so much in the larger picture. He'd die here, but not before honoring the trust of a truly good man. Niko had to live. *Someone* had to.

Yasir gripped the rail and willed Niko to look over.

iko

VASILI HAD RETREATED into the cabin without a word, leaving Niko and Roksana to greet Yasir's crew.

Yasir had clearly been through an ordeal since they'd been separated in the north. Even in the fading light, Yasir's skin appeared grey, not helped by the man's drab outfit. Niko had never seen him in anything less than bright colors and rich fabric. He'd never been without his hat either. Without it now, he looked less like the loud, breezy Yasir and more like someone who'd been thrown to the wolves. Whatever he'd endured, he'd clearly survived. They'd discuss it; Niko, Yasir, and Vasili. Old friends, together. Just like it should be.

The boarding hooks struck the deck. Ropes groaned, taking the weight of the two ships.

A grumbling in the distance drew Roksana's eye. "A

storm." She dropped her gaze to the hooks looped over the rails and narrowed her eyes. "Walla and Aura have their ways of speaking, if we only care to listen."

Niko opened his mouth to ask what she meant when she turned her head toward her first mate and mumbled a command. He whistled, short and low. The crew subtly freed their weapons, keeping them hidden while continuing about their business as though nothing had changed.

Niko stared across the shortening gap at Yasir.

The two ships were close now. A gangplank had been raised on Yasir's side, his men waiting to get within range before lowering it.

Yasir's hard glare met Niko's. His smile had died sometime in the last few moments, and all the luster had snuffed out of his eyes. All at once, he looked older, harder, and stricken. A man lost at sea. Yasir gripped the rail. The sleeves of his ill-fitting shirt pulled back. The shifting light revealed red welts at his wrists.

Niko dipped his chin. "He's being coerced," he muttered.

"Yes, Niko. He is. We're about to find out why."

The gangplank slammed down, bridging the gap between the ships. Roksana freed her sword, and Yasir's expression crumbled. "They'll kill you!" he yelled. The crewman behind Yasir grabbed him by the neck and hauled him backward, through a sudden swell of men climbing ropes and swinging across the gap.

Niko freed his sword, and the world turned to chaos.

CHAPTER 29

asir

INSTINCT HAD him lurching to the side, and luck meant he somehow avoided the flash of a blade that should have sliced a new smile into his cheek. A pistol fired too close to his head, making his ears ring. The crew buffeted him from side to side, almost knocking him over. In the chaos, Necktie came at him, his face scrunched in some horrible angry mask. He slashed a second time. Yasir danced back and stumbled into another man, earning a growl.

Arms like iron bands came down around him from behind, trapping him in their crushing embrace.

"Hold the dandy! He's mine," Necktie ordered, lurid glee making his eyes glisten.

Yasir bucked, or tried to, but the only sign whoever had hold of him even noticed his struggle was a mild grunt in his ear. Scraping his heels down the man's shins did nothing. Fear and dread broke cold sweat across his skin. He couldn't fight the hold. He wasn't getting free. Shoving his head back against his captor's wall-like chest, Yasir lifted his chin. If he was to die here, it'd be with his head held high.

Necktie lifted the dagger, grinned from ear to ear, and stalked closer.

The clash of swords and sounds of yelling broke over Yasir in a wave. So consumed by his own fight to survive, he hadn't cared about the battle erupting around them. But over Necktie's shoulder, on the *Walla's Heart* deck, a hulking mass of a man plowed through a blockade of Alissand's crew, knocking them aside as though they were no more troublesome than toy soldiers. *Niko*.

A horrid little whimper fell from Yasir's lips as his heart leaped at hope.

"That's right, you'd better cry." Necktie licked his thick lips.

Niko stalked across a plank between the ships, a vicious-looking sword gleaming in his hand. One of Alissand's crewmates charged and thrust their blade toward him. Without breaking his stride, Niko kicked the prick over the side, into the water between the ships where he'd surely be crushed between the hulls.

Another ran at Niko and had Niko's fist meet his face. The man slammed to the deck, writhing in agony with a torrent of blood spilling from his nose and mouth. Another fool took Niko's blade to the gut.

With his first wave of foes down, Niko scanned the deck, eyes widening when his gaze found Yasir. The snarl on his face had Yasir near-sobbing. Even if he didn't make it over in time, the two men who held Yasir would pay with their lives.

A rough, heavy hand slammed down on Yasir's face and the dagger came up, gleaming between him and Necktie. "Where d'yah want it, eh?" The brute's spittle wet Yasir's cheek. "Slow, in the gut? Or fast, across the throat?"

"W-wait." More words wouldn't come, and by Aura, that pathetic squeak couldn't be the last thing he said. He'd always imagined he'd say something deeply moving at the moment of his death. Not whine like a babe.

Bloody fingers clamped around the brute's neck from behind. The brute reeled, torn from Yasir in one great heave. The bloody tip of Niko's blade erupted from the man's guts. Warm blood dashed Yasir's face. And the brute fell, or Niko kicked him. Either way, he was down, looking at the dark blood on his fingers in disbelief.

The man with the iron grip shoved Yasir aside, probably realizing he wasn't worth dying for. Yasir stumbled over a loop of thick rope and fell against a barrel. By the time he righted himself, Niko stood over two dying men, his hair wild and blade dripping. He reached out a bloody hand.

Without question, Yasir grabbed it.

"Stay behind me," Niko ordered, his voice a low wolf-like growl. He turned his back, and it was all Yasir could do to stay low and stay close as Niko's great blade-swings cut down every crewman in his path.

 asili

H<small>IS</small> <small>BORROWED</small> boots struck the boards as he paced. Yasir's arrival was not as fortuitous as Nikolas believed it to be. He didn't know what happened during events in Seran; he hadn't been there. He'd heard, they'd all *heard,* but the only souls Vasili had let live were those he'd controlled. All the others he'd encountered were ash. Including Yasir's lover, Liam. Dead by Vasili's hand.

He could blame his actions on the flame, but it would be a lie.

Gunfire barked outside the cabin, followed by rapid returning fire.

He reached for the cabin door only to have it swing inward, spilling a bear of a man into the cabin. A pistol —he saw that first. He grabbed it by the barrel and thrust it to the side. The brute slammed his shoulder into Vasili's chest. They tumbled, the cabin tipping in his vision. The weapon boomed, gunpowder flashing. Vasili's back struck the boards. His teeth jarred together. Panic tried to choke him. *Not on the back.* He twisted, got a hand around the man's throat, and drove him against the floor, pinning him by the neck with every damn muscle Vasili had.

An elbow swung up, cracking Vasili in the jaw. Blood laced his tongue. He spat into the bastard's snarling face —kicked out as the brute tried to smother him—and twisted onto his front.

"Come 'ere, pretty thing." Hands locked around his leg and yanked.

Gods-damn it, where was Nikolas?!

The brute dragged Vasili across the boards. Vasili scratched his nails along the floor, trying to get a hold. The pistol came into sight, resting on its side, discarded. He reached for it, fingertips skimming the handle.

Thick fingers dug into his thigh, pinching.

Enough!

He rolled onto his side and kicked his heel into the bastard's leering face. The brute recoiled, clutching the bloody tear in his cheek. Eyes full of rage fixed on Vasili. If he hadn't wanted to kill him before, he certainly did now.

Vasili grabbed the pistol, aimed, and pulled the trigger. *Click.* Useless thing! He tossed the pistol at the brute, only for it to be batted aside, and the brute stomped forward. The grizzly wound in his cheek dripped blood.

Escape was through the cabin door, but the chime of metal clashing and gunfire from outside did not bode well. Vasili's chances of survival, however, might be better out there, in the chaos, than in here with a man twice his size, who clearly had no idea who Vasili was or why he should be kept alive.

Vasili scrabbled to his feet and dashed behind the captain's desk—Yasir's before Roksana had gotten her hands on it. Vasili had spent many a night here drinking rum, boots kicked up on the desk's edge, and his thoughts fuzzy while Yasir told his tales. He knew it well. Knew all its secrets.

The brute stalked closer. Blood dribbled from his chin and trickled down his thick, whiskered neck, soaking into his stained shirt. He wasn't possessed, at least not by the flame, but he certainly had an abundance of murderous glee in his eyes.

Vasili spread his hands on the desk. He was cornered, with nowhere to run but through this prick. By all rights, Vasili knew he looked like an easy catch. Everyone made the same mistake in assuming his heart was as fair as his looks.

He dipped his hand beneath the desktop, found the cold, hard steel of Yasir's hidden knife, and prized it free. The brute tensed, about to dive around or over the desk.

Vasili launched the lightweight but lethally sharp knife through the air so fast the brute had no chance to avoid it. It punched into his eye, jerking the man back. He let out a satisfying but bloodcurdling scream and stumbled on the spot. Wrapping his trembling hands around the small handle, he pulled the blade free, revealing a bloody, weeping orb that had once been his eye. Vasili could almost sympathize.

With a roar, the brute lunged over the desk.

Vasili darted away, grabbed a heavy, iron boot hook from the floor, and swung it like a bat. The iron struck the bastard on the back of the head, and down the brute went, out cold or dead. Incapacitated, at least.

Vasili retrieved the small knife from his bloody fingers and drew the blade across the man's throat. Fools and dead men left their enemies alive.

He'd made it as far as the cabin door when the second man dashed inside. Vasili lunged from the shadows, looped an arm around his throat, and punched the small knife into the man's back several times.

Grabbing the dying man's short sword, he finally escaped the cabin.

Bodies lay scattered across the deck, some moving, some not. Pistols had given way to swords, with Roksana's skilled crew holding their ground.

Nikolas wasn't among the fallen or those fighting.

An enemy crewman lunged at Vasili. A gun boomed, and the fool dropped, sprawled at Vasili's feet.

Roksana stood across the deck at the end of the long gun, her frown more likely due to the fact she'd killed a man, not that Vasili had been in imminent danger. Another fool came at him. Vasili dispatched him with a crude swing of the blade, his reflexes faster.

The chaos had turned in Roksana's favor. Her crew finished off the stragglers, cutting throats and dumping the bodies over the side.

Vasili hung back, listening to distant thunder rumble and growl, threatening a storm. Clearly, Yasir's crew had not been friendly. But what of the man himself?

Blood sloshed across the deck, channeled into gutters, and spilled over the sides.

"Get this scum off my deck!" Roksana declared.

Slumped against the wall outside the cabin, Vasili lifted his gaze to the crew returning via the gangplank. Nikolas propped up Yasir; neither had seen Vasili. He glanced at the cabin's swinging door. There was no use in hiding. The truth would find him.

"Storm's coming. Cut her loose!" Roksana bellowed her orders, and her crew hastily withdrew from the abandoned ship, returning to *Walla's Heart* to cut the ropes tying the ships together and tend the sails.

"Head for Kaza Point!"

Walla's Heart groaned, her sails flapped and bloated with the wind, and the ship lurched, rocking atop restless waves.

Yasir pulled himself free from Nikolas's solid grip, muttering something, probably his thanks, and mustered a smile. That smile said what words alone could not. He admired Nikolas, had said as much when he and Vasili were both sharing things probably better left unsaid. It was good that Yasir and Nikolas were close. They'd need each other when he was gone.

Yasir's haunted gaze found its way across the deck to Vasili, and a change shot through the man. He straightened, finding his pride and passion beneath his weariness. Nikolas said something, his attention drifting to check on his aunt, but Yasir ignored him and marched for Vasili.

Vasili had the blade in his hand. A part of him—the cruel part that had kept him alive this long—demanded he raise it against his friend, but some other part of him must have overruled it because Yasir's vicious right hook struck fast and true, ringing heat and pain through Vasili's face. He stumbled against the wall. Yasir's snarling face was all Vasili could see, his teeth clenched and bared and his eyes mad. And still Vasili didn't move, didn't defend himself.

Nikolas was between them suddenly, tearing Yasir off. "What the fuck has gotten into you?!"

Vasili dabbed at his lip, fingers coming away glistening with blood.

Yasir lunged again, stopped only by Nikolas's bear hug that scooped him up and dumped him a safe distance away. He shoved a hand against Yasir's chest, holding him back. "Stop, dammit! What is this?"

Yasir's face said it all. Fury made his face hard, but the rage swiftly burned itself out, and, once that was gone, Yasir had nothing left to hold him up. He fell against Nikolas, the weight of grief holding him down.

Nikolas folded Yasir into his strong arms and looked again at Vasili, his woefully emotive expression already changing as he pieced the cause of Yasir's actions together.

"Where's Liam?" Nikolas asked.

Guilt riddled Vasili's soul, hollowing him out, leaving a void that could only be filled with the callousness of feeling nothing at all—because feeling all of it would cripple him. He had no other defense against his own sins. "Liam was dead the moment Yasir brought him into this!"

"You killed him!" Yasir moaned. He mustered some strength from somewhere and tried to fight from Nikolas's hold. Nikolas reeled him into his arms, where Vasili had been so recently, but might never be again after this.

Nikolas muttered something to Yasir too low to catch, and Yasir crumbled against him. The pair retreated to the cabin, the door closing with finality behind them.

Something brittle and sharp broke inside Vasili.

The crew stared, probably considering whether to cut one more throat and toss his body over the side too.

Vasili glared back. He still had the bloody dagger. Let them try.

He'd always been alone, the Caville crown made it so, and then for so long his own mind had been his only company. It was better to be alone; alone meant there was nothing to lose. Just oneself.

Careful not to run, he descended the hold ladder into the storage bays. Most of the crew was above, so when Vasili pressed his hand to the locked storage door holding his brother inside, nobody saw.

He rested his forehead against the wood grain, smelling salt and tar and timber and blood. He saw again the moment in the market square, the moment Yasir was supposed to die. Liam had been a... distraction. He'd also saved Yasir's life. Gods, this fresh agony was the very reason he'd built his walls, keeping the world at bay.

"Vasili?" Amir's soft voice filtered through the cracks in the door.

He lifted his head and stared at the grain, imagining Amir standing on the other side. They'd been brothers once, not the enemies they were now. Vasili had pushed him away, but before then, before the elves, before the flame meant anything, before Mother had died, he'd read to Amir the story of the prince in his glass palace. That one had a happy ending. Theirs, he'd long suspected, did not.

Vasili hadn't wanted any of this. He'd had hope once. But he'd been different then. They both had.

"Will you make this torture end?" Amir asked, closer now, probably pressed against the door as Vasili was. Did he hold up a hand, reaching for a brother he'd mourned years ago?

"Vasili, I know you're there. You see me now, don't you?"

He closed his eye and curled his hand into a loose fist against the door.

"When she died, I lost everything overnight," Amir went on. "My mother, the brother I idolized. Father, well, he was that in name only. I had nothing. You had another life in Alek and his farm. All I had were books, and myths, painting, and stories of magic that took me away. You were gone, lost in a fervor to save the people from the flame—I know that now. I didn't then." He sighed. "I painted portraits of you, over and over, and hung them about my chamber so I wouldn't be alone."

Vasili pressed his lips together to stop their waver.

"And then, when I let the elves take you, I burned every single one of those paintings. I'd done something terrible. I hated myself for it. You were truly gone, and it felt good, for a while... The flame wanted that. I was a boy with a power I didn't understand whispering in my ear. Maybe I still am. It always whispers. You hear it. But not now, not here. It's quiet here. I can think again, and I'm sorry, Vasili, for everything. Nikolas was yours, and... I wanted to take something of yours, to hurt you, so you'd see me. I'm not like you. The flame made me stronger, but I didn't know how it would destroy everything, even you. You don't believe me, I know, but I can't go on like this. I can't go back to who—what I was. I won't."

His labored breaths seemed loud suddenly.

Behind Vasili, stacked in one of the opposite storage bays, lay the ballast bags, and among them lay hidden the bags of spice.

Nikolas always kept his word. Even hating Vasili, as he surely did now Yasir had revealed the truth from the market square, he'd made an oath and he would not break it.

"Vasili?" Amir asked.

He swallowed, closed his eye, and spread his hand against the wood. They'd both been corrupted, used by the flame, helpless like the generations before them. But Vasili had a choice now: He could let it win and he'd never have to fight again. It would be easy to surrender. Or there was another way. Just as Nikolas believed. A better way.

And the choice was Vasili's to make.

"I see you. And we will end this, brother. Together."

iko

THE FLAME HAD MADE Vasili take those lives in Seran. It had to be the flame because the Vasili Niko knew wouldn't have chosen to kill Liam. He said a lot of shit, he was mean as a snake, but that was because Vasili *always* lashed out when backed into a corner.

Niko should go to him.

His gaze drifted to Yasir peeling his filthy clothes from his bruised body. Mottled skin was the evidence of Alissand's beating. Rage soured on Niko's tongue. Rage at it all, the nasdas, Alissand, and the fucking Yazdans. And Vasili. He couldn't go to him like he was. He'd say something in anger like he always did, and they'd fight. Vasili would lash out. Niko would just make it worse.

The deck tilted, hanging oil lamps leaning as the ship rolled on steepening waves.

Yasir steadied himself against the cot while Niko clung to the fixed chair like it was his lifeline.

"I'm sorry—"

The captain snorted. "It's not for you to be sorry, Niko."

"It wasn't Vasili."

"He didn't like Liam. Tried to frighten him off—"

There had been tension between them, but there was tension between Vasili and *everyone*. "Like I tried to frighten you off months ago?"

Yasir pulled a dark shirt on over his head. "You clearly didn't try hard enough."

"That's on you. I warned you, Yasir. Vasili made it clear to both of us. Whatever he feels inside has nothing to do with his actions. He can't afford to care."

Yasir turned, folding his sleeves up with harsh, jagged tugs. "You didn't see his face in Seran. He was *glad* Liam was dead. He thought him weak, a distraction. Liam knew it. He was trying to..." Yasir choked on the words. "He wanted to be useful. He wanted to *help*, because that's who he is, and it got him killed. Did Vasili tell you the flame killed Liam?"

Vasili hadn't said a word about Liam's death, but he'd been adamant he and the flame were one. He wasn't sure what to make of his silence. Guilt, perhaps?

Yasir had every right to be furious. But this wasn't Vasili's fault.

"You were right, Niko," Yasir tucked his shirt in and tightened his cuffs, wrapping himself in more fitting clothing than the rags Alissand's crew had put him in. "I didn't want to see it. He was so... *Vasili*. By Walla, I was blind."

The ship groaned and tilted. Niko's insides rolled. He closed his eyes and gripped the chair harder. Despite the Yazdans penchant for the ocean, Niko was beginning to realize he was not made for the sea.

"I need to get out there."

Niko opened his eyes as Yasir flung open the cabin door. Lightning flashed, washing the deck in brilliant white. Thunder roared. All Niko could do was hold on and pray to Walla that she forgave whatever had angered her so. He assumed Vasili was below deck but dared not venture out for fear of being swept into the sea.

The cabin door swung closed on its hinges, and Yasir was gone. The crew yelled as *Walla's Heart* was tossed about by the gods. If they sank at sea and both Cavilles died, would the flame be freed?

The heave and swell of the ship, the thrash of water, and the yelling crew seemed to roll on forever, and all Niko could do was grit his teeth and keep the contents of his guts on the inside, but eventually, the wind lessened and the storm stalked away.

Plucking his fingers from the chair, he ventured onto the deck on unsteady legs. Moonlight spilled from breaks in the clouds, painting monolithic jagged rocks white, and from the pale faces of those around him, they'd clearly come close wrecking on those very rocks.

Grey-faced and with hooded eyes, Yasir finally returned to Niko's side. "We'll shelter in the bay overnight." He clamped a hand on Niko's shoulder.

"That was a close one!" A smile briefly brightened his face. "Thank you, Niko. For coming for me. I'm just... Just give me some time, eh? It's been a rough few days."

"Take the cabin," Niko said. "It's yours anyway."

"It is." He grinned, some of his sparkle briefly returning. "We'll talk in the morning."

Yasir retreated into the cabin. Niko's heart ached for his friend's loss. Liam had not deserved such an end, and had it not been for the flame, for meeting Vasili, he'd perhaps still be alive.

The anchor-chain rattled through its eye and plunged into the sea, startling his thoughts. The shore-line was a moonlit silvery line, a sharp reminder they couldn't stay at sea forever.

"Niko?" Roksana's boots clipped the deck as she approached. Her grim face suggested more ill news.

He sighed. "What is it now?"

"It's best you come and see." She led him across the deck and down the ladder, into the hold. His aunt stepped aside outside the storage bay where Amir was being kept, gesturing for him to look. Given the lack of yelling and insults coming from inside, it seemed likely Amir was either dead or missing. Which begged the question, where was Vasili? Of course, the prince would pick the middle of a raging storm, while everyone was distracted, to enact whatever fucking scheme he'd been brewing.

There was no sense in delaying.

He stepped inside and pulled up short at the sight of the two Caville princes sprawled on the bed of silk, both as pale as milk. Niko dropped to his knees and pressed his fingers to Vasili's limp wrist. Vasili's pulse thumped back, strong, steady.

"Bastard!" He puffed out a ragged breath and rocked back on his heels. The telltale bag of blue powder lay open within reach of Vasili's limp hand.

He knew what this was, of course. Vasili had made him swear to take them home, but he hadn't expected it so soon. He'd hoped they might have days. Days in which Niko would try and talk him out of this insanity. Vasili had made it too late for talk. He'd forced Niko's hand. Only action remained.

Vasili's head rested to one side, his arm hung off the bed, his face peaceful. With Amir at his side, laid out, vulnerable, asleep, high on spice and dreaming fuck knew what, the pair almost looked innocent of the storm they'd both been at the eye of. "Fucking scheming Caville pricks."

Niko straightened. A niggling voice of exhaustion and doubt wanted him to land the skiff and walk the fuck away from it all.

"We'll need a wagon and horses," he said, defying the doubts.

"If we're to get these two back to Loreen in good time, we'll need something more substantial than a cargo wagon." She folded her arms. "I have a carriage and strong horses in the Yazdan stables outside Seran. We'll need them if we're to travel at speed."

Alissand would surely spot them if they entered Seran. The stables on the city outskirts would be less guarded. "How far is that from where we are?"

"The storm pushed us southward. We're not far

from where we left off. A few hours' march and we'll have our hands on what we need."

"Then we go in fast and get what we need at dawn." The thought of going north again and returning to the salt mine made him want to grab Vasili by his thin shoulders and shake him awake. Meanwhile, Amir could rot from a spice overdose for all he cared.

"Niko." His aunt touched his arm as he turned to leave and drew him back. "Keeping them under with spice will not be easy. There are risks."

He nodded. "Vasili knew them when he asked this of us."

"Is there really an end to madness in Loreen, like Vasili said?"

"There is, but it's hell." He shook off her touch. "If you were in any doubt that Vasili is worth the loyalty and honor of a so-called Yazdan, then you have it right here. He will die so we might survive. There is no greater sacrifice than that."

He couldn't stand to be near her, but he didn't want to leave Vasili either. He wanted to bundle him up and take him away, Amir, the Yazdans, and the flame be damned. He wanted to build a new life somewhere far away from it all, where the prince didn't have the weight of a crown on his head or a curse in his veins. Just a cabin in the woods, an open fire, and a burbling brook.

But those dreams were a fool's fantasy.

He'd see this done. He'd keep his word because it was all he had left to give the man he loved.

Vasili's last order would also be his own.

iko

THE YAZDAN STABLES—A sprawling collection of redbrick barns—lay nestled in a valley on the outskirts of Seran, surrounded by lush, spring-fed greenery. The main barn's windows were dark, and the fields they'd crept through appeared empty, largely due to gaping holes in the fences, but as quiet as it looked, there would likely be guards nearby.

A handful of Roksana's elite crew headed toward the large, pitched-roof, open-fronted barn with the gleaming black Yazdan carriage tucked inside.

The crew split, with four men sent to retrieve horses. The remaining three guarded the carriage. Niko hung back, eyeing the carriage from across the yard. It had windows and bore the same dark flame insignia as all the Yazdan carriages.

Vasili would hate it, but if all went well, he'd be unconscious for the entire journey. Still, none of this sat easy with Niko. The carriage lying untouched in an open barn felt too convenient.

The clop of hooves signaled the horses' arrival. The crew quickly fixed the stocky beasts to the carriage under Roksana's guidance.

Niko kept low and scanned the fields. Birds tweeted, and a soft breeze stroked the grassheads. In the calm and the quiet, his fingertips itched. The flame's icy touch tingled, aching to be free.

He'd hoped, after being at sea, that he'd miraculously step back on land and the flame would be absent. It wasn't. With every stroke of the oar toward the beach, the power had warmed his veins, and as soon as he'd left the boat for the wet sand, the weight of it had come roaring back.

There was no escaping the curse, not once it was in the blood.

With the horses finally tacked, the whole rig rattled and clanged over cobbles, loud enough to startle birds from the trees. Niko broke from cover. "Let's go!"

Movement near the back of the barn caught his eye. A squad of four men sprinted up a path, Yazdan blades gleaming in their hands. Alissand's men, all likely possessed.

"Niko!" Roksana reached down from the carriage. "Climb on!"

Power sizzled through his veins—a lust needing to be sated. "I'll meet you at the beach." He thwacked the lead horse on the rump to spur it on.

"Niko, you don't need to do this!"

The carriage clattered off, and Niko started toward the approaching squad, lowering his hands to his sides. He spread his fingers and willed the flame from its hiding place. It came easily, spilling free in smoky tendrils, and with it came a huge wave of relief and the knowledge that this was *right*. It must be right because it felt too good to be wrong.

Alissand's men bore down. Surprisingly, they weren't possessed, but they were intent on stopping him.

Power burned in his veins, desperate to be unleashed after its forced silence at sea.

Bushes rustled, snapping his attention behind him. A shout rose from Roksana. Two more squads darted in ahead of the carriage, making the horses rear. An ambush. Taking the carriage *had* been too easy. They'd been waiting.

Kill them. Kill them all.

The voice in his head sounded like Amir's, but also like his own, like this was some twisted dream his addled mind had concocted in the *between* place. A twitch, a memory. Amir's laughter. The pieces of the past tumbled through his thoughts. *There's a good dog. Take it all.* Some were memories, some were lies. He couldn't make sense of it. But one thing was clear. The carriage must be protected.

Kill them.

Foreign words spilled from his lips as the flame spilled from his fingers, coming alive under his control. A gesture, a word, and the flame galloped over them, consuming them, turning lives to dust, and it wanted *more*.

A needle of fear tried to push through the flame's will, but Niko moved on, and more lives turned to dust around him, until the carriage sped down the track and vanished out of sight.

Niko wasn't finished.

The more lives it stole, the stronger it became, and the stronger *he* became. Around and around. Laughter tickled his mind, sending the pieces of himself scattering. That needle of fear stabbed at his madness, warning him to rein it back. But he was so damn tired, and it felt good to let go.

Ash swirled at his feet, but there were other souls nearby; he sensed them like beacons in the night.

He drifted *between*.

Kill them all. There's a good dog.

He was tired, broken, battered, and bruised, but freeing the flame made all the hurt fade.

A white horse stood stark against the darkness.

Niko stopped and blinked at the creature.

A simple beast. Easily consumed. The animal snorted as Niko approached through the grass. *Kill it, dog, and move on.*

Niko raised his hand. The dark flame licked about his fingers and snaked up his arm. The horse shied some and shook its head, then instead of fleeing, its velvety nose nudged his palm, nostrils fluttering. Its ears flicked.

Consume it.

The horse whinnied softly and snuffled his hand some more.

"No carrots today," he heard himself say.

Adamo.

Like a stretched band breaking, the flame's freedom and control on his mind savagely snapped, lashing back, whipping through him. He gasped, suddenly drowning in sensation—in fear and hate and sickening guilt.

He blinked awake, gasping into the wet grass, fingers clutching at the soil, anchoring himself where he'd unwittingly fallen.

The horror of his actions boiled at the back of his thoughts, threatening to spill over and scorch all reason and sense from his mind. This madness... He should have known it had been waiting, should have been able to recognize it sooner. Almost hadn't. If not for Adamo, he might have gone right on to Seran...

Adamo nudged him in the shoulder and nibbled on his sleeve, tugging at it as though trying to uproot him.

Adamo... it didn't seem possible that the horse was here.

He sank his fingers into Adamo's mane, and, with the horse's help, staggered to his feet. A saddle hung half-off, and his reins were tangled with twigs. Niko set the tack right again. Each familiar motion of looping leather and buckles together helped settle his mind too.

A knot of something like despair tried to choke him. He swallowed it and leaned against Adamo's warm neck, breathing in the solid and real smells of leather and horse. "How are you here?" Yasir had fled the north on him. The captain must have brought him to Seran, and

275

when Alissand's men caught Yasir, they left Adamo at the stables.

Adamo nibbled on his sleeve again.

"You're a survivor too, hm," Niko mumbled. "We have to go north again." He stroked Adamo's neck and rested his forehead against him. "One last time." He just had to cling to some sanity long enough to get to Loreen. He had to, for Vasili.

Adamo being here, finding him now, was surely a gift from the gods.

Niko tilted his head and peered at the pale blue Seranian skies. If they had the gods on their side, then perhaps they'd make it safely to Loreen. Swinging himself into Adamo's saddle, he clicked his tongue, geed Adamo into a trot, and headed for the bay, the carriage, and the prince who relied on Niko to hold it all together somehow.

 asir

HE HAD YET to decide if the goods inside the gleaming Yazdan carriage were the most valuable he'd ever hauled or if he should just run the damn thing over a cliff and be done with it. At least the driver's seat was padded and comfortable, and covered, which would keep off the snow once they got north of the desert plains. The four horses kept up a decent pace, even now, with the road having cracked and broken up under the midday sun.

Roksana was inside the carriage with the two princes, seeing to their needs, and Niko rode alongside on Adamo. How he'd found Vasili's horse, he hadn't said. In fact, he hadn't spoken much since they'd begun this fateful journey.

If there was any sense of justice in the world,

perhaps marauders would raid the carriage and steal Vasili away... Although, he didn't really wish for that. Mostly not. Perhaps a little.

Alissand would by now be aware of the stolen carriage and its likely cargo. They weren't to stop, not for anything. Niko had been clear on that. They had just days to make the journey that had taken weeks in Yasir's trader wagon.

He wasn't even sure it was possible, but Niko was in no mood for discussions. He simmered atop Adamo like a thundercloud. Yasir had glanced across a few times and thought he'd seen the flame in the man's already dark eyes. But he'd been seeing strange things since Liam's death. Creatures in the dark and in his dreams. They were all watching. Waiting. Staring at him and gathering in numbers, like they knew this nightmare would be over soon, one way or another. There was more riding on this journey than the lives of two princes. Perhaps *everything*.

Which was why he hadn't run the carriage off a cliff. Yet.

They were under a day north of Seran when one of the rear guards trotted up to Niko and mumbled something in his ear. Niko nodded and shifted Adamo's trotting pace alongside the carriage. "We're being tracked."

"Oh, well. That was inevitable, I suppose." Yasir briefly glanced at the salvaged long gun on the seat beside him. They'd taken it from beside a wagon that had been burned to a shell at the side of the road.

"I'm going to drop back and take a look. Keep the carriage rolling. Do not stop *for anything*."

"Yes, yes, Niko." He damn well knew the orders. To emphasize the point, he clicked his tongue and urged the big draft horses along, keeping their heavy hooves clopping. The carriage trundled, occasionally skipping over loose rocks but staying steady on its six large wheels. The Yazdan carriages were better made than most. They'd hold up well on the old track. He hoped.

Niko dropped out of sight. Yasir stared ahead. None of this damn journey felt right. In the past, he'd ventured north with a wagon full of silk and come back a rich man. This time he'd be lucky to return at all. And what was there to return for?

The miles rumbled beneath the carriage wheels. Niko reappeared as the sun began to set behind huge jungle palms. He made no mention of what had been following them, and the troubled look on his face kept Yasir from asking.

Daylight faded and the lead rider lit a lamp to keep them on the road in the dark.

"Yasir." Niko reined Adamo alongside, their progress slowed by the night closing in.

"Hm?"

"You're quiet. It's not like you."

"Well, there's not much to say, is there?"

Niko's face darkened and his lips pinched.

And now Yasir felt like a prick. None of this was Niko's fault. "The books..." he began. "Liam and I... We, well, he was studying them."

"Did he find anything useful?"

"Possibly. It spoke of the nasdas like a living thing. It has desires and needs."

"How does that help?"

"If it desires, then it can be tricked."

Niko pondered his words a while and said, "But how, when it's inside us?"

"In Loreen, when Vasili was supposed to have killed his brother, it left him then, though only briefly," Yasir said, thinking aloud.

"In the palace, the flame left the dying king to possess his sons," Niko agreed. "It leaves its vessel when expecting a new one."

"When it leaves a vessel, that's when it's vulnerable, don't you think?"

"Possibly. But if there are no Cavilles to anchor it, it goes free."

"I don't think it's that simple. If it were just a matter of all Cavilles being dead, it would have seen to it they all died long ago. It's using them to kill, to make itself stronger, like a parasite. Once strong enough, it will kill its vessel or take complete control, but not before."

Niko's cheek fluttered. "Yes. That seems... likely."

"So, then we can assume it's currently not strong enough. Which means it believes it's vulnerable to something."

"The salt chamber."

"The prison, yes. If we get it inside, and we say the words—"

"Words?"

"The words on the chamber floor, remember? Sorcerers' words. The books said they're the words Etara spoke to appease her sisters and weaken the nasdas. If we use those in the salt chamber, perhaps that's enough? At least, that's all Liam was able to decipher before…"

They fell quiet again. Yasir's mind wandered to the moments he'd shared with Liam in the gardeners' cottage. Those memories were warm and safe to return to, like a fire in a hearth.

"Do you hear it sometimes?" Niko asked after a few more miles had passed beneath them.

"Hear what?"

"The flame?" He glanced over, rocking with Adamo's stride. Niko appeared relaxed, but he clutched the reins so hard his knuckles glowed white in the dark.

"I don't know," Yasir admitted. "I dream… things."

"The dreams, do you ever see them in the day?"

"I… No." He frowned. "Do you, Niko?"

Niko faced ahead again. The glow from the lead rider's lamp barely illuminated his face, casting much of it in shadow, and now Yasir was looking, he saw the gathering of fine lines around Niko's eyes and at the corners of his mouth. "Amir forced a great deal of blood in me." He paused, either losing his train of thought or believing he'd said enough.

"I'm sorry that was done to you. It wasn't right. None of it was right. I should have listened before, when you said for me to leave and about Liam, but I thought… I don't know what I thought, maybe that the four of us were strong enough to beat anything." How wrong he'd been about that. He blinked and glanced at Niko, but the soldier gazed ahead, giving no indication he'd heard a single word. "Niko?"

He blinked, coming back to himself. "What?"

"You were speaking of Amir and blood." Yasir tried to slow his heart's nervous fluttering. Niko was a rock. If he crumbled, what hope did the rest of them have?

"I was?" He looked stricken briefly. Adamo tripped, startling Niko into tightening the reins again. Once he had his balance back, he turned Adamo around and slipped out of sight behind the carriage somewhere, saying no more.

Yasir shifted uneasily. Niko was as dangerous as Vasili and capable of killing every single one of them with little more than a gesture and a few words.

iko

As NIGHT CLOSED IN, it dragged a bank of fog with it, making progress intolerably slow. Thick, rolling whiteness swallowed the sound of carriage wheels crunching over desert grit while the lamplight from the front and rear riders penetrated only a few strides ahead.

He should have Yasir stop the carriage.

It wasn't safe to continue.

But any progress, even inches, took them closer to Loreen. Alissand was surely following by now. The princes might wake at any moment. They could not afford to stop.

The fog was quiet and the thick air tasted damp. His skin itched, as though they were being watched. He twisted in Adamo's saddle to get a look at the rest of Roksana's crew.

The two crewmen posted at the rear had vanished among the fog. They'd been there moments ago...

"Form up," Niko growled, keeping his voice low. Yasir jerked his head up. The lead rider slowed his horse enough to bring it in line with Yasir. "Keep rolling," Niko added. He grabbed a hanging lantern from the carriage hook and caught Yasir's gaze.

"Be careful. I've never seen fog so thick in these parts," Yasir said. "Easy to get lost in."

Niko nodded and brought Adamo to a halt, letting the carriage slowly roll on by. Banks of fog closed in behind it, and the rattle of wheels faded into the night.

There was no sign of the missing men, but there wasn't a damn sign of anything, just more wafting mist. "Ho!?" It seemed unlikely they wouldn't hear him.

Adamo snorted and tossed his head, shaking his reins. "It's all right." Niko patted his neck.

The small hairs on Niko's arms began to rise, skin prickling, and Adamo shifted restlessly, chewing at his bit. The horse's instincts were good. The missing men likely hadn't gotten lost in the fog. Whatever had been tailing them during the day, the thing that had avoided Niko, had likely lured them away.

Niko softly nudged Adamo forward, toward the distant clatter of wheels, keeping the lamp high, for all the good its small halo of light was doing. Fog was just fog. There was nothing in its shifting veil but the ghosts from his own head.

A growl bubbled to his left, the sound thick and heavy, rumbling from something huge. Adamo twitched and danced to face the source of the growl, only to be met with shifting mists.

Niko raised the lamp.

More growls rumbled nearby, behind him now. Moving through the fog. *Circling*.

Adamo whirled, tossing his head and tail. More growls sounded, bubbling up from all around.

Shadow beasts.

Adamo reared. The saddle slipped, and so did Niko. The ground rushed up, slamming into his shoulder. The lamp shattered, spilling flaming oil across cracked and parched ground.

Red eyes lit the gloom. Six pairs, at least. Niko scrabbled onto his hands and knees. More eyes glimmered in the shifting mist. Everywhere. All around. Adamo bucked, slamming his huge hooves into the ground, narrowly missing Niko.

He grabbed for the sword at his hip, thoughts ragged and clumsy. The spilled lamp flame simmered, fading as its fuel soaked into dusty ground, and the beasts stalked closer.

He knew how to stop them.

But it meant freeing the flame, and the last time he'd let go, he'd barely been able to wrestle himself back under control.

A beast sprang forward, leaping for Adamo's neck. The horse reared, teeth bared and ears flat, screaming. The beast's teeth clamped into Adamo's flesh, tearing gouges from his neck. A second beast lunged, and a third came for Niko. Madness boiled red in its eyes, so full of rage it knew nothing else.

And then it occurred to him, the flame had no body of its own, no skin to command, no physical presence. It *needed* Niko more than Niko needed it. The flame was not his master. He must master it.

He flung out a hand and spoke a word in a language he barely understood.

The beast dropped to its belly. A heavy weight slammed into his side, sending him sprawling, and the beast he'd commanded was up again, snarling through its teeth.

Adamo galloped into the fog, the sound of his thundering hooves quickly fading.

The beasts closed in. Eight of them. All as large as a man.

He couldn't do this. He wasn't strong enough. He didn't *know* enough. The flame was inside him and all around, and he didn't know how to damn well stop it, or the beasts, or Vasili from damn well dying when it all ended. "Etara, help me!"

The words.

Etara's words.

He knew them.

Amir had buried them inside him.

They fell from his lips again now. Strange sounding words. Words that no human should wield. *Stolen* words. The beasts slowed their approach and hunched low. Niko spoke louder, barely pausing for breath, and slowly climbed to his feet. The beasts hunkered down, shrinking back. The words took on a strength of their own. Each one was a weapon. A way to control the flame, to hold back the dark. The words were its weakness.

The beasts turned away and retreated into a swirl of fog.

The words died upon his lips, heeding to the thick quiet. He waited for the growls, but none came.

Adamo had gone, he couldn't hear the carriage, and the lamp flame was spluttering its final light. He'd seen them off but lost the carriage in the process. Turning on the post revealed only more soup-like mist. A gloomy, shadowed figure walked toward him, impossibly leading Adamo by the reins. Niko frowned at the vision, unsure if any of this was real.

"Lasher?"

The elf grunted something Niko had come to translate as either a greeting or *fuck off* and held out Adamo's reins.

This damned elf just didn't quit. "If you keep helping me like this, people are going to think we're friends."

Lasher stared back, either oblivious to the meaning of his words or just not giving a shit. "End nasdas."

"Yeah, yeah." Niko took Adamo's reins and ran his hand down the horse's neck, wincing at the gouges the beast had torn out of his skin. They weren't deep, but they bled and would need attention to stave off infection. There was no way he was losing Adamo.

"I don't suppose you know which direction my companions are?"

Lasher pointed into the fog.

Niko mounted again and eyed the persistent elf. If he mentioned Lasher to anyone, they'd think him mad. Niko didn't believe it himself. But he couldn't deny Lasher had helped. The elf dipped his chin and melted back into the fog.

Niko clicked his tongue and set Adamo plodding in the direction he hoped the carriage had gone, picking up its tracks in dirt grit moments later. The beasts should have returned to their maker, and Alissand would know they were not an easy target. When he tried again, Niko would be ready.

THE FOG LINGERED into the day, changing to a lighter grey but still hanging thick about them.

"This is folly," Yasir grumbled loud enough for Niko to hear. "We must stop. We've been traveling for almost two days. Adamo needs care. The cart horses need water, feed, and so do we. My ass hasn't been this numb since a memorable night in a pleasure-house. We can't continue this pace."

Standing still felt like handing Alissand seconds in which he'd gain on them. "We haven't traveled far enough."

"Because of the fog! I can't damn well see where we're going. For all I know, we've gotten turned around and are walking in circles." He gestured helplessly at the thick blanket in front of them.

The burble of a stream distracted him a moment.

He reined the carriage to a halt. "We're stopping." He dropped the reins and jumped down, "Right here." Stretching his arms, he winced. "I swear to Walla, Niko, you will have to pick me up and force me onto that damn seat yourself, and neither of us wants this to get that personal."

Niko pulled Adamo to a halt. "Yasir—"

"I'm the driver." Yasir glared. "It's my job to see we arrive safely! If we do not rest, we won't make it at all. Forgive me, but you haven't been thinking clearly since we started this damned march north. One of us must see sense. Throw me in the back if you like, but I'm not taking these horses another step in this horrid pea soup."

Perhaps he had a point. They were hardly making progress anyway, and the horses were no good exhausted.

Adamo snorted and dropped his head to munch on grass. If Niko tried to move him, he'd likely find him as helpful as Vasili.

"Fine," Niko grumbled, though it was clear the decision had already been made.

Yasir untethered the horses and walked them to the brook's edge. Niko did the same with Adamo and knelt at the stream to splash water over his face.

"The two of them are well," Roksana announced, offering him a rice cake from her traveling bag.

He stayed crouching at the water's edge and stared into the mist rising off the water's surface. "They'll need more spice soon, Roksana."

"I've dealt with that."

He glanced back at his aunt. She wouldn't hurt Vasili. She knew the risks as much as he did, but all of this was one last risk, wasn't it?

She knelt beside him and handed him a flask. He ate and drank quickly, glancing back at the gleaming carriage wrapped in swirling fog.

"A damn shame we lost those men to Alissand's beasts."

It was, and it had reduced their numbers to just three guards, not including Niko. He slumped against a tree. "Do you think we're going to make it?"

"I do, actually." She smiled. "Why don't you rest up?" She must have seen the refusal on his face before he could speak because she quickly added, "You're no good to anyone if you can't think for tiredness."

Yasir had said the same. But rest wasn't going to clear his head. Only the salt beneath the Caville palace could do that.

"There's room in the carriage," she suggested.

He didn't trust himself not to slit Amir's throat or open a vein, especially with his lapses in control.

"What of Vasili?" Roksana pushed.

"What of him?"

"He may be unconscious," she replied carefully, "but he's likely aware. You care for him, and he for you. You should sit with him."

"Coming around to the idea of loving a Caville?"

"Coming around to the idea of ending this madness." She smiled sympathetically. "Sit beside him.

Rest. I suspect these quiet moments will be few and far between on the road ahead."

"I'll consider it." It wasn't long before he pushed from the stream's edge and climbed into the carriage. Two low oil lamps lit the interior, softening the edges around the two sleeping princes on twin cots. Both lying on their sides, breathing softly. Roksana had cleaned Amir up some, and at the sight of his peacefully calm face, Niko's emotions twisted into a tangled mess he had no hope of escaping.

He knelt by Vasili, turning his back on Amir, and took his prince's hand in his. Vasili's lean fingers were delicate compared to Niko's large, rough digits. His silky, silvery hair lay over the scarred side of his face. Niko tucked a lock of hair back and stroked his knuckles down the prince's soft cheek. All of him seemed achingly delicate, like a glass ornament placed somewhere to be admired but never touched. Of course, the delicate facade disguised a deadly whip-like mind and a man with the mental strength of forged steel. It was that complexity Niko loved so fiercely, among many other small revelations that all conspired to tangle Niko's heart in knots. Had he been told years ago how he'd love Vasili Caville so thoroughly he'd die for him, he'd have laughed like a madman. Fitting, perhaps, that madness stalked them both now.

Niko shifted to lean against the bed, keeping Vasili's hand in his. He rested his head back, letting his eyes close. He could rest, just for a little while.

He dreamed of a cabin in the woods and a prince bathing in the stream.

Roksana roused him sometime later, leaving him alone for a moment with Vasili. He kissed the backs of the prince's fingers and admired his peaceful face. "I won't leave you."

Outside, he mounted Adamo and nodded for Yasir to get underway.

 asili

Snowflakes twirled and dallied, enjoying their freedom until the river's inky black waters devoured them. There was no use in attempting to cross from one bank to the other; the water would drown him as surely as the flame had tried to. So he waited, perched on a boulder, the world around suffocated in fog.

This was a dream, of course. Or some form of one, brought on by spice. He wasn't by a river. The princely blue clothes he wore had burned in the palace fire long ago. He touched his face, fingers trailing over the scar, and sighed. Even in a dream he was still marked.

"My son," a familiar voice said.

Vasili lifted his gaze. Talos stood on the opposite bank, leaning heavily on his cane. A silver crown sat neatly in his greying hair. His blue eyes were as sharp and cruel as colored diamonds, and his chin was mottled with silvery whiskers. The buttons on his finely embroidered court attire gleamed.

Vasili dropped his gaze to his father's reflection in the shifting water and saw only pulsing black smoke where his reflection should have been.

"What is it you hope to accomplish, boy?"

Boy? He looked like one, he supposed, to an ageless immortal entity. Vasili picked up a pebble and weighed it in his hand. "Isn't that obvious?"

"Surrender," it said with his father's voice. "And survive."

He stroked his thumb over the pebble's coarse surface. "A life as a puppet is no life at all."

"What do you have in this world that's worth dying for?"

He had one thing. A dream of a cabin in the woods and a man whose strength was endless and honor was true. A better man than Vasili. A man who would fight that *thing* across the river until his dying breath.

"You forget," the flame said. "The soldier is mine."

Vasili half smiled and looked up. "He really isn't anyone's."

"He has a hunger within him, a rage, like yours. With every death we take, his rage grows."

Vasili tried to hold on to his smile but felt it slipping. He had hoped Nikolas would resist the flame. If anyone could, it would be him. But his descent into madness was as inevitable as the flame itself.

Vasili narrowed his eye at the flame masquerading as his father. "Why are you here?"

"I am everywhere," it replied flatly.

"No, you are not that. I know what it is to be confined within invisible walls. If you were everywhere, you would not be here, wasting time by speaking with me."

"What is your intention, boy?" it asked again, worded slightly differently, as if hoping Vasili wouldn't notice its persistence.

Vasili smiled. "Don't you know?"

Talos took a step to the water's edge. *"I am the blood in your veins, the thoughts in your mind. All that you are belongs to me."*

"Apparently not." The flame couldn't cross the river. It was trapped on the other side, just as Vasili was trapped in this dream. For all its power, its weakness was its vessel.

Talos's facial features twisted and flexed, melting like a mask held above a candle. *"Serve me."*

Vasili climbed from the boulder and approached the water's edge. Cold rage from the flame misted his breath. Vasili knew that rage. He'd spent years drowning in it. Scratch a little deeper, and it wasn't rage at all—it was fear. The flame was *afraid*.

Laughter tickled his throat. He set it free, and the flame fled in a swirl of smoke, leaving snowflakes spiraling in its wake.

He watched the snowfall melt on the river's surface again and smiled.

It would be over soon, and the flame knew it. For the first time in forever, Vasili dared hope to be free.

iko

PILES OF SNOW had been banked alongside the road-side. Pink rock salt glittered about its surface, keeping the supply route to the north clear of ice. The salt was too patchy to have any real impact on the flame crawling through Niko's veins, but he welcomed the satisfying crunch of it beneath Adamo's hooves.

They'd been on the road nine days. Three days ago, desert fog had given way to swirling snow. Loreen was close.

He'd spent some days in the carriage, watching over or dozing alongside Vasili, or driving the wagon while Yasir and Roksana rested. He'd expected more beasts, but none came. Expected elves too but saw no sign of them. The endless hours on edge, listening for an elf whistle or the growl of beasts in the fog, were beginning to take their toll.

Alissand must be on their tail, so why hadn't the shah attacked?

Niko trotted Adamo ahead, leading the carriage while Roksana's three remaining guards stayed close to it. His mind wandered, lost in the swirl of snow, and he almost rode under three bodies slung from trees without seeing them. "Hold," he called.

Yasir's "whoa" and the clink-clunk of the cart horses tack sailed through the quiet.

Trotting Adamo back to Yasir, he reined up alongside the carriage, seeing Yasir's wide-eyed expression at the grizzly display.

"Get the carriage off the road," Niko said quietly. "I'll deal with those. And we'll wait here until the weather breaks. Stay quiet. Just a small fire. The smoke will be lost in the snowfall." Yasir blinked. "Understand?"

"Yes. Yeah."

Corpses were a sure sign of elves staking their claim. If there were elves nearby, they'd need to abandon the noisy carriage and continue on foot.

With the bodies dealt with and the carriage hauled off the road into the brush, Niko crept through the spindly undergrowth, listening for the crunch of snow or the rustle of branches. Elves had used the tree canopy to ambush him before. He'd not fall for the same tactic again and kept his gaze trained on the above as well as the below.

After scouting the immediate area and finding no elf tracks, he returned to camp. "We walk from here."

"How far to Loreen?" Roksana asked, gathering sticks for Yasir's small campfire.

"A day's fast riding," Yasir said. He crouched by the fire, gently coaxing the flames to life with dried leaves. "It'll be slow-going with our... cargo. Cut through the steep valleys and we can maybe shave off a few hours?"

"There's something else." Roksana dumped the pile of sticks by Yasir and brushed dirt from her hands. "It's taking more and more spice to keep them under, Niko. Too much and they'll seizure, but too little and they'll wake. They both have a higher resistance than I anticipated, and our stocks are low."

Really, their resistance shouldn't have come as a surprise. Amir had more spice in his veins than he did the flame, and Vasili had no choice but to take it to ease the pain from his scars. "How long do we have?" Niko asked.

She glanced at the carriage. Its once gleaming black panels were grey now, splashed with sludge and salt. "They could wake at any time."

For either prince to wake before they arrived at the salt mine and chamber would be a disaster. The flame would come roaring back, kill its counterpart, and consume everything. "Then we must continue now."

"How do we move them if we can't take the carriage?" Roksana blew into her hands, then crouched and warmed them by the measly flames.

"The cots can easily be made into sleds with timber

from the carriage," Yasir suggested. "You and Niko won't have any trouble pulling them on snow."

"Me?" Roksana frowned. "What's wrong with your muscles, Yasir?"

He gave a dismissive snort. "This body is clearly made for dancing, whereas yours, Roksana, could lift a barrel of boulders and carry it ten paces."

She nodded. "Goodness, we can't damage that dancer's physique."

Yasir pointed a finger at her. "*That*... is very true."

"We'll use the horses to tow them, but if we stumble into a band of elves," Niko said, cutting off their banter, "there'll be no escaping them with two sleds."

The mention of elves had the pair falling back into silence.

"I'll check on them. It gets damn cold in the carriage." Roksana climbed into the carriage, and Niko's heart flipped, urging him to go inside too and sit beside Vasili. They were all tired, hungry, and frozen to the bone. This last push to Loreen was all that stood in their way, but it would be the hardest part.

Niko crouched beside Yasir's little campfire and helped strategically place a few sticks to feed the flames. "I'll scout ahead, perhaps as far as Loreen. Get a look at what's waiting for us."

"Leaving me with your aunt, her three monosyllabic crewmen, and two spiced princes?" Yasir grimaced. "Fine. Go."

"You'll be all right. And you like the big, quiet types."

The captain laughed, but the sound was brittle and

soon broke apart into sobs he had no hope of holding back. Niko grabbed him by the shoulder and pulled him close.

"I lost him, Niko..." Yasir mumbled. "I damn well lost him."

He let the man sob, tucked against his chest, and even after his convulsions stopped and he wiped his face on his filthy coat sleeve, Yasir didn't seem inclined to pull free. Words alone couldn't ease his grief, but company could.

"I don't know if I can do this," Yasir finally said, easing himself from Niko's hold to toss a few more sticks on the fire.

"Neither do I, but here we are."

"Part of me hates Vasili."

Niko braced an arm against the thawing ground. "He's an easy man to hate."

"Harder to love?"

"Something like that."

Yasir sighed, rubbed a hand over his face, and reapplied his smile. He tried to keep it there but failed. "I'm so fucking afraid. The war, the flame, the elves, all of it. When do we get a break? Something? Some hope that this isn't all for nothing?"

Yasir was usually the one full of hope and laughter and color. Seeing him broken pulled Niko's heart deeper into the dark. But it wasn't all for nothing. It couldn't be. "Not all elves want the flame freed. Some want it to end."

Yasir looked at him like he'd lost his mind. "What?"

"Just..." He drew in a deep breath. "Trust me, we're not alone—"

"Trust you?" Yasir laughed. "How can I trust you, Niko, when I see the flame in your eyes? I needed you in Seran—Vasili needed you, and you weren't there. Had you been there—"

Liam wouldn't be dead. Niko's thoughts reeled. He'd gone with Roksana to secure Amir. Had he known... "Yasir, I tried to stop Vasili in the desert—"

He laughed again, but the sound was empty. "You didn't bloody well try hard enough, did you! Vasili killed those people like they were nothing, like the marauder, you remember that? You remember the look on Vasili's face. He had no idea what he'd done then. If you'd been there, Niko..."

"Had I been there, what could I have done?" Niko hissed. "Killed him?"

"Yes. No. I don't know!"

He understood why Yasir blamed him, even as it cut him open. If Niko had killed Vasili before he'd reached Seran, Liam would still be alive, as would the hundreds he'd killed in Seran. But half the flame would have gone free and Alissand would still have Amir. "Yasir—"

"Go to Loreen." He stabbed a stick at the fire. "Hopefully, we'll still be alive when you return."

The accusation was unfair, but Yasir was hurting. They all were. Niko returned to Adamo, his heart heavy, and mounted up, pushing regrets aside. Adamo trudged through the deep snow, circling outward from the camp. He was going to Loreen, but he had another reason for lingering nearby first. Keeping his hood up and head bowed to the lazy snowflakes, he whispered, "Where are you?"

A clearing opened up. He twisted in the saddle, searching the eerie stillness through the trees. "Lasher? You there?"

Adamo pawed at the snow, trying to get to the frozen grass beneath, and shook his head, rattling his bit and bridle.

"Come on, you bastard. Show yourself."

The cloaked figured emerged from the grey, stirring the flakes around him. "Butcher," he growled low.

"I'm scouting ahead to Loreen. Will you watch the carriage? Keep them safe while I'm gone?"

The elf grunted, whatever the fuck that meant. He wouldn't hurt them, Niko knew that much.

With a click of his tongue, he urged Adamo into motion again and headed north.

LOREEN LAY MUFFLED in a vast blanket of snow. The palace's enormous towers thrust from the white, like stalagmites poking at the thick clouds. Virgin snow crunched beneath Adamo's hooves as he maneuvered down a side street. Clouds of vapor puffed from the horse's nostrils.

Loreen had been lost long ago. When Niko had returned from the war, he'd laid the blame firmly at the prince's feet, but the true blame lay with forces far greater than any man.

The palace loomed larger with every step. Its towering, blackened walls and broken windows told the story of an empire crumbled. He reined Adamo to a stop. There was no use in going further. The elves had accomplished what thousands of soldiers had died trying to prevent. The Royal Cavilles and their centuries-old seat of power were gone.

Pulling Adamo around, he started back along their disturbed path in the snow. There were no elves here. No people either. Nothing but houses jutting from the snow like tombstones.

If the spice held out, there was nothing left to stop Vasili from returning home and fulfilling the destiny King Talos had spoken of: dying for his people—dying for everyone. Time was running out to find another way.

ROKSANA GREETED him on the road. "Dammit, Niko, did you see my men—Mykos, Jesaph, and Luca? We heard a whistle, so they went off to check. They haven't returned."

The whistle was an elf sign. Lasher had probably dealt with any rogue members of his kin but would have known to avoid Roksana's crew. "No sign of them, Roksana. I'm sorry. We can wait a little while, but if there are elves nearby, we should get moving."

Two sleds were rigged to two heavy cart horses, with the princes bundled in blankets and strapped down upon them. There was no time to inspect the ties.

Should Amir's come undone a few times, a tumble in the snow was all the bastard deserved.

Wrapped in furs, his face calm, Vasili looked the picture of serenity.

"This was your idea," he told the sleeping prince. If Vasili woke to find himself tied to a sled, it would surely earn Niko a lashing. "Hate me later, Your Highness." *Or better yet,* he thought, *love me later.*

With no sign of the guards, Roksana rode the horse pulling Vasili's sled, Yasir took Amir, and Niko led the way on Adamo.

Nobody spoke. Just the hiss from the sleds and the thump of hooves accompanied them. The snow had ceased its relentless barrage, and the air had cleared, expanding the view through acres of naked trees, toward the palace far in the distance. The cold nipped at Niko's fingers and misted his breath. He missed Seran's constant heat, its vibrant color, and its noise. Loreen was a carcass in comparison.

They marched on. The palace hovered behind the spindly branches, like a mirage, glimpsed here and there.

The weak winter sun had begun to drop behind the palace by the time they approached the city outskirts. Niko spotted small halos of light near the palace gates and thrust out a hand to stop their march. Too distant to make out any details, but the city wasn't nearly as empty as he'd believed.

"Get them out of sight," he said. "I'll take a look."

"Hurry," Yasir puffed into his hands. "Roksana is freezing her balls off."

"You lost yours years ago," Roksana drawled.

Niko left them trading good-natured insults and steered Adamo between abandoned houses and into a narrow side street that meandered closer toward the main gates. Leaving Adamo loosely tied to an old post, he crept closer and crouched behind a low stone wall and its mounds of snow.

Two men flanked the palace's entrance, torches held aloft to fend off dark and the cold. The snow, so pristine when Niko had first visited, had been churned to slush through the palace gates and into its grounds. Two men hadn't done that.

A dozen more torches illuminated the palace gardens.

As he watched, a squad of three men marched from the palace promenade through the gate, and any hope they were civilians quickly faded. The Yazdan crest gleamed on their armor like the Caville crest had once adorned Niko's. They didn't appear possessed, but he wasn't close enough to know for certain. Yazdan guards. Men he'd helped train during his brief stay with the family.

Alissand was here.

Niko hunkered down and muttered a curse. All this time he'd feared they were being tailed, but the shah had never planned to attack on the road. The shadow beasts were just a distraction. He'd known exactly where they were headed and beaten them here by hours.

Keeping low, Niko retrieved Adamo and returned to

the concerned faces of Roksana and Yasir. "Alissand's here," he growled, dismounting Adamo to check Vasili's ties. "Gods be damned!" He flicked a curl of hair from Vasili's cheek and pulled the furred hood tighter to his face. They were so close... If Vasili were awake now, he'd slide a thin, lopsided smile toward Niko and demand to know what he planned to do, *Nikolas*. Vasili *always* had a plan.

The weight of Yasir's stare drew his eye.

"Niko, I... I fear this is my doing." He glanced at Roksana, who only had her own sad smile to offer, before looking back to Niko. "When Alissand caught me in Seran and forced me aboard his ship, that wasn't all he did. I said some things... He demanded to know about the books, and the..."

He didn't need to say anymore. The truth was all over Yasir's pale face and shameful slope of his lips. That and the missing fingernails he'd tried to hide.

"Dammit, Yasir."

Yasir flinched. "It was after Liam, and I... I wasn't thinking. I didn't care—"

"Stop, it's all right, Yasir. I'm not angry at you." He sighed at Vasili and wished the bastard were awake to scowl at them all.

Alissand was the thorn in all their sides. He had guards, the flame, and generations of sorcerers' knowledge. He wanted control of *everything*, but how much of that was the flame's whispers and how much the man himself? If the princes woke now, the flame would rise up and command Alissand's men, and probably Niko too.

"Take the sleds to the tunnel," Niko told Yasir. "You remember how to find it?"

"I do." He lifted his chin and gripped his reins fiercely.

"What are you going to do?" Roksana asked with a note of concern. She'd dismounted her horse to check on Amir's ties and gave them a few rough tugs.

"What I always do, ride right through the front gate."

"And take on all of Alissand's men alone?"

"I don't intend to take on all of them." Alissand wouldn't expect him to just trot into the palace grounds.

"Niko—" Her tone scolded, like a caring aunt's might. She planted her hands on her hips.

"Get the princes inside the salt chamber," he said, cutting her off. "I'll find you there."

"What if you don't make it?" Yasir's grip tightened on his horse's reins.

"I will."

"But what if *you don't*?"

He looked at the sleeping prince bundled in furs. Vasili had asked for this. His last order. Nothing short of the gods themselves would stop Niko from standing beside him. "I will see him safely inside that chamber." He held Yasir's gaze. "You have my word."

A soft groan slipped from Amir's lips.

Roksana leaned over him and pulled back one of his fluttering eyelids. "Shit! He's waking up. We have to go, Yasir. Now!"

"Go." Niko swung himself into Adamo's saddle

again. If Amir woke, rousing the flame within him, their journey would be for nothing.

Roksana quickly mounted up.

Yasir's stare lingered on Niko.

"I'll be there, Yasir. Now go!" He jabbed his heels into Adamo's side and launched the charger from the brush onto the wide, main road leading to the palace. Yasir would get them to the salt chamber. And Niko *would* join them there. But first, he had to play by Vasili's rules, and there was one thing the prince excelled at. Lies.

"Yah!" Adamo raced into a gallop, his massive hooves rapidly clapping against the slush-covered cobbles. The palace loomed atop its mountainous slopes. And the torches glowed at its gates, like targets in the dark.

Faster.

Niko kicked Adamo on, hunkered down, and relished the vicious bite of the cold air burning his face and the race of his heart.

The guards had seen him. More men appeared with their torches held high, forming a blockade. They'd clearly never met Adamo before.

"Yah!"

Go, Adamo! Adamo spurred on, a racing, charging, fearless force sent from Etara herself. Nothing could stop Vasili's devil horse once he found his stride.

"HALT THERE!"

Adamo was almost on them when they flung themselves aside. He galloped into the palace grounds, among a whole throng of men. Niko pulled back on the reins, and Adamo abruptly reared, screaming his rage at being held back. Niko clung on, leaning into Adamo's neck. Soldiers formed up, closing in. Adamo dropped, circling and stamping his hooves, keeping the guards at bay. Around, he danced.

"Alissand!" Niko bellowed. "Come out, you fucking coward!"

Adamo tossed his head, stamped, and snorted, half-wild.

"Alissand!"

"Nephew." The shah emerged from among his men. The Yazdan crest glimmered on his breastplate. "Where is the creature you love, your beloved prince?" He waved his men back and approached. "I shall take his pretty head as payment for the death of countless Seranians and hang it from his palace gates." His eyes were the same glossy black as the flame in the crest.

Niko bared his teeth behind a snarl. "You don't care for Seran or its people. You never have. It's all about blood. Power. Control."

Alissand's pantomime smile cracked. "You think you're a better Yazdan? You're nothing but Leila's mistake."

"Without the flame, you're a weak and greedy fool. A coward hiding behind pristine armor."

"How dare you, boy!"

Niko laughed. "You claim to stand for honor. Where is yours? Roksana is twice the shah you are."

"Roksana is a traitor to the flame!" he roared, striding from his circle of men.

Adamo startled and danced back. Alissand tore the

straps from beneath his armor and dropped the metal breastplate in the snow. He pulled his blade free and tossed the scabbard aside, brandishing the recurve Yazdan sword as a clear threat.

"Free your blade then, and let us end this," his uncle demanded.

The old lust for the fight had Niko's heart racing. "As men? No flame?"

"No flame." Alissand blinked and the flame touch cleared from his eyes.

Niko regarded the crowd. Forty men, maybe more. Good.

He dismounted Adamo, let a guard take the horse, and freed his blade.

"Rules, Uncle?" Niko asked.

"To the death."

CHAPTER 37

asili

THE RIVER HAD DRIED up and the snow no longer fell. The dream was coming to an end. Nikolas had either succeeded, meaning Vasili would wake inside a metal cage beneath tens of thousands of tons of rock and salt, or Nikolas had failed. In which case, Vasili would wake a puppet in his own skin while the flame consumed the world.

"My mother told me many tales before she died," Vasili began, fully aware of the shadowy presence across the dry riverbed. "The flame was born of the gods, she said. Etara—the goddess of earth and war—poured all of chaos into the making of her son and set him free upon the land. She was proud of her creation, and her creation was proud to be hers. But Etara's sisters, Aura and Walla, wanted peace and balance, not chaos, and so

313

the flame, whose only crime was to exist, was discarded." Lifting his gaze, he found the figure made of dark flame. It wasn't a man, despite adopting the outline of one. But it did feel, Vasili knew that as much as he knew his own heart. "It had no choice in its birth and no choice in its fate."

Vasili climbed down from his rock and stopped at the riverbank's edge. The shadowy figure stood at the edge of the opposite bank: a dark, flickering, faceless reflection.

"She didn't tell me of its fury, but I know it intimately, like I know my own." He couldn't tell if the words had any impact or if any of this mattered. "Freedom is a choice."

The flame rippled and stepped from the bank into the riverbed, beginning its approach.

Vasili lifted his chin and whispered, "I have chosen my ending. Will you choose yours?"

 asir

AN ITCHING TIGHTNESS returned to Yasir's veins as he cantered his horse and sled across moonlit fields and down into the narrowing furrow that would eventually lead to the cliff face and the palace's tunnel entrance.

Roksana rode close behind, her face full of grim determination.

The princes were secure in their sleds. Amir just had to stay asleep for a little while longer and this would all be over.

Their pace was forced to slow by the track's narrowing and heavy snow.

Approaching the cliff face, when the track opened, the snow ahead had been churned to slushy mud. Yasir lifted a hand to halt Roksana.

An arrow whispered past his head and twanged against the wall of rocks. His cry lodged in his throat. He dropped the reins and yanked the long gun from the saddle, lifting it to his shoulder to scan the tree line—and saw them.

Elves.

They poured from the trees. So many, it seemed like all the elves in the world. Their front line dropped to their knees, arrows nocked, ready to fly from their longbows, while the second line came forward, freed blades catching moonlight. Yasir had one shot. It would take too long to reload a second. He had to make the first count. But felling one elf wouldn't slow the wave of them. Nothing could stop that many, only Niko... and he wasn't here.

He raised both hands in surrender, catching Roksana's eye. Her gaze skipped manically from elf to elf as they closed in. An elf barked a harsh sound, and she thrust her hands up, away from her holstered pistols.

An elf jabbed Yasir in the leg and grunted, gesturing for him to dismount. He climbed from the saddle, watching more elves swarm in. Some peeled off toward the sled. "Wait. Stop. Leave him!" He lunged toward the sled. A blade kissed his throat, freezing him still. His gun was plucked from his hand and dropped at his feet with a soft *thud* in the snow.

Elves descended on Vasili's sled. Their sharp knives cut through his ropes, and the bundle that had kept the prince safe spilled open.

Panic turned Yasir's heart to ice in his chest. He

couldn't allow them to take him, or either of them, but especially not Vasili. *Not him*.

"Wait!" The elf-blade pressed harder into his neck. "We're here to stop the flame!" They wouldn't understand. But he had to say or do something. *"Please."* It couldn't end like this, with the elves taking the princes, bleeding them all over again, setting the nasdas free. It was all coming undone. They'd gotten so close, and to fail now...

A murmuring rose from Vasili's lips.

Yasir stilled, panting hard. If Vasili woke, they'd all be ash in seconds, including himself. Vasili would kill his brother with the click of his fingers, and then maybe it wouldn't be so terrible that he was dead, because he wouldn't be alive to witness the end of all things.

A soft, rolling laughter filled the clearing. The sound was almost lost beneath the elves' snarling growls and the deep thud of Yasir's heart.

Then, suddenly, and with no fanfare, the two elves who had descended on Amir's sled vanished in a blink, turned to ash and swept away by the wind.

Gods, no...

The knife vanished from Yasir's throat, and the elf holding him back shoved away, rocking Yasir on his feet, but Yasir could no more run than he could stop Amir from rising.

Amir swung his legs over the side of the sled, cocked his head, and pushed to his feet. He rose to his full height—seemingly taller than Yasir remembered him being—and rubbed ash from his tattered sleeves.

The elves backed away, arrows nocked in readiness.

"Well," Amir said, running a hand through his shaggy white mop of hair. He studied his audience as though he were a king upon his dais. "How very unexpected." He staggered, seemingly intent on moving forward but struggling to coordinate putting one boot in front of the other. "So many elves!" He laughed, but this time, the sound was far from the smooth, bubbling laughter of the flame, instead sounding like the wracked sobbing laughter of a man in despair. "So many lives to feed the flame," he added softly. His trembling hands shot to his head. He took a step and collapsed, knees sinking in the slush.

Yasir was witnessing a man fighting himself, or rather, fighting the poison that had claimed him as its own. Amir didn't stand a chance. Yasir grabbed his gun from beside his boots, shouldered the stock, and aimed at Amir's bowed head.

Pull the trigger. To end him now, before the flame took him. But wouldn't it then all weigh on Vasili's shoulders?

Amir looked up. Tears glistened on his stricken face. Bright blue eyes begged. His bottom lip quivered. *"Kill me?"* He rocked back into a crouch and curled a fisted hand to his chest, as though fighting some great pain around his heart. "Kill me!"

Yasir fixed the prince's forehead in the long gun's sights. His finger pressed against the trigger.

Amir sprang from his crouch and sprinted forward.

"No!" Vasili's shout came too late.

Yasir tugged the trigger. The gun boomed and

kicked back. Amir flew backward off his feet and fell, sprawled, unmoving in the snow.

A vast, hungry silence filled the space around them, swallowing all sound. Yasir lowered the gun, panic racing through his heart and mind.

Vasili was braced on an arm on the sled. He swung a look back at Yasir, his face white with terror.

What had he done?

Amir's leg twitched. The silence choked, the air suddenly thick with a great weight of dread.

Black liquid flame bubbled from underneath Amir, staining the snow as it crept outward. Vasili tumbled from the sled, got to his feet, and stumbled again.

Yasir rushed in. "Look out!"

The dark flame surged across the snow, flowing like the great expanse of night had funneled into a river.

Vasili bolted toward the cliff face and its tunnel opening, sprinting hard. Slithering tendrils chased him. He ran—ran so hard, not glancing back. Elves watched, Roksana screamed something, but it didn't matter.

He almost made it...

A few steps more.

The flame lashed down Vasili's back like a whip. He missed his footing and sprawled into the snow. The river of black washed over him—into him—drowning Vasili's prone body. Until vanishing. Moments passed. The night breathed again, and the pressure eased.

Vasili pressed a hand into the snow beside him and levered himself to his knees.

"He's all right..." Yasir staggered forward. Oh gods,

he'd thought the flame had killed him, but he was getting up; he was all right!

Roksana grabbed Yasir's arm and shook her head.

Vasili was on his feet now. He turned.

The veins and scarring on his face simmered black under the moonlight.

Vasili opened his all-black eye.

The nasdas was whole.

CHAPTER 39

iko

ALISSAND HELD his sword low at his side, comfortable with the weight of the blade. He was no stranger to battle, despite Niko's earlier insult regarding the unmarked armor.

Niko swung his sword experientially and rolled his shoulders, then lowered his stance, spreading his weight.

The audience looked on, curious. Some had even sparred with Niko in the past. A few jeers bubbled up, hitching Alissand's smile higher. He had the crowd on his side, was well-rested, and clearly thought he'd win.

The shah was heavy. Well-muscled. A match for Niko, physically. His age lent him more experience too, though slowed his reflexes some.

Niko swallowed. It wasn't often he'd fought

321

someone who posed a real threat. It was almost a shame Vasili wouldn't be here to witnesses this. He had as much reason to see Alissand dead as Niko.

"You think you can best me, nephew?" The shah rolled his sleeves up and began circling, like the wolf from Niko's dreams. He had the look of a predator. Someone who believed themselves better than all others. "And for what? The Caville bitch who killed his own family and almost killed mine?"

Niko circled too. *Just keep the egotistical fool talking.* He almost heard Vasili speak in his ear. Lies. Misdirection. This was the Caville way.

Alissand grinned as they circled. "He makes a puppet of you, even now. A fool. Is any thought your own?"

"Are we going to talk or fight? I know which I'd prefer."

"Well, I would, but you see..." He straightened. "We're no longer alone." Alissand gestured for his men to part. The circle of men broke open, opening a path straight to the palace, where a stream of elves descended from the palace doors, approaching calmly.

What fresh madness was this?

He stared again at Alissand. "Elves?"

"Surprisingly accommodating when promised a prince."

There were dozens, and they kept on coming, a small army. No... Gods, what had Alissand done? "You think they're... working *with* you?" Could he be so foolish? "Are you mad, Alissand? They'll kill everyone—"

A twitch toppled Alissand's grin, making way for a

vicious snarl. "No Yazdan will ever kneel to a Caville again." He pointed the tip of his sword at Niko's chest.

Niko batted it aside with the edge of his blade. "They will kill *everyone* and hang you by your own guts from trees."

Alissand's men shifted uneasily.

More elves left the palace and approached Alissand's smaller contingent of men. They were all armed, and all wore the narrow-eyed sneers of vicious killers. They weren't allies, no matter what Alissand had convinced himself of to get this far. He'd promised them a prince, but they didn't want just one. They'd take everything and burn the rest to the ground.

"You've brought these men north to die," Niko said. He threw his sword down. It was time to end this nonsense now and return to the salt chamber. "This pantomime"—he flung a hand at the restless crowd—"is over."

The shah chuckled, but his laugh quickly cut off. "Your princes are mine. You can't hide them from me. If you think to bury them inside that chamber you found —oh, I know all about that thanks to the talkative Captain Lajani—think again, nephew. By now, the elves have them both, assuming you were foolish enough to drag them here together." Alissand laughed. "There's nowhere left for you, Nikolas." He curled his right hand into a fist and presented the Yazdan ring. "Surrender to the Yazdans. Or die by elf."

Niko's snarl twitched. "As much as I despise the wretched fucker Amir, he had one thing right."

Alissand tilted his head. "How's that?"

"He freed the most dangerous weapon in this war." The moment he tossed a gesture toward Alissand, the flame came roaring to the forefront of his mind, possessing body and mind, but with Etara's words on his lips—he *controlled* it. And control was everything. "Me."

Raw power rolled over Alissand. The flame tore over him, lighting him up inside its darkness, ripping mortal strength from his body.

He fell back, but the shah's reflexes kicked in, and the same power in him simmered alive, shielding him from the worst Niko could do. "You can't throw the flame at me, boy!"

Guards moved in, flickers in Niko's peripheral vision. He spun, whipping the flame over them all, muttering the old words, keeping the power leashed and controlled. They wouldn't die, they weren't going to make the flame stronger. He held it by the reins. As they fell, gasping, clawing at the filthy snow, he wondered if he truly had been made for this.

You gave me the greatest weapon there is in this war...

Amir's words came back to him now as the fragmented pieces of his memories stitched together. The prince telling him he'd killed his parents, deliberately sought out the Buclands, destroyed pertinent pages from ancient books, turned Niko around and around to prevent him from understanding the power within him. Chaos and control.

He'd been born a weapon, forged by a history he didn't understand, and thrown into a war he had no wish to fight. But fate had brought him back to the shadow of the Caville palace, where his destiny waited.

The chamber, the power, two powerful bloodlines combined in him. Mah hadn't been alive to tell him his path, but he had found it all the same.

Power.

Control.

He breathed in, filling his lungs with cold Loreen air, and as Alissand tried to fling the same power back at him, Niko merely smiled. He absorbed the hit and drew flame back into himself, drawing it from Alissand until the fool shuddered to his knees. All around, man and elf knelt, gasping in the snow. But alive.

Alissand's fingers twitched around the handle of his sword.

"Don't."

The shah looked up, eyes as black as Nikolas's surely must be.

"I've killed better men than you," Niko warned. "And I don't need the flame to do it."

The elves were shaking off their weakness, reaching for their arrows and blades. Niko should kill them. They wanted to do the same to everyone here. But not all elves wanted destruction, and if someone didn't stop the killing, it would never end.

He could stop it. Here and now.

Stop it all.

A pair of elves were on their feet, arrows nocked and bows drawn. He could kill them with a thought, but the others would swiftly move in and nothing would change. More ash would fall. But it didn't have to be that way, not now he had a choice. He wasn't the monster Amir almost made him out to be.

A high-pitched whistle soared over their heads, alerting the elves to a new presence.

Niko whirled at the sound.

A stocky elf approached through the palace gates and lowered his hood. Lasher said nothing, just walked toward the nearest elves, ignoring Alissand's weakened men in favor of meeting his people. A visible change rippled through them, sweeping away their tension and softening their bloodlust. Every elf Lasher passed by dipped their chins, and the two who had their longbows trained on Niko lowered them under Lasher's glare. This was not Alissand's army, but Lasher's.

Kings and queens did not win wars, Niko realized. Good men and women and, apparently, good elves did that.

Lasher turned and met Niko's gaze. There was no satisfaction on the elf's face, just mutual respect. Lasher was like him. A soldier caught in a war he did not want. He'd chosen another way. And he wasn't alone. The elves who stood behind him wouldn't attack first.

Niko eased some of the power running through him and offered the elf his hand. "I have to find him and end this."

Lasher gripped his hand. While they did not speak the same language, his hand in Lasher's was understanding enough.

Alissand might have had something to say, but as Niko turned toward him, movement at the palace gate caught his eye. A lone figure approached. He might have been unrecognizable if not for the tousled white hair, so stark against a cloak of dark flame.

Power swelled before him, creeping outward.

No. It couldn't be... Niko took a few steps toward him but stopped. Black veins had cracked his pale face, shattering his perfection.

The flame held all of Vasili, and Vasili held all the flame.

His single black eye scanned the crowd—the nasdas reading each soul.

"Vasili?"

But it wasn't Vasili. The nasdas's gaze snapped to Niko and struck like a physical blow, ripping through mortal flesh and blood. The control he'd fought so hard to find was torn from him. The ground tipped and his mind spun.

"Kneel," the nasdas ordered, Vasili's voice twisted and wrong.

Agonizing heat burned through Niko's veins. *Kneel, kneel, kneel.* The voice echoed over and over inside his head, lashing at his consciousness like whip blows. Again and again, driving him down to his knees. It was too much. He couldn't breathe around the pain, couldn't think to find the words that might control it. *"Vasili."* That was the only word he could find, the only word he had strength enough to voice.

Moans and cries from the men rose and then fell away, silenced forever.

No... Gods, Vasili...

Niko clutched at his head, trying to stop the immense pressure to *obey* this creature.

Amir had been killed. Roksana and Yasir? He didn't know their fates.

But Vasili's fears had been realized.

The nasdas had won.

Cold tears wet Niko's hot face. The burning onslaught continued, as did the moans and cries of men in their final moments—so like his nightmares, but now the beginning of the end.

His sword lay in the slush beside him.

He'd failed Vasili. The man whose trust was the most precious thing of all. The man who had sacrificed his freedom, his life, his love to stop this.

Niko hadn't been able to save him, not in the way he'd wanted. But he could still be freed.

The final order.

Niko's final act.

He folded his fingers around the blade's handle.

Agony thumped through him. *Kneel-kneel-kneel*, striking his mind like hammer blows on hot steel. He pulled his burning body to his feet and started forward.

"Kneel."

Never.

He found a smile on hearing his Vasili from his memories ordering him to kneel and dragged it to his lips. He recalled watching the prince tip his face to the sun, loving the warmth of the Seranian sun, the same prince who'd laughed freely at Yasir's scandalous jokes and stroked his fine fingers across Niko's face.

Vasili's only wish was to be free.

An arrow flew at the nasdas, but the thing in Vasili's skin batted it aside and thrust out a hand.

Niko followed the lash of flame as it wrapped around Lasher, swallowing him down.

"No!" Niko lurched forward. "Vasili, you viperous prick! Look at me, damn you!"

He had to be in there somewhere still. He was... Niko knew it.

The nasdas's head ticked, tilting sideways, and its dark-eyed attention speared into Niko again. *"Kneel, and serve me."*

The heat of the nasdas's enormous power throbbed through Niko again, over and over. Worse than the heat in the hottest of forges. He gasped and staggered. He was supposed to fall like the others. Supposed to succumb, surrender, kneel, and die. But he had Bucland blood in him, the blood of the three. He could resist. Another step. The heat beat harder, trying to drive him back or down to his knees.

He hissed every breath through clenched teeth. "Never. Surrender."

The nasdas's face—a twisted mockery of Vasili's—contorted with rage. "KNEEL!"

The heat spluttered, weakening behind the nasdas's rage. The old families had trapped it before; it wanted to make sure all threats succumbed to it. Vasili had said its rage was real, and maybe that rage was its weakness too. Whatever it meant, Niko used the nasdas's moment of weakness to stagger forward.

Vasili was close now. His entire body burned with dark flame. He'd likened the Cavilles to a candle. Everyone had expected him to burn out long before now. But he hadn't. Because Vasili Caville didn't fucking surrender to anyone or anything, least of all some ancient curse. Vasili still held on, somewhere, somehow. Niko believed in him.

"Come back to me, you son of a bitch."

The heat beat harder, and the skin on the backs of Niko's hands flaked and peeled. Pain was temporary; it would all be over soon. There was no force in this world strong enough to keep him from reaching Vasili.

He pushed his left hand through the flame, reaching out. *"Take my hand,"* he begged, not to the nasdas, but to the prince trapped within. Black flame boiled Niko's flesh. The nasdas looked down at the hand, its face a cracked mockery of Vasili's.

He knew pain, but this was an agony like no other, like the flame was trying to scorch his soul into submission. Blood burned his tongue. *"Take my hand..."* Niko forced the words through cracked and splitting lips. *"Or I'll throw you over my damn shoulder, Vasili."*

The nasdas still raged and burned in all its fury, but the smallest of cool flickers briefly chased the black from Vasili's beautiful eye. Between one blink and the next, the Caville bright blue suddenly shone through.

Vasili grabbed Niko's hand.

One last order.

Niko pulled Vasili forward—onto his blade. Hard steel met little resistance and sank deep into Vasili's skin and flesh. Vasili fell into Niko's arms. His gasp fluttered at Niko's ear.

The nasdas's terrible burning power collapsed, almost taking Niko and Vasili to the ground with it.

But he stayed standing, stayed strong, holding

Vasili's suddenly limp body against him. "I've got you. You're not alone. I have you, Vasili. We're safe."

Vasili's short breaths sawed from between his lips and fluttered against Niko's neck. "So... cold." His fingers gripped Niko's arm, holding so damn tight.

Niko bit back a sob and clutched Vasili's head against his shoulder. "I have you, you hear me? I'm not letting you go."

"My assassin." The whispers were so quiet now, they might have been imagined.

Yasir sprinted into sight at the palace gateway, his expression falling. "Niko... Vasili—the flame..." The sight of him blurred, lost through Niko's tears.

Niko turned his head away from those watching, from everyone who would wish this man in his arms dead, and he whispered against Vasili's cheek, "I gave you my word, and I'd give it a thousand times again to save you from this."

"We had," Vasili sighed, and the last vestiges of his strength drained away, "the cabin." All his weight, what little there was of it, slumped into Niko.

Niko pulled the sword free of his gut and tossed it away. He scooped Vasili into his arms. Warm blood—so much of it—soaked Vasili's clothes, plastering them to him.

He was dying... There wasn't much time. Maybe no time. Grief and exhaustion conspired to trip Niko, but he wasn't damn well faltering now. He turned and found a small army of elves blocking the route to the palace doors. Lasher stood at their front, barring his way.

"Let me through, damn you!"

They didn't move.

"I'm ending it, like you said! Do not stand in my way when you know this is right. You've always known, that's why..." His voice cracked. "That's why you came, why you're here, why you've never left. Let me through, let it end." The next word came out with a tremor. *"Please."*

Lasher stepped aside.

Niko fell into a staggering run. He stumbled by the elves, up the steps and into the palace's gaping entrance. Snow or ash spiraled from holes in the roof. He ran down the moonlit halls, remembering another time when Vasili had worn cruelty like armor to protect himself inside these walls, when he'd demanded Niko serve him, when he'd stood at his chamber window and stared out at the world like a man staring through prison bars.

Niko hadn't known him then. Nobody truly knew Vasili because he'd never been free to discover who he truly was.

Darkness tried to pour in from the shadows. He couldn't see, couldn't find the kitchens, the tunnel to the salt mine! *Why must he fail at every turn?* He fell against a wall, muscles burning from exhaustion.

"Niko?"

"Yasir!"

The glow from his torch warmed the halls, chasing off the dark.

He could do this... he had to do this. "Yasir, here. Help—"

Yasir's hand came down on his shoulder and the man's soft face shone in torchlight. "I'm here."

"Roksana?" Niko muttered. He hadn't seen her outside, but she'd be nearby.

Shaking his head, Yasir raised the torch high. "This way."

Then Roksana had fallen. It was just them against the full weight of the dark. Despair weakened his knees. He'd trudged through mud, he'd slaughtered enemy after enemy, he'd stood to a king, and fallen to a prince. He could do this once last thing. One last order.

Forcing his body to move, he carried Vasili toward his fate—the fate that awaited them both.

$\mathcal{N}$iko

THE SALT CHAMBER'S icy air nipped at Niko's face, and salt crunched underfoot. The air smelled of minerals and metal, like blood on steel. The cage lay ahead, in the glow of Yasir's torchlight. Niko carried Vasili toward it, hating every wretched step.

They'd come this far.

He had to see it through.

Vasili stirred in his arms. His blue eye rolled, pupil wide but unfocused. The flame's dark poison had faded from his veins, leaving him pale again, but for how long? "Where?" he groaned.

"The cabin, remember?" Emotion clawed at the lie in Niko's throat. "Just you and me. We'll be safe here, Vasili."

Yasir opened the iron clamps. Old metal creaked and groaned, then clanged in the vast space.

Vasili stared up at Niko. His brow pinched. Beads of perspiration gleamed on his pale skin. He knew the lie for what it was, but a soft smile touched his lips all the same, and Niko's cracked heart shattered. How could he do this? How could he condemn Vasili to this metal prison when the only crime he had committed was being born into a destiny he had no choice in.

Vasili's glassy-eyed gaze held the answer; Niko had given his word.

He carefully lowered Vasili into the structure—a prince upon a throne of iron bars. Vasili lowered his trembling blood-smeared wrists into the clamps. He flicked a glance at Yasir and nodded.

Yasir folded one clamp over. It clicked into place.

"I'm sorry," Vasili whispered, his gaze on Yasir.

Yasir hesitated, the second clamp raised. He swallowed and nodded. "I know." The second clamp clunked into place.

Vasili's brow was still pinched, his face ashen. "Say the words, Nikolas, then go."

Yasir handed the flaming torch to Niko.

Even restrained in metal, pinned down and wounded, Vasili still looked like he'd defy the world. Like all of this was a temporary inconvenience, but there was nothing temporary about dying alone, and Niko couldn't leave him. He stepped up to the cage.

"Nikolas," Vasili hissed.

"I'm not leaving."

"Don't be stubborn." He coughed lightly and

winced. "Your love is worthless. It's your hate I need..." He smiled at the echo of the words he'd spoken so long ago. "You do not die here."

Niko rested his hand on Vasili's arm, between the iron frame. "I don't take orders from Cavilles."

"You agreed to my last."

"Your last order was to get you here, not to leave you here."

Vasili's thin brows pinched together. "Bastard."

By some miracle, he found a smile. He would always find one for his prince. "I'm not leaving."

Vasili let his head fall back. He blinked quickly, dislodging a tear. "You vowed to live, Nikolas," he whispered. "You vowed to find someone. To take him away to a life you'd build for him. You gave me your word in this. You are a man of honor. Do not go back on your word now." Rising anger clipped at his words.

Niko turned and knelt at Vasili's feet. He laid his hand over Vasili's inside the cage and then looked up. Vasili Caville might be the bravest damn soul he'd ever met. He'd do any damn thing for him. And he wished he could take him away, like he'd promised. But as Vasili had always said, that was not their ending. "You were always that man."

The corners of Vasili's mouth twitched, digging in. He forced his lips together and squeezed Niko's fingers. "I do not want this to be our end," he whispered, his hard mask and its anger crumbling, leaving just a terrified young man behind.

Niko squeezed his hand, holding on for the both of them. "I know."

 asili

FEAR HAD him in its icy grasp, its weight like the cold iron cage holding him down. The nasdas thrashed inside his head, desperate for freedom. It sensed its end, like Vasili sensed his own. Tiredness crawled over him, numbing the pain.

Nikolas just had to speak the words and leave, sealing this nightmare away. Vasili would die, and the nasdas would forever be trapped here, in this crypt— where it was always supposed to remain.

"Go, Niko," he begged. It hurt too much to think of Nikolas wasting his life when he could go on and live a better life. "I can't be the cause of another lover's death." Niko deserved to love again. Which he would, because the fool fell in love all to easily.

Niko rose. His rough hand cupped Vasili's wet face,

and his dark Yazdan eyes were suddenly all Vasili could see. He'd infuriated Vasili, frustrated him, confused him, and distracted him. He had not planned to love Nikolas Yazdan, but he couldn't have made it here without him.

"As Etara as my witness, I will forever stand beside you, Your Highness."

It was the first time he hadn't used Your Highness as an insult, and, of course, it crippled Vasili's determination to send him away. He hated him for that but loved him too.

Nikolas kissed him then—so softly, so simply. It was nothing, really. A brush of the lips, but if it were the last thing Vasili felt, he'd gladly take its touch with him to meet the gods.

"Rest now." Niko pulled away. His dark eyes brimmed with unshed tears. He stood proud, with the torch in his left hand, raised against the dark. His Nikolas. His sorcerer. His lover, and finally, his assassin.

Tiredness pulled Vasili's strength from his body, made him want to rest, but gods, the fear that if he closed his eye, he'd never see Nikolas again... He didn't want to die. He never had. He had too much still left to do, too many places left to see, but mostly he just wanted to lie back in a field somewhere and stare at the stars, tomorrow his own. That was all he'd ever wanted.

Nikolas's murmuring began. Old words. Sorcerers' words. Words from the gods, and Nikolas whispered them as though they'd always belonged on his lips.

The nasdas stilled its mental thrashing and watched through Vasili's eye.

Nikolas's voice filled the chamber, echoing over and over, chasing itself into the dark, until finally diving inside Vasili's soul, finding its target. Down, they pulled. Vasili could no longer keep his eye open. The dark rushed in, smothering him, taking him under. But its rage at being repressed was too strong a thing to contain. He could hold it no more...

With Etara's grace, he might die a free man.

The words rolled around and around, spiraling higher and faster, and the nasdas, for all its hunger and power and rage, was suddenly defenseless.

Hundreds of Cavilles had died before him, mad and lost, and each one had surrendered to the flame. But he'd fought it, fought them all, the elves, his father, his brothers. Fought them and finally won.

The weight of the ageless curse lifted from his body and mind, the nasdas fleeing its human trap. And finally, as death came for him, Vasili was free.

 iko

THE NASDAS TORE from Vasili's body as a vast torrent of dark, like it had Talos in the palace chamber somewhere far above, but this time there was no Caville for it to jump to, no vessel for it to fill, and no freedom to find inside the prison of salt.

Etara's words fell hotter and harder from Niko's lips, as though each one was a blade, striking the thunderous power as it swirled and howled its rage. Its whirling threw up shards of rock salt. Grains dashed Niko's face and rained against his lips and tongue. His torch sputtered and died, the heat and light blown out. He dropped it and saw how the markings etched into the chamber floor glowed, lighting him, Yasir, and Vasili up inside an eerie blue hue.

The nasdas howled and raged above, like a living storm.

Niko rarely prayed, having given up on the gods, but he needed the extra strength now. *Etara... help me, damn you. Make right your mistake and help me save him. Walla, lend me your strength, and Aura, guide me in the dark.*

Yasir pushed through the lashing storm, his arm raised against the onslaught of burning salt. Niko nodded, still speaking the words, still forcing the nasdas out of Vasili and keeping it out. It wouldn't return to Vasili, not now the prince was too close to death.

Yasir turned his head toward Niko. "Now?" he yelled.

Niko nodded, and Yasir opened one of the cage's clamps.

There was a man's word, his honor, and then there were the things that mattered above anything else. Like love. He wasn't leaving Vasili here. Fuck the prince's last order, and fuck destiny.

The ground beneath his feet trembled. Salt danced and skipped. A sound like thunder cracked somewhere high above the nasdas's enraged swirling storm. Niko stood firm and poured everything he had left into forming the words and chasing the creature made of chaos into its raw form.

A new power burned through him now. This one didn't hurt. It soothed, washing through him, coming alight and filling the chamber. Salt crystals sparkled, like a reverse rain of blue stars rising from the floor.

Yasir unlatched the second clamp and scooped Vasili's limp body over his shoulder.

A slab of salt-rock broke from the chamber ceiling. Its enormous shimmering bulk plunged through the nasdas. It slammed into the floor, shattering the glowing swirl of Seranian writing and exploding, raining huge blocks of salt in all directions. Several punched into Niko. He staggered, and the words on his lips faltered. The blue light spluttered, and its shining stars blinked out.

Yasir whirled. *"Niko?"*

"Run!"

More huge slabs of salt rained from above, hammering into the chamber floor. The air and ground trembled. The nasdas howled and whipped up the salt into its form, blasting Niko's skin, making it burn. His eyes stung, his vision blurred.

He glanced back. Yasir had Vasili. He ran... stumbling around fallen chunks of salt. They would make it.... they *had* to make it.

Power surged in Niko's veins, but the wrong kind. The nasdas had noticed their retreat. The sudden swirl and weight of the dark rose, filling the chamber. The soft blue light lifting off the broken floor did nothing to penetrate it now. More salt rained, ripping swathes through the dark, but not enough to stop it. And in one great push, it lurched toward Yasir's small, fleeing figure.

"Oh no you don't..."

Control.

He stood in the path of the plunging wave, thrust out a hand and defied that *thing* that would take their last hope away from them all.

Etara!

Ice and fire tore through Niko, burning him up from the inside, but still he stood firm and, with the words, demanded the nasdas *hold*. The air sizzled. Pressure thundered inside Niko's skull, threatening to break him apart.

It could not be allowed to escape.

Control. He had it in his blood. He was the only one left who did. He was made *for this*.

The greatest weapon in this war...

It all came down to now.

The nasdas reared up, towering like the mountain of salt surrounding them, and crashed down.

Cool, calm Bucland control tightened his veins, and Niko staggered, gasping. Everything burned. His sight, his skin. The chamber blazed with blue light, each tiny fragment of salt suddenly sparkling like diamonds under the sun. He'd defied a prince, defied a king, defied everything to bring him here, to this moment, and he'd damn well defy the nasdas too. It could not consume him. Its vessel was gone, it had no anchor, it was vulnerable, and when the words left Niko's lips this time, the nasdas's enormous storm twitched, contracted, spiraling ever smaller around Niko. A howl rose, and the tight maelstrom grew faster still, stirring the glittering salt in the air. Salt and light burned its flailing edges, pouring *into* the nasdas. Its rage was all-consuming. The cage twisted and warped, coming undone bit by bit. The nasdas tore it from the floor and consumed it. The salt... so sharp, so bright, it consumed that too... and *screamed*.

With nowhere to flee, no vessel to inhabit, and no way out beyond Niko, the nasdas was consuming *itself*.

Niko staggered under the weight of the endless howling, the brittle light, and the suffocating power. Rocks slammed into the ground left and right. The claps of thunder weren't thunder at all. Enormous, jagged cracks zigzagged through the chamber ceiling. A massive segment of ceiling tore free and violently slammed into the chamber floor.

The nasdas's power spluttered within Niko's veins, turning jagged, like hooks sinking in, but something else was happening too.

Under the onslaught of salt and control, it was *fading*, burning itself to nothing.

Slowly—too damn slowly—the weight bearing down on Niko lifted.

Horrible, jagged groans sounded. He looked up. Salt rained into his eyes, and among the drifting light, great jagged forks zagged through the chamber ceiling, splitting the chamber in two.

The ancient palace foundations and the mountain it sat on were coming down around him.

He ran, tripped. Rocks pummeled his head and shoulders and exploded all around. A vast, horrible, yawning sound moaned all around. He ran harder, sensing the weight of the mountain coming down... There was no nasdas now, no burning in his veins, nothing, just his own weak body and the tunnel a few strides ahead.

All at once, the earth heaved, a wall of air threw him off his feet, and the world went black.

 asir

THE GODS themselves had come to Loreen. The ground shuddered back and forth, and a strange kind of brittle thunder cracked the air above the city.

Yasir stumbled and fell, dropping Vasili under him in the snow. "Gods... gods..." He flung a glance back, almost too afraid to see what monster would be rising out of the earth, and saw instead the Caville palace crumbling apart tower by tower. Clouds of snow and glittering rocks rose to devour it. The sharp, spear-shaped towers curled in on themselves like a hand closing into a fist. Etara herself had taken it back, and the nasdas with it, where it belonged.

He choked on a sob.

Nikolas was surely dead. Roksana was surely dead

too; he'd lost her in the chaos when the elves had ambushed them.

Yasir crawled to Vasili's side. The prince's face was as white as the snow they lay on, his lips icy blue. Dead, his head told him, but his heart would not believe it. Even if no man could look as pale and limp as Vasili did and live. Fingers trembling, Yasir reached for the pulse at Vasili's neck. He didn't want to know. Because if Vasili was dead and Niko too, and Liam was gone, then why was Yasir still here?

A pulse fluttered under his fingers, so faint he may have dreamed it. He pressed harder and felt it beat. "Vasili?"

He lived?

But the blood, his hollow face, he was surely seconds from death, and Yasir had no idea how to save him. He scrunched a hand in the prince's clothes and buried his head against his chest. "I tried... It wasn't enough."

Footfalls crunched through the snow. Yasir blinked up at the huge, horrible looking elf and almost laughed. Because of course an elf would kill them now, that was the fucking way of things, wasn't it?

The elf knelt beside Vasili's head, but instead of cutting his throat with the dagger in his belt, he ran a hand over the prince's chest and peeled back the torn, bloody shirt, revealing the horrid, gaping, three-inch wound near his navel where Niko's sword had sunk in. The elf scooped up snow in his other hand and bizarrely packed it into the wound.

Yasir had clearly lost his mind. He giggled and

maybe wept at the same time. He really didn't know anymore. Was this even reality?

The elf scooped Vasili limply into his arms, like the prince was one of his own kind, and jerked his head for Yasir to follow.

"This is insanity... I'm insane," he muttered. "Or dead." Both options were equally plausible.

He clambered onto unsteady feet and trudged after the elf. Behind them, great clouds hung in the space where the grand Caville palace had once dominated the skies. Its absence felt like a wound on the world.

Niko had always planned to save Vasili—he'd told Yasir that when the time came, in the chamber, he'd know what to do. And he had. Vasili had a skill for slithering through the cracks of any plan not his own, so they'd kept it from him.

But Niko was supposed to be right behind him. Niko was supposed to *live*.

Numbed, he bowed his head for the soldier who'd saved them all in the end. "Goodbye, my friend."

He waited a moment, listening to the breeze and the quiet.

A coughing, spluttering ghost drifted down the street, stumbling about. No... not a ghost. Salt sparkled on his ragged clothes. He coughed again.

Yasir started forward, a dangerous flutter of hope in his chest. "Ho there..." He fell into a jog. Dare he pray?

The man hunched over, bracing his hands on his thighs, and spat in the snow.

Yasir broke into a staggering run. "Niko?"

He looked up—his face masked with salt and grit—pushed himself upright, and grinned.

"You bastard!" Yasir stopped himself from throwing his arms around him, seeing as he looked like he might collapse in the next breath.

Niko grunted and warded him off with a hand. "Careful. Everything's broken."

Yasir swooped in and scooped an arm under his, helping to hold him up. "How?"

"Vasili?"

"I... He's in a bad way—but he lives."

The soft sound from Niko made Yasir's heart swell all over again.

"Where is he?" Niko croaked.

"An elf took him—but we can follow."

Niko said a word, perhaps a name, and stomped on. "Show me."

THE ELF HADN'T GONE FAR. His footprints in the snow led through Loreen to an abandoned townhouse.

Yasir followed Niko inside and expected Niko to threaten the creature, perhaps another fight for their lives to ensue. Instead, Niko's relief at the sight that greeted them was almost palpable. Instead of coming to blows, Niko mumbled his thanks to the elf, as though they were *familiar*.

Yasir again wondered if this was all some kind of hallucination. Perhaps he lay dying in a ditch somewhere and all this was some attempt for his mangled thoughts to make sense of it all.

The elf, whose name appeared to be Lasher, had laid Vasili on the floor in the house's small main living area. Yasir watched, shocked into silence, as the elf took a salve from his traveling bag and applied it to Vasili's wound. He then retrieved some leaves from the pack, twisted them, and poured their oil over Vasili's lips. And he did all this without Niko threatening to rip his limbs off.

Niko did hover close by, breathing hard around whatever wounds he carried himself, like he might at any second shove the elf out of the way and wrap Vasili in his arms. But he refrained.

As it appeared they were staying, Yasir broke up an old chair to use for kindling, found some dry logs in the rear courtyard, and started a fire in the living room's small fireplace. The adrenaline had long ago worn off, leaving Yasir wracked with shivers. He also felt like he might throw up. If this were a dream, he wouldn't feel like he'd been dragged behind a horse for a hundred miles.

He slumped by the fireplace, occasionally glancing back to where the elf tended Vasili. The elf's cloak laid over the prince in a startling display of caring that perhaps unsettled Yasir more than anything else he'd seen lately. And he'd seen a lot of shit.

The fire blazed, and the elf dosed against the wall as Niko tore himself from Vasili's side and sat beside Yasir.

"I'm just going to come right out and ask... How are you friends with an elf?"

Niko blinked, coming around from his distant thoughts. "It's a long story."

"Oh, then do tell it."

Niko stretched out a leg and dusted the powder-fine salt from his clothes. His gaze quickly traveled back to Vasili.

The prince breathed, his chest rose and fell with the rhythm of it. Which was something. Whether he'd survive the next few hours was surely in the hands of the gods. Yasir had said a few prayers and would say some more before the night was over.

Niko began his tale, talking quietly, his attention often drifting back to Vasili and his huge elf guardian, making Yasir prompt him now and then. The tale could have waited, but it took Niko's mind off Vasili and *everything* else. Apparently, Lasher was something of an anomaly for an elf. He was certainly no ordinary, blood-thirsty, human-eating elf. As unlikely as all this was, if Niko said it was true, then Yasir believed him.

When the tale was done, Niko dozed a while by the fire, exhaustion finally claiming him. Yasir hunted through the house for more firewood, and by dawn, the house was at least warm and dry. He slept too, only to be startled awake when the elf crouched a little too close for comfort. Lasher had skewered something small and skinned and suspiciously cat-like on a metal rod and held it over the fire, roasting it. The elf saw Yasir staring and smiled—at least, it was perhaps a smile, or a mockery of one, full of teeth.

Maybe Yasir could decline breakfast?

Niko had moved to Vasili's side in the night and slept slumped against the wall.

Yasir stretched his aching muscles and moved to sit on the opposite side of the prince. Vasili still had a sickly pallor, his lips the color of slate, but the fact he hadn't died yet had to be a good sign, didn't it? It seemed too much to hope that he'd survive all this, but he hoped anyway.

He'd been wrong to blame Vasili and wrong to accuse Niko of failing them.

Whatever happened, he had one hell of a tale to tell. All it needed now was its happy ending. He took up the prince's slim hand in his own and sent a silent prayer to Aura to save a lost prince.

CHAPTER 44

iko

Despite Yasir's attempts to distract him, Niko's thoughts didn't stray far from Vasili. Lasher had tended Vasili's wounds with concoctions that appeared to be doing some good. The horrible wound in his gut had stopped weeping. As for any damage done inside his body, only time and the gods would tell if those killed him. With stomach wounds, it wasn't the incision that killed, but the damage done inside. Men had writhed for days in agony from such wounds, only to die in their sleep.

Niko wasn't without his own issues. He'd broken a rib or two when the chamber collapsed and had woken sprawled in the tunnel where the blast had thrown him. His right ankle was fractured, made worse when he'd dragged himself free of the rubble. The constant ache in his chest throbbed like an angry second heartbeat, but his leg had helped itself by turning mostly numb. He'd swallowed so much salt that he was sure his lungs had shriveled to dust, leaving him gasping whenever he moved.

At least Vasili lived, for now. He didn't dare hope he'd wake. Because hoping led to tragedy, and he couldn't take another hit.

Yasir cleared his throat, rousing Niko from his thoughts to find the captain by the fireplace, holding out his hand for Lasher to shake supposedly. Niko fought a smile from his lips.

Lasher looked at Yasir's hand, puzzled by the empty gesture.

"My name is Yasir."

When it became clear Lasher had no idea what to do with an offered hand, Yasir lowered it and frowned sheepishly at Niko. "I feel like communication is a problem."

"He's not big on talking."

"No mystery why he gets along with you then."

Lasher then attempted to share his breakfast of roasted cat, which Yasir promptly declined, looking a little green in the face.

Niko declined too, unsure if he could keep anything down. With his meal quickly devoured, Lasher wrapped himself in his cloak and left the house, probably to find supplies—although it was difficult to know whether the elf might leave and never return.

Yasir approached Niko's side and crouched beside Vasili. He quietly observed Vasili's peaceful face. They both knew the chances of him waking were slim. The nasdas had left this body *because* it had been courting death for too long.

"It's gone..." Niko said to both of them. Perhaps Vasili could hear him too. "With nowhere to go, and trapped inside all that salt, it consumed itself and then... if there's anything left, it's under a mountain of salt."

Yasir merely nodded.

It seemed like it should be over, but Niko had lived so long with the threat of the flame hanging over him, with the Caville princes and their scheming, with the Yazdans and their greed, that when he thought of all that being done with, the urge to laugh or cry almost overwhelmed him. He couldn't think on what it all meant now, could focus only on Vasili's next breath.

A day and night passed by, with Lasher applying his ointments and feeding Vasili a liquid that was perhaps keeping him asleep to help mend his body. When the elf spotted Niko struggling to stand, he insisted with a snarl and a shove that Niko sit his ass back down and accept help. Niko would have argued before but didn't have the strength now. He let Lasher fiddle with his ankle but drew the line at letting him apply the salve. Niko did that himself.

Friends was not the right word for an elf. But they definitely had *something*.

Dawn crept into the quiet city the following morning, spilling red sunlight through the filthy windows. Lasher was out searching for supplies again. Niko got to his feet and hobbled into the next room. He had to keep his muscles moving or he'd grind to a halt. The prince hadn't passed during the night, but he was running a fever, his face wet with cold perspiration. Niko couldn't do a damn thing but sit and fucking wait, and every slow, wretched second was damn well killing him.

He wiped condensation from the small window and stared out at the snow-covered street. If the nasdas was truly gone, what happened now? Would the elves retreat to their lands? Would the people return to Loreen? He wasn't sure he could find it in him to care.

Lost in thought, it took too long to register the heavy thud of hooves in snow. A rider outside.

Limping into the main room, he ordered Yasir to stay quiet beside Vasili, threw his cloak over his shoulders, and flung open the door, heading into a blast of wintery air.

Sunlight sparkled on ice. The white horse stood in the glare from the sun, its rider in shadow. Vapor puffed from the animal's nose. Niko raised a hand, shielding his eyes from the sun.

He'd know Adamo at a thousand paces, but his being here could only mean one thing...

Alissand sat atop the saddle. In the shadow of his hood, Niko could make out blood crusting the man's rough beard. Bruises blackened his face. His eyes were as cold as ice.

He slid from Adamo's back and immediately went down to one knee in the snow. "Nephew." He coughed, spitting blood into the snow.

Adamo jerked his head, pulling free of Alissand's grip, and danced backward.

Good boy...

Niko limped a step closer to the Yazdan who'd neglected his people, the Yazdan who'd tried to kill his own nephew, who'd treated Vasili like an object to feed his desire for blood. A Yazdan with no honor.

"Niko. I thought... you lost, but here you are." Alissand chuckled until his spluttering cough returned. He sank his hand into his pocket and held out a closed fist. "Your mother would want you to have this," he wheezed.

His fist trembled, held out, waiting.

Niko had half a mind to leave him in the street. The cold would finish him off and the rats could pick his bones clean.

Adamo whinnied softly and plodded to Niko. He nudged Niko in the arm. Hungry, probably. Niko tickled his velvety nose. "Shh, you..." The gods had brought him Adamo before, when he'd needed him the most, and here he was again. A sign, surely. After everything he'd witnessed, he was beginning to believe.

Alissand lifted his head. Pink drool dribbled from his chin. "Please, Niko. Take it. For Leila." He opened his fist, and there in his palm lay his Yazdan ring. Mah's ring. Every time he threw it away, the damn thing came right back. Alissand blinked wet eyes. "Taken from Captain Lajani... You did alone what none of us could with whole armies. It's yours."

Niko limped to Alissand and crouched to meet his uncle's hard gaze. "I wasn't alone." He plucked the ring from his uncle's hand and examined it in the bright sunlight. A black flame on gold. Perhaps he should toss it in Walla's ocean like Vasili had done with the boots he'd taken a disliking to. But this was a new dawn, a new day. The nasdas was gone. Could the Yazdans stand for something different now?

He folded his fingers around the ring—a legacy ended. A fate fulfilled. Dare he hope for change?

He lifted his gaze to Alissand. A slow, deliberate smile crawled onto his uncle's lips, a smile full of malice that said *nothing* had changed.

Alissand thrust out a hand—a dagger flashing. Niko lurched back, miraculously avoiding the blade's tip. His boots slipped, his wounded leg buckled, and he fell backward on his ass in the snow. Alissand reared up, dagger raised to plunge down, his face a hideous mask of madness. Niko uselessly thrust out a hand. Sudden and icy fear froze a gasp on his lungs. Sunlight blazed, searing Alissand's dark silhouette into Niko's vision.

The dagger plunged down.

He couldn't die here, like a pointless afterthought.

A blur struck Alissand in his side, knocking him clean off Niko. The pair tumbled in the snow. Niko twisted onto his side and froze. Roksana pinned her brother beneath her and slashed his throat in a swift, savage arc of her blade. He gurgled blood, the bent fingers of one hand going to his throat as though to stem the flow while the other grabbed uselessly at Roksana.

She slapped his hand aside and got to her feet, then spat in the snow.

Alissand's mouth gaped, forming silent words. His blood seeped into the snow, turning it dark. And then he moved no more. The hand at his throat fell to his side, and all the life snuffed out of Alissand Yazdan's eyes,

Roksana only then seemed to notice Nikolas. She wiped the dagger on her thigh, tucked it back into her boot, and offered her hand.

Niko took his aunt's hand. As he accepted her help to pull him to his feet, he spotted Yasir in the house doorway, a chair leg in his hands. He promptly dropped the leg and slumped against the doorway. "Oh... Roksana. There you are." His shrill laugh ended in a sob.

She touched her forehead and smiled. "Captain." Then looped her arm with Niko's and said softly, "The Yazdans look after their own."

CHAPTER 45

*N*iko
Four months later.

SERAN'S DOCKS and harbor were hives of activity, with the sounds of clanging hammers, rapid orders, and the constant background murmur of men and women at work.

Niko walked among the traders, occasionally stopping to lean on his cane as the persistent ache crawled up his leg.

A few people nodded as they passed him by, recognizing him by sight from the public council meetings. Some steered out of his way entirely, preferring not to make eye contact. These people barely understood the events that had almost caused the collapse of their beloved city. They just knew the Yazdans had been a large part of it, the good and the bad. Tales were being spun in the bars, on the long, hot Seranian nights, of how a great darkness had tried to rise up and swallow the world, and how a Yazdan soldier and a heroic Caville prince had impossibly triumphed in the north, where the gods were said to still roam. The prince had given his life for their freedom, and the name Vasili Caville was spoken of only in whispers, lest the curse be woken again.

Yasir might have had something to do with those tales. He'd certainly helped to spin them in a way that meant the people didn't form a mob and tear down the Yazdan house and burn Niko and Roksana on stakes.

Walla's Heart sat low in the water against the dockside, her belly full of silk cargo—and likely some less legal cargo too. Niko eyed the ramp and considered his bad leg, wondering if it was worth hobbling aboard.

"Don't fret it, old man!" Yasir called. He appeared in a splash of color, like an advertisement for every silk he sold. Wrapped in his peacock finery, there was nothing Niko could do but grin at the fool as he jogged down the bouncing ramp.

Yasir tipped his new wide-rimmed hat back and offered Niko a cocky sideways smile. "Did you change your mind? Three months at sea, Walla's endless freedom, rum to warm your belly, and"—he dramatically swept his hands down his frock-attire—"the finest company in Seran."

Niko chuckled. "I just came to see you off."

"Your loss, my friend." He grinned, flashing white teeth, but his wide smile failed to hide the haunted look in his eyes. No doubt Niko had the same look. Yasir's first love had been taken from him, but his second—the ocean—would save him, Niko was sure of it. He'd return happier for having been away, trading silks, earning coin, and visiting his distant family.

"I'm going to miss you," he admitted gruffly.

Yasir thwacked him too hard on the back. "Of course you are! Just keep my seat warm at the Whispering Pearl for my return, eh?"

"I will."

His mood turned sober, and the hand on Niko's back gripped him by the shoulder. A knot lodged in Niko's throat. He really was going to miss him. The last three months had been hard. Roksana's rise as shah, the people's demands that the elves be curtailed even as their numbers dwindled to nothing, the forming of a council to balance out who held the power in both the north and the south. Yasir had been a ray of sunshine through it all.

Yasir's sad smile ticked into his cheek. He nodded, not needing to speak a word, then tugged Niko into a quick embrace.

It was a good thing he didn't speak because Niko wasn't sure he could find the words to reply. Yasir stepped back, dramatically took his hat from his head, and bowed with a flourish, then jogged back up the ship's ramp. "Don't fucking wait for me, Niko! You hear?" He didn't look back because he'd *be* back.

Niko lingered, if only to clear his throat and head. It was tempting, the ocean, the freedom... new worlds. But he was a man of the land. He waved down a carriage. "Where to?" the driver asked.

"Yazdan house."

The journey took him through parts of Seran where fire had gutted districts that once glittered like jewels. Many of Seran's sprawling houses lay empty, their occupants never to return. There was a long way to go before the wounds of war healed. The scars would always be there. But scars made the person stronger for surviving them.

Staff bustled about the Yazdan house. Niko walked among them, nodding at those who dipped their heads at his approach. Roksana, the Yazdan shah, had bestowed him a position equivalent to a lord, giving him a seat on her new council. He'd tried to refuse, but Yazdans did stubborn like the Cavilles did cruelty. His position would take some getting used to. He was due to meet the council at dusk to discuss the permanent settling of refugees from Loreen.

Niko tucked his cane under his arm and walked through the inner gardens. The patch of oxeye daisies caught his eye. On a whim, he plucked one, limped up the steps to the inner courtyard—refusing to use the cane because he damn well wasn't about to rely on it— and passed through the open-sided corridor.

Cool, salty sea air breezed down the corridor, and Niko slowed his pace before rounding the corner and abruptly coming to a halt.

The sight in front of him never failed to steal his breath. His heart skipped a treacherous little beat.

Vasili leaned against the balcony balustrade, his back to Niko as he faced the sunlit, glistening ocean. His loose white shirt was pinched beneath a boned corset, accentuating the prince's narrow waist. Dark linen trousers appeared to be painted over his ass, and given how he leaned against the balustrade, the curving line of that ass down to his thighs conspired to trip Niko's thoughts. The knee-high, heeled boots finished the kind of portrait Yasir would have many pretty words for. Vasili truly was a work of art. One made of razor blades.

The prince half turned his head, showing his sharp face in profile. "Missing your tongue, Nikolas?"

Niko's smile tried to tick into a grin, but he held the urge down. The spell broken now he'd been seen staring like a fool, he approached Vasili and leaned a hip against the balustrade. Every day with him seemed like a dream, like he might blink and find Vasili gone.

He wore a crisp white-lace patch over his scar while a dark hint of kohl accentuated his left eye. A touch of gloss softened pale pink lips. Three little gold hoop earrings glinted in his ear. Niko's black satin shirt and velvet-hemmed trousers were dull and unimaginative in comparison. But Niko was content as his shadow.

Vasili noticed the daisy between Niko's fingers and raised an eyebrow. "Is that for me or did you intend to crush it between your rough fingers so there's nothing left?"

He'd forgotten he'd picked the flower and now felt like an idiot for even considering that Vasili might wear it in his hair. He stared at the drooping thing.

Vasili's lips twitched.

He was screwing with him. Again. Niko was all too aware how fucking with him was Vasili's favorite game.

Well, this game, two could play. Niko narrowed his

eyes. "Made anyone cry today, Your Highness? The maid, perhaps, who dared wake you with breakfast?"

He fluttered a hand. "The day is not yet over."

In truth, Vasili did no such thing, because Vasili Caville was dead. The cursed prince who had harbored the flame and so cruelly attacked Seran had perished in the collapse of the Caville palace. The stunning man standing before Niko now was Varian Adino, a guest of the Yazdans while he recovered from a terrible stomach wound. Few had survived the flame's encounter to recognize Vasili, and those from Loreen would struggle to compare the dashing, colorful man he'd become with the icy menace that had been Vasili Caville. Varian was a farmer, some said, though most agreed he did not dress like one. Other rumors from the docks suggested the mysterious Varian was a spice-running pirate—thanks to Yasir's tall tales. Those rumors Niko quickly nipped in the bud, lest it attract more trouble.

Vasili was free of more than the flame; he was free of his name too.

Only recently, he'd recovered enough to walk about the house, but he still tired easily. They'd stayed mostly apart, in some silent understanding that Vasili needed time to heal. In the last few days, Niko had begun meeting him on this balcony—neutral ground.

"Yasir's leaving on the high tide." Niko stopped short of saying any more. Vasili needed no encouragement to spend time with Yasir, and perhaps selfishly, Niko would prefer he spent the time with him.

Vasili cocked his head and side-eyed Niko, his smile ticking. "Perhaps I should go with him?"

Niko wet his lips and leaned both forearms on the balustrade, rolling the daisy between his finger and thumb. "Are you well enough?"

"I think so."

"Then, perhaps you should." His heart thudded in his ears.

Vasili loved the sea, of that there was no doubt. He also loved Yasir, in the same way Niko loved the captain. Niko wouldn't dream of keeping them apart. He didn't care for the ocean like they did, but he'd never stop Vasili from going to sea for months, if that was what he truly wanted. He was free to make that choice.

Vasili leaned a hip against the balustrade. The weight of his gaze sizzled against Niko's face, making him look up. "I no longer need to go to sea to be free," Vasili said. He reached out and pinched the daisy stem between his fingers, taking it from Niko to tuck behind his ear. "You brought freedom to me." His fingers slipped between Niko's, capturing his hand, and drew him close.

Niko's heart pounded behind his ribs. He wasn't sure he deserved the long look Vasili was giving him. What had he truly done? Followed Vasili's orders, like the soldier he was, and somehow survived by luck more than judgment. Vasili had been the one to guide him, even when he'd fought him at every damn step.

"Besides," Vasili purred, so close now the temptation to kiss him was almost too much to resist, "if I go to sea, I cannot have my griffin on his knees where he so desperately wants to be."

They hadn't been intimate since their rushed moments aboard *Walla's Heart* before events had taken them back to Loreen. Vasili had been recovering, and Niko had given him time and space. Vasili had to be the one to reach out first. And now, with a flower in his hair and a smile on his lips, he was. His look was an invitation, his touch his permission.

Niko skimmed his fingertips up Vasili's cheek. The prince's lashes fluttered. His neat little teeth bit into his lower lip, and it took every measure of restraint Niko had not to shove him against the balustrade and kiss him like he wanted to kill him.

Vasili's smile turned predatory. His light touch skimmed down Niko's chest and then plunged lower to capture the increasingly hard evidence of Niko's desires through his trousers.

"Hm," he purred. Warm, soft lips brushed Niko's. "You've avoided me quite long enough."

He stopped short of breathlessly surrendering his soul to Vasili Caville, but only because he'd forgotten how to speak. "I haven't been avoiding you, just giving you time to heal."

Vasili suddenly stepped back, leaving Niko reeling, clutching the balustrade. *Fuck.* He was as hard as a rod, teased to within an inch of restraint, and Vasili had the balls to flick his hair and shrug him off.

"If I want time, I'll ask for it. What I want, Nikolas, is you."

The way he spoke his name was the last straw. Niko lunged, grabbed him by the back of the neck, and thrust a kiss on his teasing lips. Vasili yielded immediately, perfectly molding his body against him. He'd have much preferred the prince's lips were around his cock, but a balcony in full view of the staff was not the best place to lose his mind. Although... Vasili blazed to life, kissing him back—shoving into him—until Niko found himself pinned against the balustrade, Vasili's slim but strong fingers clasped around his wrists, holding him firmly under Vasili's control.

Vasili broke away, gasping, his blue eye bright and piercing. "Bastard," he snarled.

"Prick," Niko flung back.

The prince's slash of a smile danced. His rigid stance softened. He leaned in, plastering himself hard against Niko's chest, no longer afraid to close the distance between them. His thigh pressed between Niko's, making it clear who had trapped whom. "If we're quick, the staff won't notice, and if they do,"—he wet his lips —"they'll have more gossip to spread about Varian Adino."

With his wrists still caught, Niko couldn't hold him like he wanted, but perhaps that was a good thing, because he was free to see how Vasili's precious face was open, so full of wicked glee that it made Niko's heart ache to think he'd almost lost him. "This house is not a cabin, and Seran is not a forest, but will you stay and build a life with me, Vasili?"

The words were out, and suddenly he couldn't breathe or think or take them back. If Vasili refused, Niko might die inside.

Vasili's eye widened, then narrowed. His lips parted, but no words came.

Oh, this was torture.

Niko wished he'd never said it.

Vasili looked down; then, freeing Niko's wrists, he pulled away. Niko caught his chin, forcing him to look. "Don't think you don't deserve it, you son of a bitch. There is no man more deserving of freedom than you."

"Nikolas." He pulled his chin free and took the flower from his hair to roll it between his fingers. "Changing a name does not change the man. I am widely despised, with good reason."

"Not by me. Not by Roksana, or Yasir, or the people who matter."

"You deserve more."

Niko refrained from grabbing him, knowing he'd shut down. "You are the bravest soul I've ever met. You fought and bled and lost everything, and still you stood on the edge of death, knowing it was your end, but you fought on, because it was right. Vasili, you're beautiful in ways I don't know how to describe, but I do know I love all of you. If anyone isn't worthy, it's me."

Niko had told him everything now, and if he threw it at Niko's feet, so be it. But he couldn't have him thinking he didn't deserve the life he'd always dreamed of. The life that was within his grasp. He just had to take it.

A hint of red touched Vasili's cheeks. "I'd call you a liar, but I know how poor a liar you truly are."

"Then will you be with me?" Niko pushed from the balustrade. He took Vasili's hand in his. The Caville and Yazdan rings glinted side by side. He only ever wore it when he was alone. "Will you, my prince?"

"Prince of nowhere," Vasili scoffed.

"You're a prince where it matters. In here." Niko touched Vasili's chest, over his heart, and then touched his own. "And here." He lowered himself to a knee, ignoring the ache in his stiff leg, and looked up. "Build a life with me? Don't make me beg, because I will."

Vasili's brows pinched, and instead of smiling, he looked pained. "I am free, but I do not know how to begin that life."

No home, no family, no life to call his own. Vasili had nothing, but perhaps that was the best place from where to start. "One brick at a time."

His frown only marginally softened. He knelt too, facing Niko at the same level, then taking his hand back, he pulled the Caville ring free. Niko looked at the ring now offered to him.

Niko took his Yazdan ring from his finger, took Vasili's, and handed his over. They both applied their family rings. Vasili took Niko's hand in his, and now he did smile. It was still tentative, unsure, but it was real.

A new beginning. A new alliance. A new future. Together.

Niko grinned, and, finally, Vasili's true smile grew, lighting up his face. "A new life, Varian?" Niko asked.

"A new life," Vasili agreed.

 asili

EXQUISITE QUIET.

The sound of the distant ocean rolled in through the open window and the occasional shuffle of shoes from staff passing by the chamber door, but those were the only sounds filling his head. His thoughts were blissfully his own. Vasili raised his glass of wine in silent thanks to the gods and to the memory of all those lost, Amir and Carlo among them, and brought it to his lips. "It has ended, brothers." His only regret was that they would never feel freedom like he did now.

Only in death could any Caville truly escape the curse in their blood.

And he had died.

Or came as close to it as any man could. Killed by

Nikolas Yazdan. As he'd made sure would happen since their first meeting. He'd managed to nudge the stubborn soldier onto the correct path, shoving him left and right whenever Nikolas had careened wildly off course. And in those final moments beneath the palace, when Nikolas had stood against the dark flame—held it controlled in the palms of his rough hands—he had defied Vasili's orders one final time. He'd killed Vasili *and* saved him too.

A knock came at the door. Vasili waited, breathing slowly. His heart thumped faster, waves still rolled in the distance, and the peace in his head held.

"I'll kick the door in if you don't open it," Nikolas warned.

His killer and savior.

Vasili leisurely finished his wine, set his glass down on the side, and tugged the corset down a little over his loose shirt, making everything just so. He glanced at the bed and the strips of silk left there for later and then at the door.

"Vasili?"

Nikolas would absolutely kick the door in. A delightful shiver of lust fluttered Vasili's heart. He almost wanted to wait for it to happen, but it would only tip Nikolas's impatience over into anger. He opened the door.

Niko stood braced against the doorframe. He lifted his dark eyes. The rabid wildness in him stared through Vasili, heating his veins and warming other interested parts of him. "Come in, Nikolas." Vasili left the door open and crossed the room to refill his glass.

The door closed with a telling *clunk*.

This was the first time Nikolas had entered his chamber. Vasili had spent too long lain up and recovering from the blade to his gut. But that was over. He'd survived, he was free, and he planned to thoroughly enjoy having a choice in everything he did—beginning with Nikolas.

Vasili observed Niko discreetly from the corner of his eye. Nikolas dropped his hand to the door lock and flicked it over. The same breathless fluttering that always accompanied Nikolas's arrival skittered low in Vasili's belly, stirring more interest.

There were powerful men, with strength of body or mind, but few had strength in both.

Earlier in the day, on the balcony, they'd somehow agreed to this evening together without saying the words. Meetings and duty had separated Nikolas from him all afternoon. But now it was night, and there were no responsibilities demanding his attention. No wars to fight. Scouts had reported to the council the elves had withdrawn from Loreen's lands and the front line. If they were truly gone, he did not wish to go chasing after them. Yasir had spoken of how an elf had been instrumental in Vasili's healing and of how Nikolas had formed an alliance with the creature. The whole thing sounded like one of Yasir's fanciful tales, and Vasili mentally kept it that way. He did not forgive easily, but he might be capable. With time.

More importantly, the Caville crown and name had been consigned to history, the royal line dissolved. He really was a prince of nothing. And now madness didn't stalk the hallways and whispers didn't seduce him toward the dark, he fancied being nobody for a little while. Being Varian.

But the days ahead were almost more terrifying than those behind. How did one plan for freedom?

He looked at the Yazdan ring on his finger and then up at Nikolas beside the bed, staring at the silk ties laid out like foreign and fascinating objects. He often stared at Vasili the same way.

That was quite enough brooding. Any more and Nikolas would talk himself into leaving. Vasili scooped up both wine glasses, drawing Nikolas's heavy gaze.

Nikolas had enjoyed being tied before, after some convincing. Vasili had every intention of having him enjoy it again. His sultry eyes suggested it would take less convincing this time.

Nikolas took the wine and swallowed its contents in one gulp, then crossed the chamber to the cabinet and poured himself a second glass. "Roksana insists I attend the council meetings—that my being there is *stabilizing*. I would rather be here." He talked some more about the meeting as Vasili propped a hip against the bedpost. The position gave him an excellent view of Nikolas's ass.

After Loreen, he walked with a defined limp, but it did nothing to lessen his presence. If anything, the limp made him more foreboding. He had a body the gods would admire, clothed in Seran satin and linen now, but when naked, he was scattered by small, fascinating imperfections. Battle scars. For a killer, he could be infuriatingly gentle and ridiculously naïve. Not a fool, just hopeful.

"Lost your tongue, Your Highness?" Nikolas asked, focusing on refilling his glass.

Vasili considered telling him how he planned to have him bent over the bed, his hands tied behind his back as Vasili fucked him hard enough to make him bite the silk he'd be gagged with. He'd bend Nikolas over that cabinet too. And the windowsill. But that would all come later.

"Come here."

Nikolas's broad shoulders stiffened. Slowly, he turned and leaned against the cabinet, presenting a picture of stubborn insolence.

Vasili sipped his wine, smoothing his voice. "Did you not hear me?"

"I heard something, but it sounded so very like an order that I must have been mistaken," Nikolas replied, echoing Vasili's lofty tone. "You're no longer a prince, Your Highness." He sipped his wine with a smirk.

The bastard's smile was the same as he'd flaunted in the past, when they'd been enemies. The smile had been cocky then; now it was a playful tease. Vasili was going to enjoy turning that grin into a gasp.

He reached behind his head and pulled the silk tie from his hair, spilling the locks free. He tossed the thin ribbon on the bed with the others. Nikolas's gaze stayed fixed on Vasili's face, and seeing as he hadn't asked him to stop, Vasili reached behind his lower back and tugged the corset ribbons undone.

With a sideways shift of the hips, he dislodged the garment, pinched it between his fingers, and dropped it at his side.

A glance revealed Nikolas still hadn't moved. Well, the majority of him hadn't. His arousal was quite apparent, lodged inside his trousers.

Nikolas was stubborn enough to have Vasili strip, but he was also hopelessly desperate to fuck. He wasn't alone in that either. Every time Vasili had sampled Nikolas, the experience had left him hungry for more. Especially when Nikolas had revealed a penchant for submission, surprising them both.

He'd be like breaking a wild horse. There was still a long way to go. The whip would stay safely in a drawer for now. Until Nikolas was ready. And if he never asked for it, it wouldn't matter. The fact they had these precious moments at all was more than Vasili could have hoped for.

But right now, Nikolas would come to him. Vasili just had to tempt him over the edge.

"Ask me," Nikolas said, voice rough with want.

When he did snap, and it would be soon, he'd be unhinged and rough and *everywhere*. That was when the ties would play their part, restraining him.

"Ask you what?" Vasili sipped his wine.

"Fucking tease," Nikolas muttered, shaking his head. He set his drink down and folded his arms, holding himself back.

He had a rough mouth too. Less a lord, more a barbarian. Gods. Vasili hastily took another gulp of wine. There was no hope in hiding his own aroused interest. His trousers were too tight to conceal his need.

Vasili began loosening his collar. He let it gape and pulled the hem from his trousers waist, freeing the layers. Nikolas continued to observe, determined to draw this out. Vasili set the glass down on the bedside cabinet, and, after straightening, he tore the shirt over his head and discarded it behind him. He'd never shied away from displaying his scars, but having Nikolas's gaze roam them brought its own eroticism. Vasili picked up a length of silk from the bed and slid it between his fingers. A remarkable fabric. Supple. Cool against the skin. But once tied, it would hold someone as strong as Nikolas.

Nikolas broke his statuesque pose and strode forward, stalking Vasili like a wolf closing in on his prey's final moments. He half sneered, half smiled, and scooped Vasili into his arms, cutting off Vasili's small gasp with a kiss. He was wildness, like the sea, and Vasili would willingly drown in him.

He gasped free, shoved him in the chest, and down Nikolas went onto the end of the bed. Before Nikolas could open his mouth to voice whatever doubts he'd found, Vasili straddled his thighs, pulled the silk between his fingers, and pressed its length taut to Nikolas's lips, instantly silencing him.

Nikolas frowned, keeping his lips firmly sealed.

"Trust me."

One of his dark eyebrows arched. His hands came up, and Vasili tilted his head, about to warn against touching. Nikolas's hands promptly dropped again and clutched at the bedsheet instead.

Nikolas reluctantly parted his lips and the silk slid in. "Good..." Vasili tied it off and straightened to admire his now silent ex-soldier. His expression bordered on irritation. He was a long way from accepting this game.

As a reward, Vasili made quick work of Nikolas's trousers ties and eased his hand inside to find the prize they'd both been waiting for. He circled his fingers around Nikolas's thick erection. The man's dark eyes blew wide, his pupils swelling. He moaned around the silk, striking Vasili's lust, heating his blood.

He'd planned to savor this, to draw it out and make Nikolas beg, but he hadn't anticipated how delicious a moment this would be. The overwhelming desire to have Nikolas submit was a revelation. Vasili had fucked around with a handful of men before he'd been *absent* for years. None had excited him the way Nikolas did now—while looking at Vasili in equal parts love and hate. Alek had been his first, and the freest. After his return from the elves, there hadn't been time to engage in anything sexual. Most of the palace staff had quivered in fear like Vasili was some rabid animal. He'd raged at them instead.

He grasped Nikolas's face in his hands and listened to the man pant through his nose. "You'll kill me again like this." Vasili sucked on his lower lip and nipped, making Nikolas flinch.

Nikolas's hands clutched at Vasili's waist and yanked him close. His hardness dug into the valley between

Vasili's thigh and hip, exquisitely eager, and with Nikolas's hard chest pressed close to his own, memories simmered alive, and Vasili's thoughts began to spiral. By the time he felt the tingling of old wounds, it was too late to fight the memories back and suddenly, *anything* pressed close was too much.

He got to his feet, pulling away too quickly. Of course, Nikolas frowned.

Vasili waved off the inevitable concern. There was still this weak part of him that sabotaged his every effort to be normal. The scars were nothing. He didn't care, but his body wouldn't let him damn well forget how he'd gotten them.

Nikolas removed the silk gag himself.

Vasili quickly dashed back in and pressed a finger to his lips, stifling what would surely be an apology for something that wasn't his fault.

Nikolas's lips parted. His tongue flicked at Vasili's finger. Taking the opportunity offered, Vasili angled his finger deeper, accepting Nikolas's sucking mouth.

He might have to change his plan to bury himself in Nikolas's ass because his mouth was so very accommodating. So many choices, so many ways to have him, and he truly was Vasili's in all of them.

A new life.

He'd promised it.

Each day was his own.

Just the thought of such a thing made his heart leap, but also made him fearful. The only thing he'd ever had to call his own was Adamo. Never a *life* of his own.

Never the freedom to walk out a door and have nobody and nothing stop him. Never the freedom to love whom he wanted.

Nikolas pulled his hand back, freeing Vasili's finger. "Vasili?"

"What?" Vasili blinked.

"We don't have to do this, if it's too soon..."

His thoughtful, worthy griffin. Nikolas wasn't escaping him now. He snatched up a silk strip. "Hands."

Nikolas braced both arms on the bed behind him and leaned back. With his trousers open, his erect cock stood eager and obvious, inviting Vasili's hand or mouth to seal tightly around it. But Nikolas's hands were out of reach, holding him up.

That defiant streak had Vasili smiling. "All right." He flicked his hair over his shoulder. "I can see you're going to make me work for your pleasure."

"Tit for tat, Your Highness."

And really, it wasn't a chore. Vasili straddled Nikolas once more, pressed a hand to his chest, laying him down, and took the straining length of cock between his lips. Nikolas immediately spat a curse and arched, feeding himself deep into Vasili's mouth. Vasili greedily took it all, running the head over the roof of his mouth and toward the back of his throat.

A new life of fucking and frivolity, of returning to a bed each night with Nikolas waiting between the sheets.

It sounded like a spice-induced dream.

Vasili applied a finger to the valley behind Nikolas's

cock and stroked from there to the tight ring of muscle. They'd need oil for any deeper exploration, but from the pitch of Nikolas's ragged breaths, he'd be willing.

Vasili straightened, letting the cock slip free from his lips, and, to the sounds of Nikolas's reluctant moans, he retrieved a bottle of oil from the bedside drawer.

Nikolas's scorching gaze dropped to the bottle in Vasili's hand and back up to Vasili's face. There were other painful memories in the room with them. Spice had likely stolen much of what Amir had done to Nikolas, or numbed it, but it wouldn't have erased it completely. He'd been fucked over countless times, most of those times by Vasili.

"You're thinking again," Nikolas said.

"Another curse of mine." Vasili perched on the edge of the bed. Nikolas rolled on his side to prop his head on his hand. Had there been other men since Amir had touched him? Had he and Yasir—

"Don't," Nikolas warned. "If I didn't want to be here, I wouldn't be. If I didn't want you, none of this would happen." He pushed up onto his knees and met Vasili face-to-face. He tilted Vasili's chin up and whispered across his lips, "I surrendered to you long ago."

Vasili grabbed his arm and twisted, bending his arm behind his back, and shoved him facedown against the bed. Nikolas let out a muffled cry, more from surprise than hurt. Vasili looped the silk around his wrists and yanked it tight, earning a grunt. He leaned close, firmly driving his cock against Nikolas's pert ass. "Comfortable, Nikolas?"

"Fuck no."

"Good."

Finesse would have to come later. Vasili's lust was too potent for more teasing. He hauled Nikolas's loose trousers down around his knees, splashed oil between his palms, warming it, and slickened Nikolas's hole, stroking downward, toward his balls, and back again.

"Tickle me or fuck me, Your Highness. But damn well pick one before I make you."

Vasili tightened his hold on Nikolas's wrists and yanked, rearing Nikolas upright onto his knees. Now with his chest to Nikolas's back, Vasili reached around with his free hand and slipped his oiled fingers around Nikolas's straining length. "No demands for me now?" he whispered into his ear, pumping fast and hard enough to stutter Nikolas's breathing and have his body twitching.

Nikolas stayed silent, his body talking for him. To have a man as powerful as Nikolas panting at each stroke of Vasili's hand had to be one of the most exquisite joys in life. A life this stubborn, strong, beautiful man had given him. A life he'd willingly share with him. Forever.

~

Niko

THE STROKES of Vasili's hand, his whispers in Nikolas's ear, it all conspired to tip Niko far over the edge of control into mindless ecstasy. He'd been lost to pleasure before the prince had pressed the hardness of his cock to his ass, but now he was its slave, and, gods, he'd never wanted to surrender more in all his life. The intimacy of it... the sensation of Vasili's careful hands gripping his thighs, the fullness of his cock, filling him up and stroking over that most sensitive part inside him. He'd never been so gods-damned hard in all his life. He ached to come but didn't want it to end. He moaned for things he'd probably later regret. And having his hands tied, his face pressed into the bed with each of Vasili's rhythmic thrusting, made him want everything *more*. He desperately needed to touch him but could only twist to get a glimpse of the prince's rapt expression.

His mask gone—it might never return now he was someone else—and his face flushed with ecstasy, he was a fucking delight to witness. His heavy gaze snagged Niko's, and something wicked sharpened the lust in his eye. He fell forward, grabbed Niko's cock in his slippery fingers, and unforgivingly pumped him to a blinding orgasm.

Vasili spat a curse, hissed between his teeth, and spilled his climax, and by the gods, the sight of him so fucking free and full of life had Niko squeezing his eyes closed and swallowing the wretched knot in his throat.

Vasili fell against Niko's back, tugged his shirt collar down, and sealed a kiss on the back of Niko's shoulder, then nipped. Niko opened his eyes to find his playful prince watching him. If he was going to look at him like that every time he fucked him in the ass, Niko would bend all day and night for him.

"Untie me," he croaked.

The silk around his wrists was gone in an instant. Niko flopped onto his side and dragged Vasili into his arms before the prince could overthink the touch and withdraw. Niko tucked him close, spooned against his back like they had on Yasir's ship, and at the cabin—like he'd dreamed a thousand times. He still couldn't believe he was here, in his arms, and safe.

"It was never about the cottage," Vasili said, speaking softly.

Niko propped his head up on a hand and tucked Vasili's hair behind his ear, so he could admire the curve of his pale shoulder and neck. He stroked that curve beneath his fingertips and smiled as Vasili shuddered. "What do you mean?" he asked.

"Your cottage, the cabin. They were remarkable because you'd made them."

"Hm..." He stroked some more and earned a light, playful slap. "I thought you hated my cottage. You were happy it burned."

Vasili turned his head, looking up. "What made you think that?"

"You sneered at everything. You even rearranged my pans in the kitchen because they offended you."

Vasili's light chuckle made Niko want to fold him closer.

"I loved every stone because you placed it. I couldn't imagine creating something so wonderful. If I sneered at it, it was from jealousy."

Niko snorted. "Jealous of a blacksmith?" That

earned him a heel in the shin. Niko growled against the back of his neck and slid a hand down his hip. Vasili laughed and rolled onto his side to face Niko and prop his head on his hand, mirroring Niko's posture. The sudden sight of him happy and soft wrapped warmth around Niko's heart. This so desperately damaged prince was his entire world and had been for far longer than he'd realized. Maybe since that first kiss in a starlit field.

"Do you want a cottage?" Niko asked, awed at the idea of a future and spending it with Vasili.

"Ah... but I'm far from the good man you promised you'd save."

Niko gathered the prince's hand in his, their rings glinting side by side. "Who wants a good man when they can have a vicious prince?" He drew Vasili's hand to his mouth and kissed the backs of his fingers.

The warmth from Vasili's smile reached his eye, and the prince laughed.

He'd build him a cottage, if that was what he wanted. Build them a simple life, perhaps with a little spice-running with Yasir on the side, because Vasili would never be content with "good." This was who they were now. The prince and his assassin. Caville and Yazdan, defying the gods, defying fate, defying anyone who dared doubt them, together forever.

Nikolas would have it no other way.

The End

~

Thank you for reading the Prince's Assassin series. If you enjoyed Vasili & Niko's adventure, please leave a review on Amazon.

Flip the page to discover more Ariana Nash adventures.

ABOUT THE AUTHOR

Born to wolves, Rainbow Award winner Ariana Nash only ventures from the Cornish moors when the moon is fat and the night alive with myths and legends. She captures those myths in glass jars and returning home, weaves them into stories filled with forbidden desires, fantasy realms, and wicked delights.

Sign up to her newsletter and get a free ebook here: https://www.subscribepage.com/silk-steel

"A story of star-crossed lovers, of two men, two enemies, who should never have fallen in love."

Angels and demons fight for love over London's battle-scarred streets.

Primal Sin, Primal Sin #1

Eternal Sin, Primal Sin #2

Infernal Sin, Primal Sin #3

ABOUT THE AUTHOR

Born to wolves, Rainbow Award winner Ariana Nash only ventures from the Cornish moors when the moon is fat and the night alive with myths and legends. She captures those myths in glass jars and returning home, weaves them into stories filled with forbidden desires, fantasy realms, and wicked delights.

Sign up to her newsletter and get a free ebook here: https://www.subscribepage.com/silk-steel